Praise for The Rice Birds

"Like the hunted rice birds of South Carolina's Lowcountry, two desperate women — an Irish indentured servant and an enslaved servant — flee antebellum Charleston in this meticulously researched and beautifully crafted race to freedom. *The Rice Birds* is an atmospheric, unforgettable novel that dives into the tumultuous years preceding the Civil War to reveal the determination, perseverance, and courage of remarkable women in search of self, family, and home. I loved it."

— *Mary Alice Monroe,* New York Times *bestselling author of more than 27 books*

"In a poignant story of two runaway servants who befriend each other in 1849 Charleston to survive, *The Rice Birds* will steal your heart. The starving Irish immigrant and the enslaved house servant battle a common enemy while trying to find their loved ones snatched from their arms. Lindy Keane Carter's transportive prose will carry you through this compelling and splendid story."

— *Patti Callahan Henry,* New York Times *bestselling author*

"Lindy Keane Carter is a captivating writer of historical fiction and a powerful storyteller. *The Rice Birds* has tension on every page, truth that shocks and exposes, and characters we come to love. Carter's Irish brogue is transporting, and the pages are littered with magical phrases: "No bigger than a penny's worth of soap" and "A big-eyed waif folded up like a broken twig." I am a big fan of Carter's writing talent, and her latest novel is a first-class winner!"

— *Leah Weiss, bestselling author of* If the Creek Don't Rise *and* All the Little Hopes *(Sourcebooks)*

The Rice Birds

a novel

Lindy Keane Carter

Keane Carter, Lindy. *The Rice Birds*
Published by Evening Post Books, Charleston, South Carolina.

ISBN-13: 978-1-929647-68-2

Cover and interior design by Michael J. Nolan

Cover image: Alice Ravenel Huger Smith (1876-1958), *Landscape*, circa 1928, watercolor on paper, 10 7/8 x 13 3/4 inches. Courtesy of the Johnson Collection, Spartanburg, South Carolina.

Dedication

This novel is dedicated to the Irish people who came to America beginning in the mid-1700's to build a better life with their unique grit, humor, faith, and loyalty.

Even though Charleston's Bishop John England warned his fellow Irishmen not to come to the hot, wild, inhospitable state of South Carolina, they came. They had little choice. Irish men built South Carolina's railroads, canals, and buildings. They fought in America's wars. Irish women sewed and tended to the sick and kept alive the traditions of their homeland.

In Charleston, a memorial to the Irish-Americans is located in the riverfront area where many of these immigrants arrived. A plaque recalls the words of South Carolina politician T. J. Withers, who said on March 26, 1855:

I know your native island has contributed a rich contingent to the best blood of mankind ... it has heightened the charms of song ... it has furnished the electric power of eloquence ... it has glorified the battlefield ... its bone and muscle have subdued the wilderness and made it to "blossom as the rose."

Other historical fiction by Lindy Keane Carter

Annaliese From Off

Annaliese, Sound and True

Visit the author at www.LindyCarter.com

PART ONE

Before the American Civil War, hundreds of rice plantations thrived along the banks of South Carolina's coastal rivers. These cruel fields built great wealth for the owners, who generally managed to fight off most threats to their enterprises. But there was little they could do to conquer one particular enemy.

The bobolink is a songbird that for centuries has migrated 12,000 miles from southern Canada to South America in the Fall. It returns to Canada in the Spring. Thus, two times a year the flocks arrived in South Carolina's rice fields. If a planter hadn't timed his planting or harvesting just right, if he'd been delayed by rain or hurricane or frost such that his tender seedlings were just rising in the fields or his milky grains were just ripening on the panicles when the birds were due, the first twitter of their advance guard made his blood run cold. Soon the sky would be black with the flock's thousands, hungry all. When they landed, rifles shot and pots beaten with spoons in the fields were pointless. The thieves were too small and too fast. When they flew away a few days later, their fortified little bodies had stolen a fortune.

So tiny but so powerful. The rice birds, as the bobolinks were called, were one of the few things that could drive fear into greedy hearts throughout the Lowcountry's rice empire. In desperate hearts, they inspired dreams of freedom.

Chapter One

At daybreak, the survivors gripped the ship's handrail as they searched the horizon. Below deck, where disease clung to every fiber and fluid, those lying in their own waste could only imagine the sweet sight of land. They prayed to hear shouts of *seaweed!* or *port!* or *shorebird!* Anything that meant this hell was almost over.

The captain came out of his stateroom looking over the manifest that was about to do him in. He'd spent two hundred pounds sterling to bribe Liverpool port agents to sign off that three hundred people were aboard his ship, but when the *Starling* put to sea on July 15, 1849, she had four hundred fifty-seven starving Irishmen packed into every moldy inch. Over the next six weeks, one hundred forty of them had succumbed to the maladies that prey upon starved bodies. The captain had been counting on that loss, but it wasn't enough.

He beckoned to four deckhands. "Seventeen," he said to them, not caring whether the Irish scum at the handrail heard, for what could any of them do about it?

They heard. Most raced below to throw their bodies across loved ones. The rest—those without loved ones down there—scrambled away to hide at the rear of the ship.

The deckhands went down into the hold.

In the crowd at the stern, two sisters couldn't get far enough away from what was coming. By now, Nora and Clare Murphy well knew the deepest hole of hell that was the captain's soul. He had shoved them into a black, airless hold after he slipped and fell in vomit, not theirs. They stayed there for three days. When he let them out, he charged them for the brown water and infested bread that were thrust into their lifeless hands. All passengers suffered from his senseless cruelty. After rough seas, he offered no aid for arms and legs broken by his poorly secured cargo. He was righteous in his indifference, loud in his opinions. The Irish had created their own woes, he bellowed. Nora and Clare saw that he was blind to the humanity of their people, as if the Irish didn't walk the earth on two legs as he did, didn't hope to scratch out a living with two sound arms as he did, didn't yearn for health and money as he did. A decent roof. A full belly.

Throughout the voyage, the sisters had stayed on deck as much as possible to escape the coughing and loose bowels down in the hold, the dying and the keening that came after, so they'd heard his rant in the wheelhouse the night before. Now that they were nearing America, he was panicked. Americans patrolling their coast would confiscate the *Starling* if they flagged her down and caught him overcrowding her.

In the hold, bloody murder chaos broke out. Nora and Clare jammed their fingers into their ears, but still they could hear people begging mercy of the men yanking their near-dead loved ones off their blankets. Two sailors dragged out a waxy-faced man hanging limp as a string between them, a bachelor with no one to fight for him. They heaved him over the rail, his only words the prayers that trailed his body all the way down to the foam. The next person was traveling alone too. The girls recognized the voice that wormed into their ears — Mrs. O'Halloran, great grandmother from County

Sligo, black-humor storyteller, entertaining curser, but wet-lunged hacker. Seconds later, her cursing stopped.

One by one, the unluckiest of the unluckiest people on earth were thrown to the waves, and while passengers boiled up out of the hatch to claw at the sailors and clutch a beloved's foot or hand for the last time, Great Britain's flag fluttered gaily atop the mainmast. The Murphy sisters counted the splashes so they'd know when to breathe again. At seventeen, when they'd opened their eyes and ears, they saw the sailors dragging one more passenger out of the hatch, the pregnant woman from Cork. In labor for hours, she'd been screeching on and off, making herself a target for the sailors who liked their passengers quiet. Her husband was wild at the men with impotent blows to their hard, brown arms. The almost-mother, writhing to hurry her child into the world, shrieked for him, for God. The sailors threw her overboard. The husband stumbled back to the hold to stuff his howls into the blanket still warm with his wife.

All across the deck the bereaved cried into one another's shoulders as loudly as they dared. Some mouthed threats at the sailors. The captain ordered one of the crew up the mainmast to the crow's nest to look for signs of New York's port.

Nora and Clare held onto each other, sickened by the violence though they'd seen plenty as the children of tenant farmers. Their father had taught them and their little brother and sisters to hide at the sound of pounding hooves on the road. Landlords and British soldiers were quick to swing their batons at heads, usually to intimidate, though, not to kill like this. Then, in the year that the sisters turned seventeen — they were twins — their terrorized lives grew impossibly, unbelievably worse. A fungus blew in from Europe. Ireland's bright green fields went black. For two years, the Murphy family lived on mottled potatoes, then rotten potatoes, then grass. Neighbors killed one another over a miraculous turnip found in a field. Gangs roamed the land stealing every cow, pig, goat, and chicken. The barns went quiet and the cottages too, but for the crying of those who had the strength.

The twins were identical—small, wren-like girls, little more than four foot ten with no hope for another inch after nineteen years. Bony as wrens too, after all the starving and now the seasickness, but they were fierce. They'd survived the walk to the port at Queenstown—people dying in ditches along the way, their lips stained green from the grass they ate, babies crying in mothers' stick-like arms—and the rickety boat to Liverpool. Nothing but hate for the English lawmakers, who'd dithered for two years and done little but talk, had kept them moving.

Nora, the elder by five minutes, looked closely at Clare to see if she might vomit. Here was the face that Nora knew as her own. Tall forehead above coarse cheekbones that overwhelmed the narrow chin. Wide space between the two front teeth. Small green eyes pinched toward the nose like God's afterthought. Black hair flowed out the back of Clare's scarf, except for the loose strands that whipped her face like sail ties in a gale. She nodded at Nora not to worry, that she was all right. She patted Nora's arm.

All of their lives, they'd taken up the space of one, had worked and slept and breathed as one. They figured they'd always live together and die together, those Murphy twins whom no one, not even Mam sometimes, could tell apart. So many times, they'd heard Mam say: "'Twas the surprise of me life when they were born, that second wee one slidin' out five minutes later, each of 'em no bigger than a penny's worth of soap, each having the same wee face."

They grew up. They were quick. With their sharp minds, Clare and Nora stood out in their hamlet full of what Mam called the bog-brains. The sisters' dreams were not identical, though. Nora was the one who stared at the hills that breathed with the Irish myths and superstitions and wondered aloud what breathed on the other side. Clare would say, "*Ach, Sister, be careful what ye wish for."* Even after two seasons of slimy potatoes, mothers watching their children waste away, and people selling all they had for food though there was none to be bought, Clare took hard the idea of leaving the farm and the families whose veins shared her ancestral blood. She challenged Nora's brave talk of leaving. *Every terrier is bold in the open doorway of its house,* Clare had said. Nora had spit on the traitorous earth. "For the lovea Jaysus, there are no farms and families anymore," she cried.

After Da buried Mam and his three younger children, he sold his tools, gave his twins the money for going to America and left for the workhouse. They watched him walk down the road, one hand behind him waving them on to America. Nora dragged Clare to Queenstown, Clare looking back between yanks, Nora screaming, "If ye feel that leaving for America is like stepping off a cliff, well, I do, too. Let go me hand then. Ye think I know how I'll land? Ye think I want to be indentured to God knows what kind of person in America? The English landholders are cleaning out the hills of Ireland, Clare, and we're the trash. We have to go."

Now they were at America's door. The huddled clump at the ship's stern heard excited cries from the crow's nest. The sailor was pointing and shouting one word over and over. *Land! Land! Land!*

Everyone rushed below to gather their belongings. The twins plucked their bags of filthy homespun off blankets and checked to make sure their biscuits were still there, one each, not to be touched until they knew where the next food was coming from. Men lifted women out of bunks and helped them up the ladder into the light. People crowded the handrail, pushing to see the ash-colored outline rising out of the sea spray. Manhattan's South Street Seaport, it was supposed to be. A blessed wind swept in, lifting the sails to deliver the Starling faster than anyone dared hope.

When the port was within rowing distance, the captain ordered the sails trimmed and the rowboats lowered. The rowers brought the *Starling* into a dock. Nora and Clare at the handrail scanned the waterfront that bustled with workers, dogs, fishermen, carts. Horses pulled wagons loaded beyond reason down the wharf. Sea gulls dropped from the sky to fight over trash in the greasy water. The only creature at rest was a man, cap pushed off his forehead, reading a newspaper beside a tower of crates. Hands behind Nora began pushing her, as if she could go anywhere. Looking back to glare, she saw a little girl in the crush. Nora had seen her before, a big-eyed waif usually folded up like a broken twig against her mother who now was trying to hang on to the child's arm. Nora elbowed people just enough to wave the woman and child in front of her. She reached into her bag and held out her biscuit to the girl. She looked at it, then at her mother, who nodded all right. The child's frantic bites made Nora's eyes go watery.

When the dockworkers had secured the mooring lines, the gangplank thudded to the pier. A man in a black uniform emerged from the waterfront chaos and boarded the *Starling*. He shook the captain's hand with familiarity, looked over his documents, and when the captain gestured toward the hatch — an invitation to inspect below — the official shook his head.

Clare poked Nora. "He's afraid to go down there," she said.

"Aye, he should be. Hope to God he's in a hurry to get off this cursed ship," Nora said. "We're days late arriving and we can't miss our next boat."

"Me brother is meeting us," the little girl's mother said as she searched the waiting crowd. Faces bright with expectation tilted up at the *Starling's* deck like a field of sunflowers turning toward the sun.

Some in that crowd weren't going to find who they'd come for. Nora wanted to get off and away before the shrieking began.

The port official began working his way through the passengers, telling one person then that one to open their mouths for a look. Every now and then he'd peer into an ear. Nora and Clare watched him with the distrust they applied to all authorities. This one was particularly rotten with this half-arse inspection, not that they were going to speak up. The sailors had told them that he'd be looking for people to send to the quarantine building, which would mean another thirty agonizing days. The twins' packet to South Carolina was scheduled to leave that afternoon.

The official tapped passengers' shoulders, one, three, seven, saying *quarantine*. The twins were in the back of the crowd. Nora pulled Clare, the mother, and her child into a crouch. They heard the man's terse words—*you, quarantine island*—a few more times and then heard his quick steps down the gangplank. Minutes later, people staggered off the boat with their cardboard valises and vacant-eyed children. Everyone ended up in a cavernous room, where men in a different kind of uniform glanced at their papers, asked them to sign ledgers, and waved them through. In fading daylight, the newcomers and their diseases disappeared into the narrow streets that flowed away from the East River.

The twins ran back to the waterfront to hurry as best they could on wobbly sea legs past offices, sailmakers, counting houses, warehouses, and towering piles of freight. Auctioneers' calls echoed down the wharves. Stevedores half-blinded by the bales on their shoulders pushed past the girls who had slowed to read the signs at the slips. The boat to Charleston was supposed to be at Peck slip.

As Nora pulled her sister away from staring at men carrying bodies off a ship, she tried to think of something cheery to say—they had made it to America!—but she was out of cheery now, having used it all up during the six weeks of boredom, terror, boredom. "Food in our bellies," she'd said more than once. "More food in the mistress's pantry," more than twice. "Honest work in a respectable home in a place called Charleston for four whole years." Those were the images that Nora had tried to lay over Clare's memories of Mam in her grave and the neighbors digging up the fields with their hands for the one good potato they were sure was out there.

Finally, the girls saw the sign overhead. *Peck.* A line of passengers inched down the pier to a waiting ship. Some of them wore tailored jackets or fancy dresses, while others wore the rags and waxy pallor of coffin ship survivors. The ship's name, *Columbia,* matched what was on the twins' tickets.

"Mother of God," Clare said. "Ten more days of sea."

Nora squeezed her sister's hand. "Just one last bit of water," she said.

"Bit of water?" Clare asked. "Ten days of — "

Nora pulled her forward.

On the *Columbia*'s deck, a man with military shoulders watched the sailor on the pier direct passengers. Despite the September heat, the man wore a black wool uniform coat and a captain's hat with black visor and fabric crown. A gold badge gleamed at its center. Behind him, a gang of sailors in frayed, mismatched shirts that had never been uniforms of any kind straightened to attention every time the man glanced at them. The sailor on the pier waved the well-dressed passengers aboard and sent the others, all women in sad skirts and wraps, to wait to the side. Nora and Clare got in that line. Young women dripping with dirty bags and cardboard boxes ran down the pier to join them.

The *Columbia*'s bell rang out. The man in the captain's hat motioned to the sailor on the pier to get the sad skirt group on board. The line began moving, Nora in front of Clare. Climbing the gangplank, she felt a nasty push — clearly not Clare — and as she turned around, she found that two women had gone around Clare while she fished in her skirt pockets for her ticket.

Finally, Clare pulled it out, waved it at Nora, and got in the line.

Nora glared at the pushy woman. "Ye want to send the two of us into the water?" she asked. "We'd sink like fieldstones and ye know it. Don't ye dare touch me again." Seconds later she stepped onto the deck where the captain was checking tickets and tapping the shoulders going by.

"Fifteen," he said as his fingers brushed Nora.

She moved to the handrail to keep an eye on Clare.

"Sixteen, seventeen," the captain said, touching two more shoulders. "That's it," he said. He waved at the next woman on the gangplank—Clare—to back up.

"What! No!" Nora grabbed his arm. "That's me sister. She has to come with me."

The captain ripped her fingers from his arm and stormed away. A deck hand stepped between the twins. They clawed at him as he pushed Clare backward. The girls behind her were shaking their heads no, no, no, pushing forward, waving their tickets with furious fists. The sailor from the pier hauled them off the gangplank one by one and shoved them toward a white-haired woman who in turn shoved them toward a man holding ropes.

The sailor's hands landed on Clare.

Nora screamed, "No!"

Someone grabbed Nora by the arms and dragged her backward. Clare fought so hard going down the ramp that she and the man nearly slipped off until he twisted her arm into a sickening angle. Nora bit the sailor's fingers hard enough to win release, but only for a second, for another sailor pinned her against the lifeline.

Dockworkers began unspooling the mooring lines from the cleats, which sent the rejected girls into full hurricane. One of them walloped the old woman and ran away. The others—six in all and not as quick—slapped at the woman, at the man trying to bind wrists, and at one another.

Several of the *Columbia*'s sailors dropped from rope ladders into two rowboats tied to her stern and began pulling her out of the dock. Nora threw a leg over the lifeline, but the gap between the pier and the side of the ship was widening quickly. She shoved her way through the gawking passengers to get to the bow. Clare screamed for her sister slowly passing by. Nora threw her leg over again, looked down at the swirling water, pulled it back. As the hard lump of the bag that held the last of Da's shillings banged against her thigh, she thought of throwing it to Clare. But the water—she couldn't take that chance. Only a few feet wide, the gap might as well have been the Atlantic. The *Columbia* was moving faster now, ripping her away from Clare, now on her knees, hands tied behind her back, screaming for her only family on yet another perilous and hostile continent.

Chapter Two

Nora pounded on the stateroom door until someone shouted to the sailor outside to let her in. The single-window cabin was dark but for the oil lamplight that spilled across the desk where Captain Robert C. Wells hunched over a logbook. Nora rushed at him like a wildfire.

"Don't," he said, not looking up.

"Me sister! She has a ticket! Why—"

His quill continued its scratchy looping and dotting. "You're on, aren't you? Be grateful," he said.

"Ye have to turn back. Ye have to—"

Wells shot her a look that sent her back a step.

"Sir," she managed, much as she hated to cower.

He dipped his quill in the inkwell and went back to the logbook.

"Sir, when will ye return to New York? When will ye pick her up? Who's that woman who took her?"

"It's September. Gale season, as is October. Schedules are impossible to keep."

"What a load of bollocks. Ye have mail and packages to deliver on a schedule." She rested her fingertips on his desk. "Every ten days. I asked."

The captain came around the desk at her, hand raised. Nora now realized the size of him, well over six feet, hands as big as an Irish Draught's hooves. After nineteen years under the thumb of a landlord, she knew how to feign submission. She looked up into his eyes, shiny and black as a wharf rat's. A ropey scar ran from one ear to his jaw, the legacy of violence on what she now knew as the lawless seas. A black anchor tattoo stained his neck. The stench coming off him—old sweat, mildew, tobacco, and an ineffable something else—made her gag.

Nora stepped backward again. "She's me only family on this miserable earth," she said quietly. "Sir."

He grabbed a handful of her hair. "Sometimes our passengers? They fall overboard? Your employers would understand that I couldn't have prevented that." He shook her by the hank. "Happens all the time."

Looking at him square on, she refused to cry. Her eyes were only as high as the gold buttons on his chest pockets. He let her go and walked back to his chair.

"At least tell me who that old woman is. What she'll do with her."

Wells flicked a finger toward the door. "Get out."

"Where will she take her?"

The captain called for the sailor outside.

As the man dragged her out, she screamed every curse she knew, but in Irish.

* * *

Seasickness, her old traveling companion, found her again in her bunk. Nora's moans joined the chorus of moans rising and falling throughout steerage. She tried to calm down, think rational thoughts. Surely the Charleston people who had hired her and Clare would be incensed. Surely they'd insist that the indenture agent straighten this out and see that Clare was delivered on the next packet to Charleston. But they wouldn't know she was missing until Nora arrived alone ten days from now. Then her employer's letter put on a packet to New York would take another ten days. A lot could happen in twenty days.

The passenger in the bunk above, a girl about her age, leaned down to point out the bucket in the corner should Nora need it. Bulging eyes ruined the otherwise appealing face. It seemed to Nora that any minute those glistening orbs would yield to gravity and land in her lap. Then she'd definitely need the bucket. She didn't want to look at the face, didn't want to talk, couldn't even if she wanted to. When the girl kept on blabbing, Nora closed her eyes. *If she starts talking about opportunity in this glorious new country, or God, or even just bloody hope,* Nora thought, *I'll strangle her.*

The girl said, "Ach, the seasickness. Ye think you're going to die. Then ye want to die. Then ye're afraid ye're not going to die."

Nora sighed.

"Me name's Margaret. From Sligo. On me own now."

Nora gave up. "Nora. From Connaught."

"Heard yer curses on the captain before the crew ran me off the upper deck. That one about weasel's piss, 'twas glorious. 'May yer obituary be written in weasel's piss.' I grew up on curses, a'course, but never heard that 'un. Have ye got more?"

"May the devil tear yer body from the funeral wagon in front of all the funeral," Nora managed to say, suddenly feeling a little better.

Margaret made rapid little claps and shared a few curses that she'd learned from her mother always moaning by the fire. After a while of nothing from Nora but labored breathing, Margaret said, "Poor Ireland. People fleeing as though running from a fire they are."

"Aye and nothing left when they turn 'round to look." Nora pressed her stomach double-fisted to see if that would help.

"Don't turn 'round I say."

"Aye."

"A daughter of the old sod I am, but so help me, now I despise it, and then I despise meself for feeling that."

"Aye," Nora said.

"It failed us. The sod killed us. How'd that happen?"

Nora closed her eyes. "Doesn't matter now."

"At least we speak English. That'll help us get work."

"How'd ye learn it?"

"The priests."

"Ah. Me too." Nora had a feeling that God was about to enter the conversation.

"Catholic ye are, a'course."

"No." Nora glanced up at the bulging eyes. Sure enough, they widened — how was that even possible? — at that answer.

"Well, I know ye're not a Protestant, being from Connaught."

"Right. I'm not. I'm nothin'. Nothin' but weary." *Weary with this chatter as well.*

"Ah. First chance I get, I'll be going to Mass. I'll pray for yer sister, left behind on that pier with that terrible woman there. I saw it all."

"Yes, ye go ahead and pray." Nora rolled over and put her shawl over her head.

* * *

For days Nora paced the deck, looking behind her as she had her whole life for Clare, the dawdler, to catch up. The crew handed out oatmeal, flour, molasses, and tea to the passengers, but the crowding around the brick cooking platform exhausted Nora. She barely ate. The irony of abundant food without appetite was not lost on her — another bitterness. When Margaret, who turned out to be a tough and practical girl despite the inextinguishable optimism, told her she needed her strength to keep her Charleston job, Nora ate. Worry churned through the digestions, resisting elimination, unlike the food. She peered at the coastline as if she'd recognize America's southern states going by. The heat grew with every mile. The days of stagnant air and empty sails were agony, and always the captain watched her with his rat eyes while she circled the deck in search of a breeze.

On the sixth day, another hot and soupy one, as she was leaning over the handrail in case her oatmeal came back up, she smelled him — that singular odor of mildew and sweat and something. Festering sores maybe. All her life she'd smelled the sour sweat of working men, but this man-stink was different. It made her stomach even worse.

The boots stopped behind hers. "You owe me for the food," Wells said.

"The packet fare covered it," she said, not turning around.

"All right," he said. "Then I'm charging you two dollars for the trouble you are."

She spun around, face afire. "Haven't a penny on me."

A trace of pleasure flashed in his eyes. "But you will."

"I'll make no wages for four years."

"Pity. You'll have to figure something out."

Curses pressed to get past Nora's lips, but she didn't dare release them, not even in Irish. Nausea rolled through her stomach and the heat squeezed the air out of her lungs, but she managed to stay still and quiet. The oatmeal, however, did not. It boiled in her belly, threatening to reverse its course. The captain's stink wormed into her nose, her throat, down to the rebellious oatmeal. Her shoulders began to heave. She leaned toward Wells and, holding her skirt out of the way, vomited all over his gold buttons. She ran away without looking back.

The next day, the sky birthed enough wind to fill the *Columbia*'s sails and the little packet ship finally flew across the indigo plane. It was on the morning of the tenth day, on schedule as if the captain cared about such a thing, that the ship entered Charleston's harbor. Again, Nora stood at a handrail squinting at an American skyline, this one of the actual city. A dozen church steeples rose into the brilliant September sky. Tidy little shops, identical but for their paint colors of blue, pink, yellow, and green, abutted the beginning of the wharves. Margaret joined her to watch the sailors drop into the rowboats and put oars to water to begin pulling the ship in. Other steerage passengers pointed and cried out in strange tongues, but Nora got the gist of it. Opportunity. Silver in pockets. Charleston was the wealthiest city in America, the crew had said.

The water teemed with boats long, stubby, three-masted, two-masted, no-masted, sleek or barnacled, nothing like the massive Manhattan vessels. She didn't know the world had so many different kinds of boats. There were no boats in her village, only carts behind shoeless feet.

The oarsmen maneuvered the *Columbia* toward dock pilings while the rest of her crew threw heaving lines to dockworkers, all of them black. Hand over hand, they hauled the ship in. Nora stared at them. She hadn't believed the sailors when they told her there would be black people in Charleston, people from a country on the other side of the world. Black as night they were, as were the men who rolled barrels down the piers and heaved crates out of the holds of other ships.

Wells arrived behind the girls, too close as always. He shoved a ragged piece of paper under Nora's nose—a bill for two dollars. A fortune. She took it and nodded.

Margaret watched him walk away and made a face. "Sweet Mother of Baby Jaysus there's something dead inside that coat of his," she said. "Why would ye pay that bill? Ye're almost off this ship."

Nora put the paper in her pocket. "Until Clare gets here, I'll have to at least look like I'm agreeing. Trouble enough she'll have with him if 'tis this packet she has to take to get here."

The girls joined the passengers picking their way down the gangplank and hurried under the arch of bowsprits that jutted from a dozen bows. After being cleared through the customs house, Nora and Margaret walked through a door to cobblestone streets that throbbed with carriages and people.

"America," Margaret said, looking left and right. "They let us in."

"'Tis a big city," Nora said.

"Huge."

"Stay with me here for a minute, would ye?" Nora asked. "Ye don't have to go yet, do ye?"

They leaned against the building, their bodies swaying as if the Atlantic was still under their feet. They stared at everything—a crimson and yellow carriage going by, its chest-out driver outfitted in a red coat and tall hat, a man black as a crow selling fish out of a cart, two white women walking arm in arm, their blonde heads tilted toward each other in carefree conversation. Fans fluttered in their free hands.

"White as cow udders those two are," Margaret said.

"Not farmers, I'm guessing," Nora said.

Margaret let out a puff of agreement. After a while, she laid her hand on Nora's arm. "Well, I'd best be goin'."

The only response Nora could manage was to clamp her hand on Margaret's.

"Ye'll be at the Manning home ye say," Margaret said after taking a deep breath.

Nora nodded. "On Meeting Street."

"I'll be at the Petigru's on Legare Street."

"Where ye'll never stop eating, ye said." Nora offered a weak laugh.

"'Tis for certain I won't." Margaret hugged her, whispering, "She'll be along soon."

As they came out of the hug, Nora was blind with tears. They patted each other's bony shoulders and Margaret said, "May the strength of the three best, Father, Son, and Holy Ghost, be with ye."

Then she melted into the crowd on the sidewalk.

Chapter Three

Nora took a deep breath of air as warm and thick as porridge and looked around. So many black people — on every corner, in every doorway. Black women in plaid skirts and headscarves pulled children white, brown, and black along, too fast for little legs. Black men drove carriages — another first — along streets paved with smooth stones, sending up a clatter of wheels and hooves. The tang of horse manure mixed with the scent of the sea. The heat was of a new order not to be believed, but Nora saw that the other women hadn't rolled up their sleeves, so she left hers at her wrists.

She walked toward the street that ended in front of the customs house and found it to be Broad Street, a wide avenue of shops and offices and the meeting place indicated in her employer's instructions. Despite being one block off the grimy wharves, Broad Street dazzled. Everything shone. Ladies in billowing pastel dresses and matching hats strolled with men in fancy coats — coats in this heat! — walking protectively beside them, none of them in any particular hurry. One couple lingered in front of a shop window. The man was staring at ladies' hats for the love of Jesus, this dandy with his gloved hand at the small of the lady's back.

Nora's village, unchanged for centuries, had no people of leisure, no shops, no taverns, no offices, no money, only barter. The villagers felt no shame in being penniless, though, for they had their dignity in their fields bright with green potato leaves, the wagon wheel well formed, the story well told, the music beautifully coaxed from strings and pipes. Her own da drew down on the fiddle with such skill that grown men cried at its sweet strains.

The memory of Da ran her through like a knife. That poor, sweet man, surviving enough tragedy for three lifetimes. He'd buried his three youngest children after the first year of potato blight. When the second season of rotten potatoes came, what was left of the Murphys—he and Mam, Clare and Nora—ate the stored potatoes, mottled with black slime but at least solid in some parts. But the hunger claimed Mam, always the one to push dwindling food to her children, and Da saw there was nothing left. He kissed Clare and Nora goodbye, entrusted them to the mere idea of America for he knew not a soul there, and went to the workhouse in the next county, a filthy, crowded place that most people didn't survive. Nora ached to smell the yeasty smoke of his pipe, hear her little sisters and brother playing outside the cottage. Now he was alone, if alive at all, and so was she. Her twin, her right arm, had been ripped away. For the second time that Nora's feet had touched American soil, the ground opened up and swallowed her. She dropped down hard at the bottom of the customs house steps and buried her face in her hands.

"Miss Murphy?" a man said.

Nora squinted into the sunshine at the voice. The man's skin was the color of coal gouged out of the earth and his matted hair was mostly white with hints of departing black. He wore a dark green livery coat, gray pants, and white gloves, one of which he put to his chest. "I'm Isaiah. Missus Manning, she sent me to fetch you." He pointed to a carriage and horse waiting across the street. "Ain' there s'posed to be two of y'all?"

She burst into tears again and kicked at the shins of the invisible Captain Wells.

"I'm sorry, Miss, real sorry," Isaiah said with a wince. If there was only one Murphy and she was crying, he should've known to not ask.

Nora looked over at the black carriage that looked vaguely like a jail cell. "I'll not be getting in that thing," she said, narrowing her eyes at it. "How far's the house?"

"You meanin' to walk?" Isaiah looked at her beat-up boots held together with twine. "Couple blocks over there to Meetin' Street, then the house be down a ways. This here's a mighty fine carriage, one of Charleston's fanciest. Mighty fine. You sure you don' want to get in?"

"I'll follow ye."

Isaiah shook his head. The gentleman in him couldn't stand this, but she was such a fierce little thing. "Awright then," he said.

She followed the carriage down Broad Street not completely trusting her sea-softened legs. It felt so good to stretch them, feel the soft muscles come to life. As she passed the people who were in no particular hurry, their whispers filled her wake. She caught a word — *disease* — and picked up her pace, sending her loose soles flapping. If Clare had been there, she would've squeezed her hand to snuff out the sting, but she wasn't, and Nora's hot tears welled up again. There came a feminine cough behind Nora, the affected kind, the kind someone issues to let you know you stink. Finally, after three agonizing blocks, the carriage turned left onto a residential street. A black woman pushed a pram with one hand and dabbed a handkerchief at her shiny face with the other.

Enormous houses rose on both sides of the shaded boulevard, their third floors reaching into the tree canopies. Front doors the size of haystacks stood dark and intimidating in the cool recesses of the porches. On her right, a pair of curving marble stairs rose to the second-floor porch. Green velvet panels hung inside the towering windows beside the door. The next house sat sideways on the lot, so that its street door was small and plain, opening only onto a porch. Nora stood on tiptoe to peek over the brick wall. Here was the grand door befitting such a house. In the middle of that porch, the door faced a garden where enormous black bugs raced across the weathered brick path. She moved on, gawking at the strange plants flowing in patterns around fountains and statues, and then the brick wall got higher, shutting her out. She slowed to take in everything, for the grandeur of the houses grew with each block. Isaiah kept looking back at her, having held the horses to a near crawl. After a while, he called to her that it was time to cross the street. He pointed to a house, the largest yet.

A wrought-iron fence ran the length of the yard alive with tall trees that had no branches along their scaly trunks, only reeds bursting forth at the top to rattle in the breeze. The home was a brick three-story structure with more windows than Nora could count and an alley alongside that revealed the house's startling depth. Isaiah turned the horses down the alley.

He led Nora to a one-room white building behind the house. Two black women chopping vegetables at a table looked up at the filthy spindly girl in the doorway. One of them, a middle-aged woman as round as a barrel, raised her eyebrows and said, "Huh!"

"I'm Nora," Nora said, stepping forward. The aroma of roasted meat nearly brought her to her knees.

"What you say?" the woman asked. "You hard to understan'."

"Nora. Nor—ah."

They stared at her, their knives suspended above their onions.

"And what is it ye're lookin' at?" Nora snapped.

"What she say?" the other woman said to the round woman.

Isaiah stepped closer to the table to whisper, "Don't ask her where's the other one."

"I'm Bess," the round woman said. "This is Pearl." She nodded across the table.

Pearl, younger and thinner, stared at Nora.

"We heard you was coming," Bess said. "We jus' couldn't believe it. We never seen white help before."

Nora pulled a chair away from the wall and plopped down. "And I've never seen black people before." She thrust one hand into the air, then the other. "And streets and fine gowns and black bugs the size of your big toe rushing across the ground and . . ." Her voice gave out. The tears that had brimmed all the way down Meeting Street finally spilled over. Her nose was out of control too. She wiped it on her sleeve. "And I've left me sister on the other end of this horrible country," she sobbed, "in the care of some horrible stranger and I'll not see her again until I talk to the lady here." She stood up. "Mrs. Manning. Where is she? I need to talk to her right now."

Bess moved to the fireplace and spooned something out of a pot into a bowl. Giving it to Nora, she said, "She's in the big house, but fuhst you got to eat."

Hunger stabbed Nora's insides, but she peered into the bowl with disgust. "Mother of God, what is this ye're giving me? Looks like maggots drowning in thin milk."

Everyone looked at her, mouths agape.

"What is it?" Nora said again.

"Gal," Isaiah said gently. "It's good. It's rice."

"You never seen rice?" Pearl asked.

"In a few days you'll see more rice than you know what to do wit'," Bess said.

Nora stuck her nose into the bowl and found a sweet and buttery aroma. She dabbed a spoonful to her tongue. *Bland. So be it.* A mouthful went in. *Oh, my.* The glory of it! Two bowls later, she said, "Now — Mrs. Manning. Where in the big house is she?"

Pearl took off her apron. "Can't just go wanderin' 'roun' in there. I'll show you," she said. Nora judged her to be in her late teens, a wisp of a girl like herself, but with coffee-colored freckles splattered across a light brown face.

"Hold on you two. Come 'yuh." Bess waved Nora toward her as she took a kettle from the fireplace. "You ain' goin' in that house smelling like yesterday's fish. Take them nasty clothes off." She poured some of the water into a basin.

Isaiah took his bowl of rice and left.

Nora looked at her skirt and her grimy hands, felt the fifty days of salt and sweat sticking to the inner thighs and the privates and breasts she hadn't been able to wipe down with so many eyes watching in steerage. She'd never been naked in front of anyone besides Clare, but she pulled everything off and kicked it to the wall.

Bess made a face as she caught a whiff of the clothes going by. "Your hair 'bout to get a good scrub too," she said.

An hour later, Nora stood in a fresh plaid servant's dress next to Pearl at the big house's back door. Bess had pinned up the hem so the short Irish girl wouldn't trip on the six inches too many. Pearl looked at Nora again with a suspicious eye, turned the doorknob, and introduced her to another black woman who was giving her the same look.

"I'm Nora," Nora said slowly. "Nor — ah."

"Huh!" the woman said. "Where's the other one?"

Nora felt her neck go warm. All she could do was shake her head.

"I'm Hettie," the woman said. "Wipe your feet."

Hettie left Nora in what she called the drawing room, saying on her way out that she'd tell the missus the Irish servants were here, one of them anyway. Nora looked around the room, stunned by the size of it, three times bigger than her family's cottage. The floor wasn't packed earth, but wide gleaming planks topped with rugs of many colors. So much furniture, so many places to rest your arse. In the center, two yellow sofas with matching bolster pillows faced each other. A plump, red cushion snuggled into a wide windowsill that overlooked the street. The windows! So many windows. What Mam would have given for just one to let the smoke out and a bit of light in. Huge wooden cabinets and carved bookshelves lined the walls. Silver creations topped every surface—candlesticks and bowls and trays—and potted plants anchored every corner.

Nora walked toward four oval frames that hung on a wall. She leaned in to see them better. Instantly, she reared back. She didn't know lamps and chandeliers, sterling silver and crystal, but she knew what this was. Hair. Human hair. Brown hair, yellow hair, mouse-colored hair, and black hair that had been formed into flowers, wreaths, angels, trees, and crucifixes. One of the frames enclosed six locks of blonde hair that curled into themselves like dead centipedes. Along the bottom someone had written with loops and flourishes: "Elizabeth Mary Manning, 1838 - 1839." The next frame encased a bough dripping with something—grains like that rice in the kitchen? Buds of some sort?—that hung over a headstone. Beneath that, "Elizabeth Catherine Manning, 1840 - 1842." The next one—a wreath with birds and nests full of eggs—read, "Robert Coming Manning, 1843 - 1844." And the fourth memorial, an elaborate ring of flowers made of brown hair, read "Elizabeth Emily Middleton Manning, 1845 – 1847."

Nora hugged her arms though the room was stifling hot. The sound of footsteps rose in the hall. She hurried to stand beside the two yellow sofas.

Elizabeth Rebecca Pringle Manning floated into the room with a spectral air. Nearly as skeletal as Nora, she gave off a vapor of frailty. Nora wanted to rush at her, but she held off at the sight of the woman's gray eyes. She recognized that glassy film. Grief.

The dull brown hair was parted in the center and plastered down but for ringlets that hung beside cheeks the color of raw pie dough. Rebecca scanned the room as if to check that the sterling silver was still there, took a deep sigh, and finally summoned enough energy to squint at Nora.

"You're not sick are you? You didn't touch anything did you?" she asked.

Nora couldn't remember what being not sick felt like, but she didn't have the headache and muscle aches of ship's fever, nor the rash, so she replied, "No."

"It's ma'am to me. You say, 'No, ma'am.'"

Nora nodded. "Yes, mum. No, mum."

"No, no, it's *ma'am*. Ma'am. Say it."

Nora gave the hard-edged word a try, producing a version neither of them had ever heard before.

Rebecca narrowed her eyes. "Dear Lord, I hope my little boy doesn't pick up your accent."

"No, ma'am."

"Or a disease. This strangers' disease all over town from all these Irish coming in. Irish orphans are everywhere, filling up the Children's Home. In my thirty years, I've never seen it this bad. You understand, I can't be too careful with you, but I do see that your skin isn't yellow. Pull your eyes open."

Nora complied and lost control of the brimming tears.

Rebecca peered into Nora's watery sockets. "No Yellow Fever. Very well, but you must stay away from my son until we're sure."

"Yes, ma'am. Now my sister —"

"So, your duties are dusting and mopping, laundry and linens. Clear the table after meals, wash and dry the dishes and mind that you don't bang them around when you put them away. Polish the silver and don't you dare scratch it. No wages, as agreed. We paid boat fares for the two of you."

"About the two of us —"

"You'll get room and board, of course, and clothes. After four years, you will have paid your obligation to us."

"But —"

"You can put your things in your room on the third floor."

"I have no things, ma'am. A woman in the kitchen house gave me this dress." Nora ran her hands down the skirt.

"Did Bess check you for lice?"

Nora didn't know about that, but she wanted to get past all these questions, so she nodded.

"After you two get settled upstairs, you can start by covering the furniture in here. Hettie will show you where the sheets are." She turned toward the doorway.

"Ma'am, me sister —"

Rebecca pivoted on penny-sized black heels. "Isn't she getting scrubbed out back?"

"No! Um, Ma'am. The ship captain left her at the docks of Manhattan." Nora finally rushed toward the mistress.

Rebecca held a flattened palm up to stop her. "We paid two fares. What happened?"

"Stolen she was. Ye've got to tell the company that wrote our contracts to go find her and put her on the next boat."

The grey eyes flared. "I heard I'd have to teach you Irish your place," she said in a steely tone. "How do you expect them to find her?"

"Well—"

Rebecca held out the other palm. "It's too late anyway."

"What do ye mean?"

"We're all leaving town day after tomorrow, the whole household. Didn't you see the crates and trunks in the hall? We're fleeing the epidemic, of course."

Fiery webs of panic raced up Nora's neck. "Leaving? For where, Mother of God?" She couldn't help it—her voice was rising.

"The plantation." Rebecca brought a trembling hand to her throat to signal that, really, this was too much from a servant.

Quick footsteps tapped across the floor upstairs. A male voice called "Rebecca!" from the top of the staircase. She pointed at the gallery of hair memorials. "Be sure to pack those up. They always go with us." Rebecca Manning drifted away like a fog.

Nora bolted for the front door. She had to escape this ghostly hag, worse than any banshee an Irish cave ever harbored, had to go back to New York, find that old woman from the dock, find Clare. But how? She took her hand off the doorknob. She had no money but Irish shillings, no ticket back. In this vast country lauded for its freedoms, she was caged.

That night in her room on the third floor, she tossed on a sweat-soaked mattress, the first mattress of her life, too soft and too big. Nora swept her hand across the empty spot that Clare had always filled. *Where's she sleeping tonight?* Nora wondered. *Is her belly full? Is someone nearby to protect her? Does she need protecting?*

Shadows of the fronds of the tall, strange trees fanned out across the walls like splayed knives and the creepy dry rattling in the breeze brought bleached bones to mind. In Ireland, the maggots had laid bare the bones in the roads in no time. Tired of flipping around, desperate for a breeze, she went to the window and found the night seething with creature noises. A sea of them out there it sounded like. Rolling waves of cries and scratching and frantic wings going by.

Nora put her boots on and tiptoed downstairs to the second-floor landing. Outside every bedroom door on this floor, black women slept on mats. One of them got up on her elbows to look at Nora, but she said nothing. Nora turned to the stairwell window that looked down upon the kitchen house and stable. Candlelight flickered in an open window. Someone was still up. Seconds later, Nora knocked softly on the door.

Pearl opened it. Behind her, the candle's glow bathed three cots. Two heads in kerchiefs lay against pillows.

"What you want?" Pearl whispered.

"It's so hot up there."

"Better go back 'fore they find you out 'yuh."

"I've never slept by meself before."

Pearl's eyebrows shot up. "Well, you ain' sleepin' with us."

"Always me sister beside me."

"You'll get used to it." Pearl closed the door.

"How do I get out of here?" Nora whispered to the whorls in the rough-hewn door.

Back at her window, Nora looked down on the sleeping city. She could barely read English, knew not one soul down there, and spoke with a brogue that marked her as one of the crowd that brought disease. No stranger would help her. She felt as if her ankles were tied together as surely as one of Da's chickens, which he always bound at the feet to keep them out of neighbors' pastures. Rather, used to.

Chapter Four

T he Manning caravan of carriages, horses, and wagons started out at dawn for Oakwood Plantation near Georgetown, a coastal town smaller than Charleston but the largest rice shipping port in the nation. Georgetown County was a sweet spot of abundant rivers ideal for the tidal cultivation of rice. Ideal because they offered fresh upstream water plus the tidal push that brought that fresh water to the fields. By afternoon, the caravan turned off the wide road everyone called the King's Highway onto a narrow, sandy path. Soon a jungle pressed in like the walls of a cave—bushes, cypress trees, live oak trees dripping with Spanish moss, riotous vines, and great ferns the size of dinner plates. When the jungle opened to reveal a clearing, Bess and Pearl jumped out. With her hand held to her forehead against the afternoon sun, Nora watched them run to a field, where black people looked up from their work in grass as high as their hips. Two women threw down scythes and ran toward Bess and Pearl, hands pumping skyward. Their skirts were looped into cords at the waist, exposing their knees, and they wore what looked like men's hats of straw. The four women fell upon one another with wild patting and a tongue-flapping ululation like nothing Nora had ever heard. Children flowed out of the fields toward the female frenzy.

This place was vast, she saw now that she was in the light—wild, flat, scorching hot, ugly, ugly land. Fertile, though, she had to give it that. Those fields were full of food.

A modest white house stood in the distance. Four windows graced the first floor and five windows the second. A plain iron handrail ran down narrow steps. Beneath the porch, four brick arches defined an open, shadowed space. As Nora walked toward the house, she saw behind it a smaller building with two windows, one door, a simple porch, a cistern out front, and a wide chimney rising at the rear. The kitchen.

Nora walked around the main house to the other side that faced a distant river. The Pee Dee, Bess said it was called. A wide creek ran past Oakwood's two docks and the landing that was bordered by hedges and trees. Terraced earth rose from this sandy slope to the house. Turning around, Nora saw that here was the side of the house that mattered, the side meant to impress with its grander entrance: a wide apron of steps, a large carved wooden door, and white fluted columns supporting the two-story porch.

The sun blistered every surface, rendered every bush and blade—anything that would've been green in Ireland—bleached and scruffy. The sky held not even a smudge of a cloud. The land, so flat and unremarkable, offered no mounds where the faeries could hide.

A black man stormed out of the rice field making angry gestures at the four joyous women. The two who'd abandoned their field work snatched their hats off the ground and went back to their sickles and sheaves. Bess and Pearl returned to the wagon. As Nora turned to join them, she saw Mr. Manning watching her a few yards away. Quiet and ghostly like his wife, Edward Manning had snuck up on her. He was a small, withered little man, no more than five foot six, who spoke in sentences as sawed off as he was. "Dawdling," he said. She hurried to the wagons to help unload.

For hours Nora swept and mopped what everyone was calling the big house, though it was but a penny's worth of the Charleston home. The heat—it was heat within heat, pulsing through the stagnant air, draining all energy. Even with all doors and windows open, Nora was suffocating. Her dress was soaked in sweat.

A central hall split the house into equal parts—two rooms on each side—and tacked onto these were long, narrow rooms, the dining room on one side and a ballroom on the other. Occasional rugs with worn-down patterns warmed the scarred, wide plank floors. Everywhere Nora moved with her lonely unpacking, she could hear laughter floating out of the kitchen house.

When Mrs. Manning sent her to fetch supper for the family, she flew out the back door. Two women stood in the kitchen doorway watching her tromp across the sand toward them. Heartened by what she took as a welcome, she picked up her pace. The women watched her walk straight for a small hill of ash-colored dirt and said nothing. She plowed through it, the fire ants launched their attack, and Nora began slapping at her naked legs, hopping and cursing. When she'd brushed off all the ants she could see, she ran for the kitchen, legs afire. As the two women moved inside, they shared a chuckle.

Bess bustled up and down a long wood table putting out bowls and platters of food. Pearl was washing a pot in a tub.

One of the women who'd stood in the doorway said something unintelligible. Nora suspected it was about her and it didn't sound friendly.

"Nora, that's Caroline," Bess said with a nod toward the woman.

Ignoring her, Nora blew on her legs. "Bess, have ye got something for these bites?" she asked.

"I heard you don't know how to wash and iron," Caroline said.

"Nora. What kinda name is that?" the other woman asked.

"And that's Lizzybet," Pearl said.

Nora shook an ant off her skirt and stomped on it. "What kind of name is Lizzybet?"

Caroline said something else, again in gibberish.

"What's she saying?" Nora asked of Bess.

"Now, gal, it ain' as bad as you think. Say it in buckrah English, Caroline," Bess urged.

"I say you talk tangledy," Caroline said. "Like that Patrick talk."

"Me the tangledy one?" Nora asked. "And who's Patrick?"

Pearl looked over her shoulder as she rinsed the pot. "You don't want nothin' to do with him," she said.

"Why the missus hire white help?" Caroline asked.

"She cheap," Pearl said. "She don't cost nothin' for four whole years."

Nora suddenly realized why Pearl had been so nosy about her contract with the Mannings.

"The missus goin' to give her a new dress and shoes twice a year like us?" Carolina asked.

Nora looked at her boots, the remnants of what she'd pulled off a corpse during her walk to Queenstown. "Jaysus, I didn't know new shoes were coming," she said.

"But she ain' no slave," Lizzybet said, followed by something else under her breath.

Bess pushed two steaming bowls toward Nora. "Go on now, Miss Irish. Take these to the house, but not through the front door. Use the steps and door under the porch. Better be whistling as you go. Hurry back to get the rest."

"The missus ain't goin' to make no white help whistle," Lizzybet said.

"Whistle?" Nora asked. She picked up the bowls of brown beans and something covered with a cloth, something with a nutty, buttery aroma.

"So you cain' eat none of this while you carryin' it to the house," Bess said.

Nora lifted the cloth, releasing a honeyed scent that made her mouth water. She snatched one of the golden, spongy squares and took a bite. As Bess's cornbread washed over her tongue, she headed out the door unable but also unwilling to form the "o" with her lips necessary for whistling.

* * *

That night, loneliness, ant bites, and heat drove Nora out of another too-soft bed to a window. A sickle moon hung above the jagged black outline of trees across the river. Insect song rose and fell in waves as if the creatures were calling to one another, retreating, and calling again from the jungle's depths. Again she went looking for humanity. She tiptoed down the stairs and arrived on the river-facing porch. To her left, little fires burned on tall stands along the avenue of slaves' cabins. They called it the street. She crept closer to hide behind a wide oak where she could make out a dozen men and women sitting in front of one of the cabins. A couple of them smoked pipes, a few swayed with singing. In her ear a high-pitched whine arrived, then the same in the other ear. Insects landed on her arms and neck like surprise raindrops. She ran back to her room and jumped into the netting around her bed, giving her flesh, if not her heart, some peace. *What's happening to Clare tonight?* she wondered. *Where's she sleeping? Can she sleep?*

Nora couldn't understand why Mrs. Manning wouldn't demand that Clare be found and delivered. She needed two house servants, didn't she? Or had she changed her mind? Was she planning to ask the indenture agent for her money back? Surely she wasn't that cold-hearted — to abandon a country girl to a city full of strangers.

In the morning, the sun woke Nora like a hard shake. She lay still for a few seconds, bleary-eyed, disoriented, stunned with the light's brilliance, so different from the light at home that came off the lush fields in moist, diffused rays. Somewhere a rooster heralded the sunrise, then another in a faraway field, then another from even farther away, perhaps behind some lonely woodland cabin, as if to show her that there were distant sentinels at their posts throughout the vast plantation. As her eyes adjusted, a truth dawned on her. Her harsh new world was going to leave its imprint on her. It would abrade away all that she had been. Who would she be four years hence? Her old life was just ashes now, for she was no longer part of the *clachan*, nor the Murphy clan, not even half of a Murphy pair. Not a farmer, not a free woman. Still a member of the Irish people, she supposed, but even that cloak she felt slipping off her shoulders. From here on, every desperate day would add up to her new American life, but after four years here in the middle of nothingness what would that look like? Four years of isolation and prejudice, degradation, sun-blistered skin, brutal heat, torment from creatures in the ground and in the air, and never-ending, soul-sucking labor. Working day in and day out for people who'd give you as much or as little as they pleased, including whether to show you the way out of this jungle when your contract was up. What could she possibly care about in this place? How would she know she was alive in the world? Nora threw off her covers and planted her feet on the sun-shocked floor. Of one thing she was certain: Only with Clare could she survive. She had to get her sister to Charleston.

Chapter Five

In the large ballroom that ran the entire depth of the house, Nora and Pearl unpacked two crates. From one, Nora pulled out Elizabeth Rebecca Pringle Manning's precious hair memorials.

"She's lost four wee 'uns, has she? This is their hair?" Nora asked.

Pearl wouldn't look at the frame Nora held out. She simply pointed at the wall where it and the other three were to be hung—four oval spots that were a deeper blue than the rest of the sun-bleached indigo walls—and hurried out the door.

Later, Nora found her in the dining room pulling drapery panels out of homespun bags. They reeked of camphor. The girls swagged them across a porch rail to air out and went back to finish unwrapping tablecloths and napkins. As Nora laid them in drawers, she studied two samplers above the sideboard. The smaller sampler, an outline of a simple box of a house, read: "Oakwood Plantation, established 1712 by Josiah White." The second one showed the house with the ballroom added on the right side. Trees, horses, and dogs dotted the yard. Threads of red, blue, and green stated: "Oakwood Plantation, 1721." Below that: "Stitched by Anna White in the twelfth year of her life,

1721." Pearl hurried out of the room once again, leaving Nora to wonder if the samplers had their own disturbing histories as well. Well, of course they did. What *wasn't* disturbing about this place?

Nora stepped into the hall to listen for the missus. Best to always know where she was. She heard the little boy outside, two and a half-year-old William, laughing as he ran from his mother who was always trailing behind him like air off a bird's wings. Then Nora listened for Pearl. She was upstairs struggling with stiff drawers.

Stealing her moment to rest, Nora found a chair in the hall. It faced a tall, narrow wooden cabinet that contained what looked like a plate with the numbers one through twelve along the rim. Two black arrows pointed at two numbers in a slightly accusatory way, surely an ominous sign she thought. As one of the arrows slid up to twelve, four chimes erupted in the cabinet base, sending Nora running up the stairs.

She found Pearl putting sheets on a four-poster bed, dark as peat. Nora ran her hand along a post's carvings — tiny scoops and grooves that suggested stalks heavy with grain.

Pearl glanced up at her. "Where is she?" she whispered.

"Outside. In the yard with the boy."

"Awright. Good. That's rice on the post. This 'yuh what we call a rice bed. Tuck the sheet in."

This was the longest string of words Pearl had ever sent Nora's way. Trying to hide her surprise, she asked, "Outside, in the fields, that's what they're harvesting in this terrible heat? Rice?"

"Yea. You be glad you not out there with 'em," Pearl said.

"How many people work on the plantation?" Nora clung to every word coming her way.

"'Bout a hundred. Plump this." Pearl threw a pillow across the bed to Nora. "Like this." She pounded hers left, right, top, and bottom and placed it against the headboard.

Nora plumped. "They stay here all the time? Without the Mannings?"

"Mas' and the family usually gone from plantations in the summer. That swamp air, it give everybody summer fever. Make 'em die sometimes. People die too from the sunstroke, or winter fever, the runs, snake bite. First thing white people ask when they come back in the winter is 'who died while we was gone?'"

"Snake bite? What's that?"

Pearl held up two hooked fingers and sank them into the pillow. "Serpent. Like in the Bible."

"Oh!"

"Shoooo … We got rattlers, moccasins, copperheads. They in the grass, the woodpiles, that marsh out there. Kill you fast, fuh true."

Nora went to a window to locate all woodpiles.

Pearl pulled a rose-colored quilt out of a crate and snapped it open. "We leave here in May, come back when it get cold. Usually around November. Only reason we here this early is to get away from Yellow Jack in town. We was waitin' for you to get into town."

"Fleeing one disease for another?"

Pearl dropped her voice. "The missus, well, she just touched in the haid. Mas' Manning, he do what she want so she won't make a fuss, all cryin' and carryin' on. This was her people's plantation, not his. So." Pearl smoothed the quilt across the bed. "She makes the rules 'roun' here. Dust the headboard." She handed Nora a cloth.

Nora wiped down the headboard. "Those hair memorials we brought from Charleston? She's lost four children?"

"Awright, awright, I heard you the last time. Yes, four and that why she worryin' so over William. But he alive after two and a half years so that's something."

"So many ways to die out here."

Pearl shook the last pillow into its linen sheath. "You wear me out." With a hand in the air goodbye, she left Nora alone again.

* * *

Bess put a bowl on the kitchen table in front of Nora. Pearl sat across from her, mouth full.

"Rice again," Nora said, looking into her bowl.

"Rice with everything," Bess said. "Rice 'n oysters, rice 'n fiel' peas, rice 'n greens, mulatto rice, chicken over rice, rice pudding."

"At home, potatoes *were* everything," Nora said.

"Rice at day clean, middle-day, and evening. You'll see."

"Day clean?" Nora said.

Pearl finally spoke. "Sun come up," she said as she tore a chunk out of a bread loaf.

"What're these?" Nora poked her spoon at pink crescents nestled in the rice.

"Swimps," Pearl said with a roll of her eyes.

"Look like grubs." Nora pictured shovels going into the ground to unearth these wriggling things.

"Swimps come from the creeks. They good. Now hush," Bess said. She sat down at a plate that was overwhelmed by a fish, breaded and fried, atop a mound of rice. Picking it up by the head and tail, Bess nibbled up one side and down the other, as if working a mouth harp. She waved at Nora to stop staring. When that side lay stripped, she flipped the fish over and repeated the trip. Soon, only pearly bones remained in her greasy fingers.

Nora lifted a shrimp to her tongue for a taste, then took a bite. "Oh!" she said. "This is good." She chewed faster. "Tell me about this Patrick."

"You don't want nothin' to do with him," Pearl said.

"Aye, ye said. Who is he?" Nora spewed rice as she spoke.

Bess licked her fingers. "The carpenter."

"Why should I stay away from him? He talks like me, ye said?"

"Go ahead, then, find out for yourself," Pearl said.

* * *

While Nora hung laundry on a line, she rehearsed what she would plead to Rebecca Manning. *Clare loves children,* she could say. *She would love to mind William.* What rot — Clare liked pigs better than the *clachan's* children ripping through the fields, the little terrors. Anyway, Mrs. Manning hovered over the boy night and day, so she might not want another woman doing motherly things for him. *If Clare and I were together I'd be happier, I'd work harder.* No, for the loveaJaysus don't say that, Nora thought. Don't make her think ye're not already working as hard as ye can. *I'll work for free.* Don't say that either. Ye already are.

Finally, when she'd decided to just ask for mercy plain and simple, Nora went looking for the mistress, but found her rocking William to sleep, so Nora hung up the last of the laundry and went exploring. She scared a squirrel up a tree, claws clattering on bark. The smell of cattle dung drifted by. On the other side of a barn, she found two cow-like beasts standing in a mud puddle. Broad-chested and hairy, they snorted like cows, but curved horns grew out of what looked like a hair part in the center of the skull. Below the horns, furry ears sprang straight out. One of the beasts flapped an ear in her direction, as if to acknowledge her arrival.

"They're water buffalo," a voice behind her said.

Nora spun around at the sound of the brogue. The man was young, healthier than anyone from Ireland could possibly be, and better-looking than the most handsome Irish lads back home, only better. *A fine head of glossy black hair on this one*, she thought.

"So, 'tis true," she managed to say. "An Irishman out here." Her ear tips were getting warm.

"'Tis," he said. "I'm Patrick."

"Nora."

"Ah, Nora. Short for Noreen."

"That's me. Short Noreen." She laughed and waited for him to join her. He didn't. *So serious, this one.*

"I'm from Connaught. County Mayo. And ye?" Patrick asked.

"Connaught as well. County Galway."

"Which village?"

"No village. Just a clachan." She smoothed her hair and then hated that she'd just done that.

"Poor Ireland. She's done for, she is," Patrick said as he joined her at the corral rail.

"Aye, and so to America we've fled. Ye're indentured too?"

"Three years, four months, and one week here. Two years to go." Patrick stared at her. "I can't believe me eyes. A fair Irish lass. Right here in this wilderness."

Fair Irish lass? She met his gaze longer than she knew she should. No one had ever called her that before, what with her horsey face, as Mam called it, and the gap between her front teeth. Nora had always felt that her entire body let her down from all angles. Even the breasts that had sprouted with promise at puberty had never grown bigger than runty potatoes.

"Ach, full of the blarney ye are," she said, hoping he'd correct her.

He leaned against the rail, offering a polite smile, just enough for her to see teeth as straight as a hedgerow, rare among her people. Impossibly white too. He was so darn healthy.

"I can't believe I'm in this wilderness," she said. "Thought I'd be working in a grand house in Charleston."

"Swept away into the harvest season, were ye? Well, at least ye'll not go hungry here, let me tell ye. No end of food here." He dropped his voice. "But these rice planters putting all of their money into growing food. Food! 'Tis a fool's work, don't they see?"

"Aye, 'tis."

"One storm blowin' in, or weevils, or birds, or rice worms and 'tis all ruined."

"Foolish."

"Wait till ye see the rice birds sweep in. Black the sky will be with them, then the flock will roll down into the fields like a sailor full of grog. If the harvest hasn't been brought in by then, they'll strip these fields in a couple of days."

"Terrible thing." Nora watched his hard-muscled hands make their gestures.

"And the rats, God the rats." He shook his head.

"Rats!"

"They burrow into the dikes makin' holes that turn into leaks, then leaks into breaks. Some of the field hands? 'Tis their only job to kill ten, twenty rats a day. Have to turn in the rat tails as proof."

Nora winced. "No farmin' for me."

"I'm the carpenter here." He brushed sawdust off his thighs.

Nora looked at those thighs, as thick and hard as the flank of a draft horse.

Patrick pointed at the water buffaloes. "Their hooves are broader than a horse's. Don't get stuck in the muddy fields."

"Ah."

"Well, I'd best be gettin' back to me work." Patrick backed away from the rail. "Welcome to America, short Noreen. Pleased to meet ye."

"Ye as well." Nora began her stroll back to the house. He walked beside her for a while, then peeled off toward a small white building that sat among the mills.

The mistress was on the porch, hand raised to her brow in search of the girl. Feeling lighthearted at finding a country-man — one who called her a fair lass no less — Nora ran up the steps firing off her rehearsed begging for Clare, not noticing the hard, gray eyes that wanted to know where Nora had been for the last thirty minutes.

Rebecca Manning snatched up a broom and swung the handle into Nora's head, knocking her to the floor. Slamming it on the girl's shoulders and back, Rebecca screamed, "I don't want to hear another word about this. Your miserable sister! Nothing I can do. You don't even know where she is. How do you expect me to find her? Probably sold into a brothel by now!"

Nora scrambled down the steps, but Rebecca was all over her. The girl fell again, curled into a ball, covered her head as blows and screeches rained down. The porch door slammed. Someone was calling stop, Miss Rebecca stop —

Rebecca still screaming above those cries, her boots kicking up sand around Nora's face tucked under in vain, the broom handle cracking Nora's fingers. Nora heard the second voice coming closer. The female was saying that the Irish girl would be no good with broke fingers. The beating slowed. Rebecca's breaths came in short, feverish puffs. The broom handle fell to the ground. Nora opened her eyes too soon. Little boot heels pivoted, sending sand into Nora's face again. She heard the porch door slam. Nora managed to get up and as she rubbed the grit from her eyes, she saw Pearl nearby, flexing her fingers at her as if to say check that yours aren't broken, and then she ran back into the house.

That night, Nora curled into a ball again, this time against new aches and the deepest despair she'd ever known. She imagined the letter from Clare that was surely in the mail, on a ship or wagon somewhere, taking such a long time on its journey in this vast country, a journey she didn't understand having never written nor received a letter. In this letter, Clare would tell her that she was all right, that she'd found a grand job somewhere and was saving lots of money for another packet ticket. Above all, Clare would send Nora her address. But Nora couldn't imagine the letter she'd write back. How could she tell Clare she couldn't come?

Chapter Six

On Lowcountry rice plantations, everyone brought in the harvest. Even the children were important cogs in the well-oiled plantation machine. While the adults swung saw-edged hooks through the stalks heavy with rice, the children trailed behind, gathering the fallen stalks and laying them across the stubble to dry. The next day, the workers bundled the stalks into sheaves as tall as a sixteen-hand horse. Women carried the sheaves on their heads to the stacking area on higher ground, the threshing yard. Crowned with the sunlit bundles wider than their shoulders, the women were a golden stream flowing uphill from the riverside field.

Nora and Patrick sat on the crest of the river bluff watching the procession.

"What happens next?" Nora asked as she took fresh laundry out of a basket and folded it.

"Some of the stalks get threshed here, but most go to a mill in Georgetown."

"'Tis hard to believe, growing so much food that ye can sell most of it."

"Aye."

"How far is Georgetown?" She tucked little trousers—William's—into a second basket.

"By wagon, half a day. By boat on an outgoing tide, about an hour. See those out there?" Patrick pointed to half a dozen wooden barges tethered to the docks. "Rice flats. The hands will stack the sheaves in them, wait for the tide to turn toward Georgetown, then ride it all the way down."

"I've seen that muddy water hurrying by first one way, then the other. That's the tide?"

"Aye. Turns every six hours. At high tide, the water curls slowly back toward the sea for two hours, runs hard for two, turns in the slack again for two, then races back."

"How do they use those gates?" Nora gestured at a wooden frame and door that stood between a creek and a field.

"Trunk, not a gate. One of the hinged doors lets water flow into a sluiceway to the fields at high tide. The other on the opposite end lets water out at low tide."

Nora studied the sluggish river. "Have ye ever ridden a rice flat?"

"No!" Patrick's head snapped around. "If I fell in, I'd be lost."

"Me too. I'll not be gettin' in a boat ever again."

"The coffin boats." He shook his head. "I know."

A rock-hard lump rose in Nora's throat. Was it too soon to tell him about Clare? Would he care? This Patrick fella was hard to read. His eyes, on the rare occasion that he let her look into them, were like dark caves where there was not one blade of illumination. He seemed to have no interest in her soul, her da, her story. But right now, she felt she'd explode if she didn't get it out. "I have a twin," she said.

"Huh." He leaned back on his elbows to watch the clouds roll by.

Pretty much the response she expected, but there he was, just inches away, within hugging distance, and she wanted those arms — or one, she'd settle for one — around her. She plowed on. "Mrs. Manning contracted for the two of us to come here, but the captain in New York pulled Clare off the gangplank seconds before she would've stepped on board."

"Huh. So where she is now?" He looked at her with no more expression than a potato.

"In New York. I mean, I think she's in New York. I'm waiting to hear from her." Her eyes pleaded for a glimmer of sympathy, of comprehension, of shared Irish misery — anything.

"If she's as strong as ye, she'll be fine." Patrick shrugged.

Nora pressed wrinkles out of folded shirt over and over, the kind of wrinkles that would surrender only to a hot iron, but she kept on pressing.

A shriek rose from the fields. The detested driver, a lumbering black man who was known for jacking up the cruelty when the white overseer was within earshot, was beating a laborer down into the stubble. The overseer ran to grab one of the worker's arms. The overseer and the driver dragged the worker from the field. They tied him to a tree, ripped off his shirt and whipped him with leather straps, each of their blows answered with screams. At first, all the other field hands stood frozen, watching grim-faced as they were meant to. Then a couple of men moved toward the beating, their scythes clenched in rock-hard fists, but others pulled them back.

Nora's hands flew to her cheeks. "Patrick, do something. They'll break his back."

"No, they won't."

She shot him a startled look. "How do ye know?"

"He's a prime field hand. They'll stop. Too young and

valuable to cripple he is, worth about fifteen hundred dollars. The planters won't cripple a slave these days. They cost too much," Patrick said. "So, they hire Irish now for the most dangerous jobs, the dike repairs and land clearing. There's a saying: Give the Irish the work that's death to field hands and mules."

"But not ye."

"No, not yet anyway. Look." He pointed at the driver and overseer to show they were untying the man's arms. The man dropped to his hands and knees, heaving for breath, his skin glistening with blood. A woman ran to him, tried to help him up. He pushed her away. "Couple of years ago, Manning had forty Irish lads in the fields building a new dike—eight feet wide, one hundred feet long, three feet high. If he lost one Paddy from the bog, or four or five Paddys, who'd care? Couple of 'em did die, I heard. Never knew what happened, really. I stayed away."

Nora stared at him. "Stayed away from your own?" He wouldn't look at her and for the moment she was glad she couldn't see into those dark caves.

"I didn't want them to drag me down there too, ye understand," he said. "Had to look out for meself."

Nora picked up her baskets and walked away.

* * *

"What'd you think this place was going to be like?" Pearl said in a steely whisper as they washed the supper dishes beside the cistern.

"I didn't know anythin'. How could I? I didn't know a town, nor castle, not even a church. I never heard the word plantation." Nora said. "Why don't these laborers run away?"

"Into that?" Pearl pointed at the maze of waterways lined

with the deep, swallowing mud and razor-sharp oyster beds. "Them flats and rowboats, they get locked up at night. Or that?" Her finger swung to the single road off the plantation, a mere ribbon in miles of jungle. "Somebody tried years ago, though, long before I got here," Pearl said. "People say it was a field hand too young and proud to bend any more. Mas' put ads in the papers and signs on the buildings in Georgetown and Charleston. Everybody waited for that man to get drug back here, get whipped, but he never turned up."

"So, it's possible he's free somewhere."

"Dead more like it."

"Ye ever think about runnin' away?"

Pearl put her finger to her mouth and stole a look at the big house. "Sshh!"

"Where did all these people come from?"

"Isaiah, he the oldest slave here. He say his people from a place in Africa where they grew rice. The men, they hollowed out trees to send water to the fields, built dikes like these here out of mud. The women knew to bury the seeds with their heels just enough so the seeds wouldn't float off when the field got flooded. Years ago, white men stole them, brought them here for what they know 'bout that. To make all this money."

Nora shot her a horrified look. "Stole them?"

"Sshh!" Pearl looked around again. "How you think so many black people ended up here?" She waved a glistening plate in Nora's face.

So, it's stupid I am then, is it? Because I've never heard of Africa? Anger burned through Nora's veins like kerosene, but for once she decided to keep quiet and just dry the blasted plate. To be ripped away from the only place you've ever known, to never see again the people who formed you and cherished you, to miss the smell of the soil of home before the rain and the feel of it softening after — bloody right she knew how that felt. Ripped away yes, because she and her people never wanted to leave their beloved green isle. She cursed the British who were happy for the fungus that had sown the famine that gave their lords and dukes a reason to cleanse the country of the sub-human race with their sloth and their pagan myths. Nora's country had been starving for four years, dead bodies on every road and field. Da was dead by now. She knew it in her bones.

Pearl saw the tears streaming down Nora's cheeks. "What you got to cry 'bout?"

"The great hunger. My family. My Da. My sister."

"You said you left her behin'."

"Yes, but not in Ireland. In New York with a stranger. We survived six weeks at sea only for me to leave her with a stranger in a strange country."

"Why'd you do that?"

"That bastard — "

Pearl pulled Nora away from the washtub and kitchen house. Behind a tree, Nora told her what had happened. "Mrs. Manning won't send for her and — "

Pearl sucked air through her teeth. "That's what that beating was about?"

"Yes."

"But your sister knows where you are. She can write to you, let you know she's all right. Y'all can read, can't you?"

"Yes, well, sort of. But she may not be all right. God help me, Pearl, she could be living on the streets."

"Lawd, Lawd." Pearl pulled her into a fierce hug. After a while, she offered a corner of her apron for Nora's runny nose, prompting more tears. Finally, she grabbed Nora's shoulders. "Why y'all run away from your home?"

"We were driven out. It began with the wettest, coldest spring three years ago, the likes of which we'd never seen. The rain kept on for weeks. The sheep shivered in the pastures against great squalls that pushed across the fields and slopes. One day, a thick fog rolled in from the sea, bringing death but we didn't know it yet. 'Twas thick as wool and it settled over the fields. Going nowhere it was. Smelled funny, too, ye know? Rotten. The dogs howled at the smell of it, trying to warn us maybe. Da walked out to check on our field. He came back lookin' like he'd seen the devil himself. White spots were on the potato leaves, he said. The blight. The next day, the leaves were brown, the stems were black. All across the fields, our neighbors dug up the potatoes with their hands, every potato oozing with the slime. The wailing and the moaning cut through the fog to shake me bones. Me and me sisters and brother and Mam ran out to fight our way through the fog. The potatoes in people's hands, they were black. People kept clawing into the ground to dig up another, but they were all black."

"Didn't you plant no other kind of food?"

Nora shook her head. "Some turnips, but the potato had fed us well for generations. We didn't know any better. The next year, same disease, more starvin'. Me little sisters, brother, Mam—all died."

Pearl's hands flew to her face.

"The landlord sent the soldiers to evict us. They threw our things out of the cottage, tore it down, left nothing but the door frame. Clare clung to it for hours." Nora burst into tears. "Clare, now dead maybe. My Da, gone to the workhouse, he's dead for certain."

"You don't know that." Pearl touched Nora's arm.

"No one survives the workhouse."

"At least you knew him."

Nora lifted her eyes. "Knew him?"

"My father lived on another plantation. I saw him once." Pearl looked over at the street, where women were gathering. "He married my mother on a Sunday, she told me." She wouldn't meet Nora's eyes. "Come on," she said, taking her hand.

Chapter Seven

The women eased their fannies onto pine straw mats that encircled a small fire. "*He'lenga* time," Pearl said as she and Nora walked up. "Sittin' time," she said, when the women talked about what had happened that day, or the month or year before, or sometimes, if the children had crept into their circle, how the world came to be.

"Aye, we had such a thing," Nora said. "We called it *bansheanchas*." Women's lore. The stories of the generations.

As the girls sat down in the second row of mats, the women in front flicked glances their way and gave upward nods. Above the distant marsh, egrets flew by, floating down like white cinders toward a certain spit of land as they always did around dusk. For such large birds, Nora thought, they were surprisingly graceful, with their papery wings lazily pumping and long legs trailing behind. They landed in twos and threes on a moss-bearded oak tree. Soon its limbs were dripping with egrets, all of them spread out evenly, like ornaments hung just so on a tree. This familiar winding down of humans and creatures at the end of the day comforted Nora.

Behind the women's circle, a few men lit fires in baskets atop stands to keep biting insects away. Children ran their sticks through the dirt and chased dogs too wily for them. A pair of elderly women drifted in, stiff-jointed and slow, and settled in the front row. Conversation began bubbling in the rhythmic language — part English part something else — that Nora loved to hear. With the way it rolled off their tongues, she found it almost musical. She yearned to understand the stories they might spin tonight, for storytelling created bonds, especially in fire-golden circles such as this. Theirs would be stories of cruelty and pain — for their caged lives here were like nothing Nora had ever seen — as well as stories of love and compassion given and accepted among themselves. She meant to learn that language, so that maybe eventually they'd trust her. Maybe one day the seeds of connection between her and them would be sown, but she'd have to be patient.

Pearl had explained the plantation's pecking order on the way over. The big house slaves, with their domestic skills that pleased the missus's palate and smoothed her sheets, their good English, and in some cases their ability to read, outranked the field hands. Big house slaves had better food, better cabins, and more freedom of movement. Most important, their families stayed whole. Their husbands and children didn't get sold without serious cause.

But *he'lenga* time took place outside — the field hands' realm — so the house servants deferred here. They weighed carefully every word and gesture. *Plus, you're outnumbered ten to one,* Nora thought. Bess and Lizzybet walked up, gave friendly nods to the women who'd looked over, and sat beside Pearl.

The men, in a caste of their own, knew to stay quiet if they were going to be allowed to listen from the fringes.

The women pulled long blades of marsh grass out of sacks and began weaving them into the half-worked baskets in their laps. Someone handed Pearl the beginning of something round — not bulbous like a basket, but flat as a plate. A spray of the pale green grass sprung from the side like a cock's tail. Pearl pinched the supple blades together, looped a palmetto strip around them, and tucked the end of it between the new coil and the one below with what looked like an animal rib. The air was heavy with the smell of the grass, sweet as freshly mown hay. Lizzybet clenched between her knees an enormous oval basket that flared at the middle. Her wrapping and tucking seemed to be turning the shape back toward narrow. An older woman with a clay pipe in her mouth was adding a shallow lip to the edge of a wide platter.

"That's a fanner," Pearl told Nora. "After women flail the rice off the stalks, they pour it into a fanner, toss it in the air. Wind takes away the husk, clean rice lands in the basket," she said.

Gossip was starting up in the front row. Nora could tell it was gossip because of the gloating and judgment that shone on every face. Also, the tempo had quickened and there was a lot of hissing and tongue clicking. Nora heard the men muttering *she-she talk* with contempt, but they were leaning in to hear better.

Nora noticed one man who wasn't leaning in at all. In fact, he slouched against a tree, engaged in the socializing only with his gaze. In one hand, he held a bulging burlap sack and in the other a fiddle. *A fiddle! A fiddle?* Nora couldn't believe her eyes. If he'd held a leprechaun by the neck, she couldn't have been more astonished. At home, traveling fiddlers had occasionally stopped by to play for their supper, back when there was enough to share. They taught her da how to play a few songs and he in turn had taught her.

Nora grabbed Pearl's arm. "That man is a holding fiddle," she said. "A fiddle!"

"Yea, that's Tobias," Pearl said with a shrug. "He'll be comin' this a way in a minute."

Tobias was already sauntering toward them, goofy smile on his baby face.

"Shoooo … he thinks he fishin' with some mighty fine bait," Pearl whispered. "But he ain't."

Tobias was a short character with sloped shoulders and stubby legs that did him no favors when female eyes were upon him. With his knock-kneed legs pumping, he looked more toddler than seducer. Nora mashed the smile out of her lips.

Tobias caught her mashing and straightened up into all of the five feet and four inches that God had bestowed. He'd always bragged that he was descended from aristocracy, the kings of Africa's Mende tribe. His listeners were unwilling to grant to him the prestige of royalty, but they did find him amusing and he was the only person — giant or runt — on the plantation who could play music, which they cherished. This he knew well. With that currency, he tried to win bed partners. "Leetle fiddle make a big soun'," he'd promised many times as he wiggled fiddle and pelvis.

Tobias dropped the bag at Pearl's feet and looked down at the top of her head. "Hey, pretty red bird," he said.

"Hey, Tobias." Pearl didn't look up.

"I pulled this 'yuh bulrush for you this afternoon down to the marsh."

"That right?" Pearl asked, still not looking up.

"Jus' fuh you," Tobias said.

"I 'spect you heard about Nora here," Pearl said, nodding in her direction.

He dipped his chin hello but kept his hopeful brown eyes on Pearl.

"A fiddle? Where'd ye get that?" Nora asked.

Finally Tobias looked at Nora. His lips parted in a broad smile, revealing a thicket of yellow teeth. "Mas' Manning chose me out of all these Oakwood people 'yuh to send to Charleston to learn how to play it. Fuh parties."

"Well, what're ye waiting for?" Nora asked.

The woman with the pipe in her mouth took it out and said two words to Tobias.

With a nod, Tobias tucked the chinrest under his chin, held the bow straight out from his shoulder, and with great flourish drove the bow into the strings. He took his time pulling the bow across one particular string to produce a long, low note, then pushed it back across another. Everyone heard that cue, and the singing took off.

Oh, Jesus, My Saviour, on Thee I'll depend

When troubles are near me you'll be my friend

I'm troubled

I'm troubled

I'm troubled in mind

If Jesus don't help me I surely will die

The tempo was a slow plod that sent people to gentle swaying. Tobias wove through the crowd like a piper, bowing and sweeping. Pearl gave him a thin smile when he looked her way. Instantly, his chest puffed up. As he finished the last notes of the song, he worked his way back to her.

"What you want to hear, red bird?" Tobias asked.

Nora stood up and reached for the fiddle. "Could I please? I know a couple of — "

Gasps went up in the front row. Bess and Lizzybet wagged their heads at this latest blunder. Every woman turned around to look at Tobias, swollen with wrath as they expected. Now at center stage, he hugged his fiddle to his chest and fixed shimmering eyes on the white fool with her hands out.

Pearl muttered, "Nora, what you thinkin'?"

At this, Nora winced and cursed herself being so stupid. She could hear the front-row gallery, really cranked up now, afire with buzzing and hissing. Feeling Pearl stand, Nora opened her eyes to see what would happen next.

Everyone — the front-row crowd, the men who were pretending not to be listening, Bess, Lizzybet and Tobias — was staring at Nora. A few of the children ran over to see what was up.

With a sigh, Pearl gave the basket back to the woman who had handed it to her. She led Nora to the street lined with doorless, windowless cabins, Nora dying to disappear into one of them and never ever come out. To her surprise, Pearl pulled her into one, the cabin with seashells lined up in a row along the foundation. Five mats made of dingy ticking sat atop mounds of the silvery moss that hung from every tree on the plantation. Pearl sat on one and patted it for Nora to join her. From behind the mat, Pearl pulled an unbleached white seed sack.

"Want to show you something," she said.

Nora waited, her cheeks finally cooling.

"My mother, she somewhere I can't get to, like your sister," Pearl said as she spread the sack across her knees. "She gave me this."

Nora tilted her head a little. "Bess isn't your mother?"

Pearl stiffened. "No. Why would you say that?"

Nora didn't have an answer and, given the heat coming off Pearl, she said nothing.

"She ain' my mother." Pearl's brown eyes brimmed with pain. "Don't ever say that."

"I'm sorry. It's just that seeing ye together — "

"She's tried to mother me since I come 'yuh. But I ain' seen Mama since I was nine. I got sold to Mr. Manning and she didn't."

Nora grabbed Pearl's arm. "He took ye from your mother when ye were just nine years old?"

Pearl's face crumpled as she ran her fingers over the sack's three tiny white patches tacked on with blue thread. The sack was lumpy at the bottom where small round things had settled. "My mother give me this right before they took me away. She said it would always be filled with her love. I never saw her again."

Nora imagined the mother's frantic hands filling the sack with whatever she could find in a hurry to sustain and comfort her baby, their agonized good-bye, the collapsing, the constant hole in the heart. Nora knew that hole.

"One day, when we together again, we going to pick last names. I'm going to embroider our names on here."

"'Twill be a glorious day," Nora said, stroking Pearl's arm.

"They give us only a first name. What y'all need a last name for when you belong to me, I guess they think."

Nora didn't trust herself to speak. There were no words that could soothe such tragedy.

"My mother will be so proud I can read and write. I learned how when I came here. The missus taught me. Said it against the law but it was her Christian duty."

Christian duty? thought Nora. *Mrs. Manning?* But all she said was, "So proud she'll be." She patted the sack. "Do ye want to show me what's inside?"

Pearl reached into the sack stained with long-ago spills and brought out ten pecans. "My mother gave me these and said not to cry, so I cry all over her chest. Said she'd find a way to come and get me. How long that be, I asked. She say she don't know. We both knew she'd need wings. Every slave dreams about having wings. Like the rice birds. And she gave me this." Pearl pulled out a tattered little dress and handed it to Nora.

A child's thin cotton plaid dress, one that a mother knew would be the last dress she'd ever make for her little girl. Nora smoothed it across her knees with reverence. It was filthy but expertly made, with tiny gathers at the top of the sleeves to make them pucker perfectly on the shoulders. Barely a yard of fabric, Nora guessed, and yet so powerful. The mother's presence still alive all these years later.

"Why didn't Mr. Manning buy your mother too?" Nora asked.

"Cost too much. Isaiah, he hears him and the missus talk? Isaiah say slave prices been goin' up for forty years since that law passed that say you can't bring Africans over the ocean no more. Rice planters all over Charleston selling slaves to new cotton plantations west of here, Isaiah say."

"So Mr. Manning bought who he could afford."

"Guess I didn't cost much."

"Like me," Nora said with bitterness.

"Least you ain't no slave. They don't own you. *Own* you like a chair or a chicken or something. You free to run down that road out there."

Nora blinked hard. She could do no such thing for four years, and the color of her skin would make little difference to those chasing her and beating her, but she said nothing.

"What's yer mother's name?" Nora asked, handing the dress back.

"Rose."

"Where is she?"

"A plantation called Millberry Place. She waitin' for me to come get her, I just know it."

"Where is that?"

"I don't know."

They sat with their sorrows for a while. Pearl wiped her nose with her skirt and put everything back in the bag. "Time fuh you to get on back," she said.

Nora squeezed Pearl's hand before she stood. This was a story shared, the most painful one Nora could imagine.

Blue shadows cast by the massive oak trees bathed the side of the big house as Nora approached it. In the dying light, she could see a woman in the dining room window watching her come, the only woman at Oakwood who could stand there with idle arms crossed. As soon as Nora got close enough to read her expression in the thin light, Rebecca walked away.

Something moved in the sky—an enormous bird circling the clearing between Nora, the house, and the creek. Churning butter, the slaves called that. Hunting. A sea hawk it was, the bird matched in wingspan and ferocity only by the plantation's eagles. It passed over her head—wings the color of burnt sugar spread wide, white underwings and belly—close enough for her to see the deadly talons. Suddenly the hawk tucked its wings and plummeted toward the dock where a scrawny kitten worried a fish head. The talons flared. The kitten darted. Too late. As the bird pumped away over the marsh, the cat's entrails fell in clotted black strings, backlit by the purple smears of dusk's light.

Chapter Eight

Edward Manning was a master on fire. He was certain that his good luck was about to run out. The crop of 1849 was on track to be his most bountiful in decades. It had survived pests, fires, hurricanes, freshets, and disease. By mid-September, he had brought in half of the harvest, but there were hundreds of acres to go. September was the worst month for hurricanes. Rice birds. Fire. Something was going to happen. So, he pulled in every able-bodied slave on the plantation, even the rat catchers and duck hunters, to wrap up the harvest. Every man, woman, and child hauled sheaves to the threshing yard, crisscrossed them in rectangles six feet high to await hand processing, or carried them to the flats to be shipped to Georgetown mills. All other tasks were on hold. Torches burned all night.

One afternoon, as the bustle in the threshing yard went on in the distance, Nora hung laundry behind the house as slowly as she dared. An Oakwood flat full of supplies was due back from Georgetown, but Nora had no interest in lamp oil, coffee, molasses, or broadaxes. The mailbag was scheduled to be on that flat. Her eyes went from creek to wet socks to creek to wet tablecloth until the laundry basket was empty, but she didn't want to go back to the house for the second one. To distract herself from the empty creek, she turned her attention to the threshing yard.

Four women slapped rice-heavy stalks against a wooden frame anchored by a trough. Others scooped the rice from the trough and poured it into fanner baskets. The tossing began. Up in the air went the grain, away in the wind went the papery hulls, and down came naked rice. With every motion, the women sang. Every task on the plantation had a song, Nora had learned, and every voice joined in. No one had to explain to her that it made the work go faster.

The women emptied their fanners into what looked like an upright log—the top third was hollowed out—and they took turns pounding wooden paddles into the rice. From time to time, they looked into the logs, eventually putting their paddles away to scoop and pour the rice into barrels. The overseer stood nearby watching this final collection of the prized clean rice, so easy to steal.

The sound of other voices floated in—men singing a rowing song!—and that meant the flat. Nora ran to the dock to fidget and squint down the creek. Finally, she saw the flat rounding a bend in the creek, slow as an old cow. Four men—two fore and two aft—steered with long poles. One sang the song's main thread and the others answered with the age-old chorus. Minutes later, they were unloading crates, sacks, and a scuffed leather satchel fastened with straps. Nora grabbed it and ran to the house.

In the parlor, Rebecca received the satchel and tried to dismiss Nora, who begged to stay and watch. The mistress took her time untying the bundles and leafing through their contents. Nora stood in the doorway shifting foot to foot. Rebecca pulled a dirty envelope out of the mix and gave it lengthy consideration. Nora could see only the back of it, but it was Rebecca's spiteful dawdling that lifted her heart. That was the letter. She just knew it. Clare was alive! Nora watched the mistress's cadaverous fingers turn the envelope over, saw the gray eyes cut over to her there in the doorway. Nora steadied herself against the doorframe. At last Rebecca held the letter out to her with an air of benevolence. Nora snatched it and ran for the back door.

"See that you finish hanging that second basket of laundry first," Rebecca said.

After the dishtowels were flung on the line willy-nilly, Nora raced to the nearest tree to hide.

September 5, 1849

Dear Nora,

Oh, dear Sister, I'm in a bad way. 'Tis a nightmare, this New York. That old woman on the dock took me ticket. I'm living in what they call a boarding house. Sleeping on the floor. Rats all around. That woman sent me off to work for a Mrs. VanDerwerker, a witch for certain. I don't know how to do anything with what she's calling toilets and fine china. Beat me she did when she found me stirring the fire with a ladle. Beat me harder when I cut up a bedroom rug to cover the stairs, me not knowing it was her favorite rug and thinking it would be grand to make the steps warmer. I can't answer the front door to suit her. I told her our cottage didn't have a door, so how was I to know there's a special way to answer one and she yelled something about not knowing she'd hired low Irish. What do ye reckon that is? She feeds me and the other maids nothing but rice, bread, and some kind of oily fish.

On Sunday, I ran back to the Seaport to ask when that captain's boat will be back. It isn't real regular, people say. I'll go back every Sunday to find him. I think he'll know me, since he knows your face. Surely the regret will be rattling his bones for what he did to us and he'll let me get on his ship with no ticket.

I have nowhere else to go. Every hiring sign says any color or country but Irish. Why do they hate us so much?

'Twas so daft of me to fish for Ticket in me skirt so them other girls could shove around me. Hope they have the runs for years.

What is your mistress doing to get me to Charleston? Hope your Letter will arrive soon. They say the boats that carry mail take ten days to get here from South Carolina. Ye can write to me at Smith's boarding house on Essex Street, New York.

All my love,

Clare

Nora's tears of relief fell on the letter in soft splats. Clare was safe, more or less, had a roof over her head, had food, bad as it sounded, but food. No ticket, but Nora had assumed as much. No imminent danger. This was as good as Nora could hope for.

That night, Nora watched for the best moment to beg Rebecca for some paper so she could write a letter — after supper, table cleared without breakage, two glasses of wine in the mistress's stomach, William tucked in bed, Mr. Manning smoking his pipe on the porch. Rebecca gave her a discarded magazine and pointed to the white spaces around the articles. Plenty of room there in the margins, she said.

September 30, 1849

Dear Clare,

I cried all over your Letter. 'Tis bad news I have. I am not in Charleston. I'm at a farm that's a two-day wagon ride from Charleston. They call it a plantation. 'Tis a dangerous, hot, watery, wild place. Wild hogs, wild cats big as sheep, deer, foxes, raccoons, possum, snakes, wild turkeys and those are just the scary things on land. The water harbors more.

Black people work in these horrible fields and waters. Stolen like ye they were, from a Country on the other side of the world, so they'll not be running away to get back to it. The master owns them and can sell them like animals. Some work in the house with me. One of them is nineteen like us. Name is Pearl. She was sold away from her mother when she was a wee lass. I think she's me friend. 'Tis hard to tell.

Dear Sister, this mistress will not send for ye and I've been beaten for begging. She says she's written to someone to ask for a refund for ye, as if ye were a lost Parcel. Does your mistress pay ye at all? Maybe ye can buy another ticket?

The Mannings might go back to Charleston in November for what they call the social season. If I hear of that I will write to ye. Maybe by then Mrs. Manning will soften and send another ticket.

Please write soon. I'm so sorry to have to give ye this news.

With love,

Nora

Chapter Nine

In early November, with the rice long gone on its way to Europe and the vegetable fields turned for their winter rest, the plantation's most dangerous work of the year began. The overseer sent the field hands back to the scalped rice fields to repair the complex hydraulic system of dikes, floodgates, trunks, ditches, and drains. Every man and every boy taller than five feet received his daily task, be it shoveling mud out of clogged ditches, rebuilding the embankments around each field, or clearing cordgrass, needlerush, bulrush, and cattails from the muck. With every sucking step, the men watched for snakes, alligators, knife-sharp oyster shells, and reckless axes.

Ten slaves had died of disease and accidents during September's frenetic harvest, so Edward Manning conscripted Patrick into the watery hell. For two weeks, as the creeks ran cold and colder, the men pushed shovels into ditches, slammed axes into rotted wood sluiceways, and dug out the splintered chunks. In the evenings, when by luck or design Nora came across Patrick on the grounds, he was increasingly bitter and aloof. One night, she found him at the hearth in his little tabby shed offering his wrinkled feet to the fire. He barely acknowledged her in the doorway — she'd let herself in — while he ranted about freezing his bollocks off and Mr. Manning having no right to do this to him, a skilled carpenter. He scared her, this angry Patrick shouting that he had to get away from this place, but she didn't want to go to her lonely attic. She said how glad she was that he hadn't been injured in that creek, how worried she was every morning when he went down to the fields, axe over his shoulder. A carpenter like him — Mr. Manning shouldn't risk such talent to hard labor. All of this she said from the doorway, staring at the back of his head, hoping he'd invite her to his hearth.

Apparently, he'd heard every word. He spun around to look at her with surprise, almost as if seeing her for the first time. Nora squirmed under such odd scrutiny. The eyes — cold as the set of his jaw and calculating something, it seemed. What did he suddenly see in her? Whatever it was, it wasn't romance. Just when she turned to go, he held out his hand and beckoned.

She sat beside him, still uneasy with the way he was looking her over, as if she was an ewe at a county fair and he was a judge. He thanked her for saying she worried about him and then he went silent again. The fire popped and hissed in its humble cove. Inches away from his eyes now, she could see tiny reflections of the fire flicking this way and that. The corners of his eyes softened as a whisper of a smile formed on his lips. He called her Noreen. He asked about Clare for the first time. Her words tumbled out and he seemed to find them fascinating. By the time the fire had died, they had driven their conversation through her village back home and his. Reaching for her hand, he pulled her up to stand. At the door they said goodnight and as she walked across the grounds to the big house, she put her nose to her hand to savor the smell of him.

The next evening, with her work completed and the mistress in bed with her vaporous ailments, Nora raced to the dock to pretend to watch the egrets on their nightly fly-by to their roosting tree. Within minutes, he appeared behind her, horse blanket in hand, inviting her to watch November's harvest moonrise.

He led her to a remote place on the riverbank where the golden orb was making its climb above the drowning marsh. A vast lake had appeared there overnight. Only the tips of the spartina grass were visible above the gilded water.

"I've never seen the water so high," Nora said. She didn't know what he was up to—horse blanket and all—but she had a feeling that more than her hand might be smelling like him later.

"They call it the king tide," he said, leaning closer to brush her hair off her neck. "Highest tide of the year."

She stared straight ahead as she absorbed the warmth of his fingers.

"So pretty ye are." He ran his hand up and down her back.

She turned toward him so his hand could cup her shoulder, which it did, then she leaned toward him so he could pull her closer, which he did, then she closed her eyes. He kissed her, not like the giddy boys at home but like a grown, experienced man, a man who savored her taste, her breath, her soft lips, like a man who meant what he said about her being pretty.

After, she felt pretty giddy herself. To tease a smile out of him, she said the first thing that came into her head, something ridiculous, something that she knew would never be true of someone from Connaught. "Ye're not a Protestant, are ye, with no notion of the occasion of sin?" She wiggled her shoulders at this hint of sin, and instantly wished she hadn't. She'd never mastered flirting.

But he did smile. "Oh, I know an occasion of sin when I see it," he said as he pressed her down onto the blanket.

* * *

The next day, Patrick's gang began digging twenty feet of rotten sluiceway out of a dike. When the disintegrating trunk bed lay glistening in the sunlight, the men laid into it with axes.

The driver ordered Patrick and two boys—adolescent brothers—down the embankment to dig out more dirt along the sides. The three of them were in water up to their knees. Mingo, the smaller of the boys, struggled with an enormous shovel. As the driver moved out of sight, Mingo squatted to rest for a moment, elbows on his knees, head down.

"Son," Patrick said to Mingo, not knowing his name. "Ye should know better than to get low like that in this creek." As he reached to pull the boy out of the crouch that made him look like small prey, he saw movement in the water twenty feet away. A gnarled black head, its two reptilian eyes barely above the surface, was splitting the water into heart-stopping ripples as it raced for the boy.

"Gator!" Patrick shouted. He grabbed Mingo's arm.

The boy looked back where Patrick pointed, a fatal delay. The alligator lunged with lightning speed. The endless teeth sank into an arm, tearing Mingo out of Patrick's grip. Mingo pounded on the hideous head as it jerked him backwards into the channel. His screams and Patrick's cries for help brought men spilling down the embankment to throw everything they had—shovels, axes, pickaxes—at the creature. From other rice fields, slaves and the overseer came running. The alligator rolled, came back up in a nauseating show that it still had the boy by the arm, and then rolled back down. Mingo's little brother dove into the churning creek, but the men hauled him back to the embankment. The alligator's massive tail whipped back and forth across the water's surface, propelling him and his prize downstream. No one could look away and no one could leave. The men paced along the dike, hands clamped over mouths. Patrick fell to his knees, heaving for breath. Finally, someone took off to find Mingo's mother. The little brother stumbled along behind.

The overseer waved everyone off the dike into the work

yard. The men milled about like dazed cattle, dreading the mother's arrival but feeling they should stay out of respect. When she came screaming toward them, five men ran away nonetheless. Fingers pointed at Patrick, who braced as she came at him, hands in the air. They landed on his chest to pound the story out of him. He told her what happened, not that she heard a word. Screaming questions that had no answers, she tore at his shirt and batted away the frantic clutches of her younger son. Patrick tried to grab her wrists to stop her, but she was a storm of claws and arms. Finally, he gave her a good shove. Stunned for a second, oblivious to the circle of men staring at her, she looked around with unseeing eyes. Then she ran for the dike, chased by her son and two wobbly-legged men.

* * *

At dusk, every soul on the plantation gathered outside a slave cabin bathed in the firelight cast by the torches. The mother sat straight-legged in the dirt while women fanned her with cloths. Rebecca Manning held the mother's lifeless hand, and with her other hand pinned William to her chest. The child looked around wide-eyed at the wailing crowd, the flames, the dogs sprawled on their bellies waiting for something to happen. Inside the cabin, the sobs of Mingo's little brother scoured the roof timbers.

"Jes' thirteen," Pearl whispered to Nora. They stood near one of the torches. Beside Pearl, Lizzybet and Caroline held onto each other, limp with grief, alert to every movement in the crowd. "Everyone's worried because he died bad," Pearl said.

"Such a terrible way to die," Nora said as she shook her head.

"No, no. Dyin' bad means he died without anybody 'spectin' it was comin'," Pearl said. "Nobody had time to help him cross the river to the promised land. Now they havin' worriment about Mingo's spirit roamin' the earth, tormentin' folks."

As if all of us aren't already tormented enough, Nora thought.

A wagon rattled up to the crowd and people moved aside to let it through. Alongside the shrouded body sat the four mud-covered men who had found it in the creek. The mother ran for her boy, and the men didn't stop her, for they had swaddled him in a tarpaulin to hide the gaping arm socket and bite marks. They'd covered his face too, pretending they hadn't seen it, to honor the custom of waiting for the mother's permission to do so. The little brother tore out of the cabin and joined his mother at the wagon. Climbing in, they fell upon Mingo's body, buried their faces in his chest. The mother started to unswaddle her baby. One of the men touched her arm to stop her, triggering her keening in the mysterious language that Nora still couldn't understand. Meanwhile, a mile away in the place in the piney woods where the eternal sleepers slept, men hurried to dig Mingo's grave before sunset to ensure that his soul would find peace.

In the morning, people drifted through the forest to arrive at the grave site and watch four of Oakwood's strongest field hands lower the pine box into the ground. They made sure that Mingo's head pointed west, according to custom. Shovels got to work and the dirt hit the pine lid in scratchy splats until a mound of soil rose above the earth like a fresh scar. People stepped forward to scatter broken dishes, pieces of mirrors, and blue bottles over the grave—to protect the boy's family from another too-soon death, Pearl whispered to Nora. Patrick stood on Nora's other side, his fingers looped through hers.

A clump of women helped the mother toward the mound of dirt and handed her Mingo's favorite things to put on top—several bowls of rice, an empty tin can with rosined strings, the hickory sticks that teased his music out of the strings, his collection of horse teeth, a felt hat.

Edward and Rebecca Manning waited on the sidelines,

Bibles tucked against their chests. When Mingo's mother had backed away with the help of steadying hands, Edward approached the grave. He opened his Bible and read a few psalms, every word mouthed by those gathered 'round.

After a minute of silence, Tobias stepped out of the crowd with his fiddle. For the moment not a showman, just a mourner, he began a slow song that sent people to swaying. The men sang the first verse, the women sang the response. Several had their hands on the shoulders of Mingo's mother, swaying and looking skyward. On the second verse, the women led. For the third verse, the men joined them, Near the end, many voices were breaking. *Such a beautiful way to honor the dead in this ugly place*, thought Nora, dabbing her apron at her eyes. Mam and Nora's brother and sisters had been dumped in a hurry into a common grave with the neighbors.

Tobias lowered his fiddle, blubbering and sniffling. People looked at him to start another song. The mother deserved another round for her boy there in the ground, taken too soon. Tobias couldn't manage another, though. He put his fiddle down on the pine straw and went to her to hug her. She was the only woman who'd never laughed at him.

Before Pearl could stop her, Nora picked up the fiddle and bow. Closing her eyes, she pulled the bow across the strings, producing a song like nothing anyone at Oakwood had ever heard, the kind of song that could be owned by only one singer at a time. Mellow and golden, the melody fell upon all hearts like a soft rain. Rebecca's face softened with surprise and a bit of awe. Nora's fingers moved up and down the neck to claim her notes that were marred by the ragged bow, but no one cared. The soul of the mournful song was clear enough. Loss. Pain. Despair. The Irish girl's music swept through the crowd, moving even Patrick to tears. When she lifted the bow from the final note, the only sound in the forest was the rustling in the wind-tossed pines.

She opened her eyes. People still swayed with the rhythm reverberating in their bones. Rebecca Manning was covering her mouth with her hand. Mingo's mother held her hands to her cheeks and Tobias, coming at her for his fiddle, was glaring at Nora with blistering hatred.

Chapter Ten

Nora stared into the upper window of what the mistress called a long-case clock. It was long all right. Taller than Isaiah, tallest person in the household. The plate with the numbers painted around the edge mystified her. One of the black arrows had just inched closer to twelve, she was pretty sure. She pressed her nose to the glass to try to catch it moving for certain.

William appeared in the hall, saw her squinting into the cabinet, and ran to her with raised arms to be picked up. Holding him on her hip, she pointed at the black arrow that she was keeping an eye on. "That hand has moved," she said. "But how?"

His brow crumpled into pudgy furrows.

"And that," she pointed at the silver medallion swinging side to side behind the lower glass door. "What do ye figure tells that to move?" she asked.

William turned his face to hers, waiting for the answer.

"I think it's faeries. They do things like that ye know," Nora said.

The boy peered into the corners of the cabinet. "Faeries?" he asked.

"But how do they get in and out is what I want to know." Nora ran her fingers along the crack between door and cabinet frame.

"Don't touch that," Rebecca said, appearing out of thin air as usual. "That clock's very valuable, nearly a hundred and thirty years old. Made in England," she said as she pulled her son out of Nora's arms.

"Sorry, ma'am. No harm done," Nora said. The little arms leaving her neck brought hot tears to the backs of her eyes.

"My grandfather brought it here from his Barbados plantation. It's one of the first things he put in this house."

"Ah," Nora said in the long, drawn-out way that people do to imply that they're impressed, except she wasn't.

"Brought his Barbados slaves, too, to tame what was a swamp out there in 1712." Rebecca stared out the open door at the distant river. "Seven years from the first cypress tree felled to the first fifteen-acre field smoothed and planted. That took vision, Nora. Vision, tenacity, and an iron will."

Slaves, thought Nora. *Greed.*

"William here, he's named after him," Rebecca said as she stroked her son's hair. "You're going to be a great man too, aren't you darling?"

"Ah," Nora said again, this time with tenderness if not interest.

Isaiah appeared in the porch doorway and held out two apples. "Mas' William," he called. "Them horses, they gin'lly hungry 'bout this time of day. You comin'?"

William wiggled to get down. Rebecca watched him leave with Isaiah then turned to Nora. "I've got something for you upstairs. You and Pearl." She took a step toward the washroom in the back. "Pearl!" she shouted

Pearl came running, wiping her hands on her apron as she turned the corner.

"Good," Rebecca said. "A little project for you two." Picking up her skirts, she started up the steps.

The girls looked at each other. There were several baskets of wet laundry to hang, linens to iron, and breakfast dishes to clear. If the missus was calling them away from that, nothing good was in the air.

They found her sitting at a table in one of the guest rooms.

"Sit down," Rebecca said with a wave at the two chairs that faced hers.

With leaden arms, Nora and Pearl pulled out the chairs. Scissors, glass beads, ribbons, a bottle of glue, wire, and several envelopes were lined up on the table in tidy clumps.

Rebecca laced her fingers together on top of the table. "You two," she said, forcing a smile across her face. "You look like two little rice birds sitting there."

The smile unnerved Nora. "Ma'am?" she asked.

"Tiny things. Their Latin name means rice eaters. The flocks arrive in the rice fields on their way north in spring and again on their way south in late summer," Rebecca said. "They cling to the plants, gorging until they can barely move, the nasty little thieves."

"But rice birds can fly away," Pearl said under her breath.

The room was too quiet for Rebecca to not have heard that. Nora didn't dare sneak a glance at Pearl.

Rebecca's gray eyes narrowed. "They get shot, too. Get their necks wrung. Get eaten."

Pearl smiled. "Yes, ma'am. They make good eatin'."

Nora attempted a blank expression and stared at the scissors on the table.

"Well. Moving on. Look at this." Rebecca opened an envelope and with the reverence of an undertaker uncoiled a ten-inch lock of red hair. "This is my sister's hair."

Nora and Pearl leaned back in their chairs.

Rebecca pushed a booklet toward girls. The cover read "Manual: M. Campbell's Self-Instructor in the Art of Hair Work."

"Hair work," Nora said.

"Oh, no, no, Miss Rebecca," Pearl said. "I don't touch nobody's hair."

"Nonsense. I've seen you plaiting Bess's hair."

"Yes'm, but that attached to her haid," Pearl said. "A hunk of cut hair is dangerous. It's the most powerful thing your enemy can get hol' of. It's mighty powerful, bein' so close to the brain. If someone evil get hol' of your hair to make a conjuh, he or she can make big trouble fuh you."

Inside her head, Nora was nodding. Having been reared on stories of the most sinister curse of all, the Irish hex, she was willing to respect the power of hair — or chicken's feet or rattlesnake skins — in the wrong hands. She'd learned a few things on her evenings on the street.

"My sister is dead," Rebecca said flat out. "Beyond all harm."

Nora fought to not smile but Pearl was panicked. Flapping her hands, she cried, "Oh, no, ma'am, that even worse."

"Pearl, you're not a conjurer, are you?" Rebecca asked.

Pearl settled down.

"Because if you are, I have a certain punishment for that.

I'll not have conjuring on my property." Rebecca's marble-like cheeks began taking on the flush of anger.

Nora knew that inside the slave cabins and in the piney woods, there was conjuring going on every time somebody stole somebody's man or stole somebody's okra from the plot out back. Haints were dispatched to sit on a chest all night to take someone's breath away and leave them weak the next morning. Dead frogs wrapped in snakeskin were left on door thresholds to make even worse trouble, but only if you stepped over it on your way out the door.

"It's important to me that you two learn how to do this," Rebecca said. "This kind of art is very popular right now and the New York prices are ridiculous. There is no one in Charleston who does this. In any case, I have no intention of entrusting these precious relics to some artist in New York. You can do it. I want you to take this and make a flower wreath out of it." Rebecca flipped to a page with flower wreath instructions and illustration. "And take this . . ." Rebecca pulled an identical hank of red hair out of another envelope. "And make another wreath. This is Adele. My sister's twin."

Pearl tucked her fists into her chest. "She dead too?" she asked.

Nora gripped her chair. Did the mistress sit at deathbeds, itchy fingers tickling the scissors in her pocket? Were the redheads really twins? Why did it have to be twins?

Rebecca drew in a breath and held it for a long time. "No, Adele is not dead," she said in a tone that said she was talking to idiots, "but she's dear to me and so you're going to make this tribute to her." She pointed at the illustration. "Two wreaths. Add a bird or two. Birds are symbols of the soul unchained."

Nora peered at the manual again as if she believed it could actually show her how to make a bird out of hair.

"Then I want you to make these in honor of someone else."

Rebecca flipped the page to a picture of a pair of earrings—a thumb-sized orb of woven hair dropped from a string of gold, topped off by a smaller gold bead. Opening the third envelope, she dumped out four short blond, curly strands. "Because these are so short, I think earrings will be best."

Pearl covered her face.

"Now girls, you must think of hair as a precious thing," Rebecca said as she pushed her chair away from the table. "Long after the flesh has melted, this hair will remain, ever the memorial, like a jewel. A little remembrance of someone you loved." She leveled her gray eyes at Pearl. "Like the dress your mother made for you, wouldn't you say, Pearl?"

Slowly, Pearl lowered her hands.

"You think I don't know everything that goes on around here?" Rebecca asked.

Pearl's brown eyes locked on Rebecca's.

"The dress I can understand, but why the pecans?" Rebecca asked.

Nora reached for Pearl's hand under the table.

The mistress shifted her gaze to Nora. "And if you don't have a dress to cherish, you might cherish the sight of a loved one's script in a letter, perhaps the stain of the tears she wept while writing?"

"Clare's letters," Nora whispered.

"Yes. Like the one you got yesterday, the second one I believe. It would a shame if you never got any more."

Nora burst into tears. "Please, no. 'Tis all I have of her."

"Better get busy then." Rebecca stood and left the room.

Chapter Eleven

On Lowcountry rice plantations, the slaves' time was their own after they'd completed their task of the day, a custom that the Mannings extended to Nora and Patrick as well. Many evenings after supper, the two went to the river bluff to settle on the horse blanket. They talked of their childhoods, back when life was still good. He sang Irish ballads off-key and wobbly, which Nora found endearing because it said that he felt comfortable enough to risk embarrassment. It spoke of trust, she felt.

When the last daylight had bled into the marsh and candle flames winked in the windows of the big house, Patrick walked her back home as if she needed protecting. Before they reached the steps, he always kissed her good night, and whispered things into her ear that made her cheeks hot.

Sometimes Pearl was waiting for her inside, arms crossed. *Watch out,* the look in her eyes said, a warning that was about as effective as spit on a forest fire. Later, in her room, it occurred to her that perhaps Pearl was jealous. Jealousy. That was it.

* * *

One morning when she should've been stripping beds and emptying chamber pots, Nora was hiding behind a tree with Patrick. She couldn't get enough of his smell, his lips, his hands moving over her body.

She pulled away to breathe. "I should go. She'll be looking for me."

"Polishing the silver so soon?" Patrick pressed his lips to her neck. "The party's not for another week."

The Mannings had sent invitations to the plantations up and down the river. William would turn three years old on November thirtieth, a milestone that none of their other children had ever reached, and Rebecca Manning meant to note it with a big celebration.

"I have to go," Nora said again as she looped her arms around his neck.

"She's happy with that hair work ye've been doing, is she?"

Nora made a face. "We've finished the two wreaths she wanted. She seemed satisfied. Gives me the woolies it does, but we're getting used to it."

"Run away with me."

"Not that again." She swatted his chest.

"I'm not foolin'. What do I have to do to convince ye? The party will be the perfect time to slip away. Think of how distracted she'll be." He pressed his hips into hers, kissed her neck, her ears, her mouth. "We'll run down the road until dark, get a good start. In the morning we'll keep going until we find a ride."

"To where?"

"Georgetown, then south on the King's Highway to Charleston." His hands slid down to her fanny.

Pushing him away in earnest now, she said, "'Twill be the first place they'll look."

"Ye said ye're worried about me working in the fields. 'Tis just a matter of time before Manning gets me killed out there."

"Aye, that I am, but—"

"Once we get to Charleston, we'll send for Clare, then the three of us will head to Georgia."

At the mention of Clare, she softened. "But that would take a lot of money."

Patrick cupped her chin in his hands. "Steal the jewelry."

Nora jerked away. "What!"

"Mrs. Manning is daft. Many's the time ye've said so. She won't even miss it for a while, so filled she is with the hysteria."

Nora thought about the mistress's hysterias and quirks. Careless with the jewelry that even Nora knew had real worth— diamonds and rubies in necklaces, bracelets and earrings spangled with gold—Rebecca Manning was careful with what most people would consider worthless, the hair bracelets, brooches, and pendants. All of it occupied one container, a pharmacy box that she kept in the back of a wardrobe, never locked. The good jewelry was dumped in a jumble in the back while the hair jewelry was organized lovingly in the front.

"Come on," Patrick said, stroking her arm. "We need the jewelry."

She rolled the idea around for a while. Stealing was wrong, but not so much in America. Clare had been stolen, hadn't she? Pearl too. For that matter, wasn't every ancestor of every slave in America stolen?

"There will be what, twenty or so people arriving in their boats at the docks throughout the morning, with the master and mistress welcoming everyone down at the river," Patrick said. "That's when ye'll be upstairs, taking the jewelry, then running it to me for safekeeping."

Nora shook her head. "She'll want to wear some of it for the party."

"All right, then bring me what's left after she's dressed for the evening. Later, after ye've served supper and everyone's in their cups, meet me by the grandfather oak at the end of the avenue and we'll take off."

"It'll be dark."

"I know the road out of here."

Such a long and deadly road back to civilization, she thought. *But young and strong we are. We can run hard for a long time, and he'll be with me all the way. And beyond.*

"I know people around Georgetown. Enough people to bribe to get us away," Patrick said.

She looked at him. Here was the partner she needed in this wretched country to show her the way. A man. Men could make things happen.

"Think of it, Nora, a future of our own making, not theirs. A future together," Patrick said. "Me and my fair Irish lass."

* * *

She knew she shouldn't, but she had to. She couldn't disappear into the night without saying goodbye to Pearl. Also, once the words were out, Nora would have to go through with it. Getting Pearl alone was the problem. Finally, Nora found a moment at the cistern behind the kitchen. They argued in furious whispers.

"You're crazy," Pearl said. "The Mannings? They'll find your lily-white hide before you make it to the first wagon on the big road. If you do make it to a wagon, people take one look at you and turn you in. The mas' will take out newspaper ads and put big signs on the sides of buildings in towns." Pearl paced the sandy ground stopping every few seconds to get in Nora's face. "His friends will spread the word to every tavern. The missus, when you get your fool ass dragged back here, she'll beat you like she ain't got no soul to save. Bein' a runaway is bad enough. Stealin' the jewelry makes you twice the thief. That Patrick, I know your eye tie up on him, but he just sweet mouthin' you. You can't trust him. Don't you see?"

No, she didn't. Hope had taken root in Nora's soul. As if consumed by Yellow Jack, she was feverish with the vision of the life she was going to have with Patrick. He'd be taking Clare in too, she told Pearl. What luck to find such a generous man.

Pearl threw up her hands. "Well, when you goin'?"

"During the party."

* * *

On the morning that the Mannings began welcoming their guests at the dock, Nora laid all the jewelry on Rebecca's dresser, that which was valuable to a normal person and that which was valuable to Rebecca. Later, while Nora pressed an evening dress in the bedroom, she watched Rebecca dithering over her choices, first this brooch with rubies, then that one made of hair. Nora nearly burned the dress watching her try four, five, six bracelets on, hold earrings up to her ear, turn her face left, right, left in the mirror. Finally, she chose a hair brooch, a ruby necklace and matching earrings. Nora helped her into the dress, smoothed its folds around the narrow hips, and closed the clasp of the necklace with trembling hands. As soon as Rebecca went downstairs to join her guests in the ballroom, Nora dropped two fistfuls of the good jewelry into a muslin sack. With her heart in her throat, she ran to Patrick's shed and gave him the sack.

"I'll see ye at dusk behind the grandfather oak, my lovely Noreen," he said, putting the sack into a leather bag already packed with clothes and food. "Now back to the house with ye." He kissed her on the mouth good and hard, which she took as a sure sign he was as in love as she was.

When Pearl and Nora had placed the last bread pudding in front of a guest, Tobias strutted into the dining room for his final performance of the evening. The girls ran downstairs to the cavernous place under the porch. Nora took off her starched white apron. Pearl grabbed her bony arms and pulled her into a hug. They gave each other a peck. There was nothing else to say.

Nora hurried to Patrick's shed to make sure nothing had delayed him. There was no sign of him, his tools, or the leather bag, so she raced down the long, oak-lined avenue to their freedom.

The grandfather oak, wide enough to hide three men, loomed in the distance. She ran, watching the road for tree roots, holes, and snakes that waited for her ankles. Her lungs burned but still somehow, she ran. She would breathe later. The tree grew larger, the evening shadows deeper, and she looked for his face to appear from behind it or his hand to wave her to him, but — nothing. At last, she arrived at the tree, heaving for air.

"Patrick?" she called.

No answer.

She circled the oak twice, straining to see in the gloom. She looked down the road she'd just come. Not a soul. She rushed to the road they were to leave on. Not a soul. *Where is he?* She ran around the tree again.

No.

He wouldn't. This isn't what it looks like, her brain screamed.

He wouldn't. Denial seared every cell, anger bit at her eyes, at him, at herself. *No!* She kicked the tree, ran down the road to Georgetown, raised her fists, shouted at the top of her lungs, "The devil cut yer head off and make a day's work of yer neck, Patrick, ye County Mayo piece of shit!"

When her lungs seized, she had to stop screaming. Hands on knees, fighting for breath, she looked down the long wide road where Patrick probably had hot-legged it while she was lighting the supper candles. By now he was miles away. Night was settling over that jungle tunnel, and Nora knew two things: she had to go anyway and she couldn't go alone.

She looked at the house, windows aglow with the party. Nora knew where she could find Pearl, knew she'd take Nora's outstretched hand in a second and never look back, but Nora stood rooted to the ground, thinking, or rather trying to think with an addled brain, because for once she'd decided to weigh what she was about to do. Pearl as a partner could be a problem. She'd want to go south to Charleston to find out where her mother was, but people all over that town knew her as Edward Manning's servant and they'd turn her in when his ads appeared. Together, one white and one black, they'd fit the description oh so precisely. On the other hand, Nora needed to go to Charleston too, to somehow get on another boat and go back to New York. But Pearl could be surly, which could get them kicked out of a wagon, even one driven by a free black man, but no — no free black man would pick up a runaway slave and risk his own freedom. On the other hand, Pearl knew the roads, the way back, the town, maybe someone who'd hide them.

"Be careful what ye wish for," Clare had warned at home. Freedom? Oh she had it now, though it felt more like more broken bones than cherished prize. She'd never planned to leave Oakwood until her four years were up, but now that she was leaving, there was only one person who could lead the way, ball and chain that she might be.

Nora ran back to the house without a thought of holes or snakes. Tobias's music floated out of the open windows. She ran under the porch to wait for Pearl and kicked the wall. *What a fool. Fair Irish lass my arse*, she thought. *I hope one of — no both, no all the kinds! — of South Carolina's poisonous snakes have already found your leg and twitching with the poison in a ditch ye are, Patrick ye piece of shit.*

Overhead in the dining room, the fiddling stopped. Conversations started up again, but it wouldn't be long before people would be pushing away from the table to return to the dock before complete darkness fell. Pearl came down the servant's steps loaded with platters.

Nora went straight at her. "He's left me," she whispered, slapping the tears off her cheeks. "He's run away without me."

Pearl didn't blink an eyelash. "Uh huh."

"I have to go. Right now. Will ye come with me?"

The platters in Pearl's hands began shaking. Her lips parted, her brown eyes narrowed, and though this took only seconds, it felt like years to Nora. Finally, Pearl lowered the platters noiselessly to the ground. She jerked her white apron off and ran to a dark corner next to one of the archways. Reaching behind a crate, she snatched up her mother's sack.

"All right," Pearl said. "Let's go."

"The sack! Ye were ready? Ye knew I'd come for ye?"

"What'd I say? Didn't I say he was just a sweet mouth? Come on," Pearl said, grabbing Nora's wrist.

They crept out of the porch's shadows and looked around. To their right, the kitchen house throbbed with light and voices, but none of the servants were on the path between the kitchen and the docks. Yet. To the left, the dirt ribbon to the avenue of oaks was still deserted.

Pearl pulled Nora toward the creek.

"No, no. We have to take the road," Nora cried, pulling toward the avenue. "Not water."

"Your head is took away. We ain' goin' to make it down that road," Pearl hissed as she yanked Nora downhill, past the kitchen, past the clotheslines to the creek. At the docks, she uncoiled the line to someone's snub-nosed bateau. "Tide's runnin' good," she said, pointing at the ripples rushing south toward Georgetown. "We'll be there in an hour." She climbed into the little boat and picked up a paddle.

"Ye know your way through all of that?" Nora looked down the creek, full of forks and loops that fed into more of the same until the main channel merged into the wide and dangerous river if you had chosen correctly and gotten that far.

In the house, candlelit forms moved as people said their good-byes.

Pearl held the other paddle out to Nora. "We'll have the full moon. I been to Georgetown lots of times on the rice flats. Now get in this 'yuh boat and sit down."

Nora couldn't take her eyes off the maze of meandering waterways. Sure death lurked in those black currents, currents as dangerous as the course of her life from here on, she knew. The bateau was already floating away from the last foot of Oakwood.

The heavy front door of the house swung open. A short man, backlit and unrecognizable, was leaving.

Nora clambered in and snatched the paddle. "What if we fall in?" she asked.

"Hush. You a rice bird or not? We'll fly."

And as the water swept the girls south, Nora looked back at the house and saw Tobias watching them from the porch, stiffening like a setter at the point.

PART TWO

RICE BIRD RECIPE

Select the fattest birds, remove the entrails, bake them whole or split them up the back and broil. Permit no sacrilegious hand to remove the head, for the base of the brain of the rice bird is the most succulent portion. Or the birds may be placed in either shape in a round bottom pot with a small lump of butter, pepper, and salt and cook over a quick fire. Use no fork in eating. Take the neck of the bird in the left hand and his little right leg in the right hand. Tear away the right leg and eat all but the extreme end of the bone. Hold the bill of the bird in one hand and crush your teeth through the back of the head and thank Providence that you are permitted to live. Take the remaining left leg in your right hand and place in your mouth the entire body of the bird and then munch the sweetest morsel that ever brought gustatory delight. All that remains is the front portion of the head and the tiny bits of bone that formed the ends of the legs. To leave more is to betray your unappreciativeness of the gifts of the gods.

– originally printed in 1901 in the booklet "Carolina Rice Cook Book," compiled by Louisa Cheves Smythe Stoney. Source: Hess, Karen. The Carolina Rice Kitchen: The African Connection. © *1992 University of South Carolina.*

Chapter Twelve

The man answering the knock at his piazza door knew exactly what the two people in the doorway were. He'd seen runaways before—escaped slaves in Baltimore alleys, a few bloodied convicts in a Pennsylvania infirmary—so he recognized the hunted look in the eyes. But girls! And a white one and a black one together? He'd not seen that before. These two wore filthy trousers and caps that had failed to convince him that they were boys. The black one, supported by the white one, held her foot off the ground.

"Heard there was a doctor here," Pearl said.

"Yes. I'm Doctor Simmons," he said.

He helped her up two steps and across the piazza, around its rocking chairs, and through the front door. Nora followed, peering in the windows, hoping to not see anyone else.

Inside, the girls looked left into a room with a fireplace and then right into the other that held nothing but a rude table and ladderback chairs. Shelves with plates and cups studded the wall. A central hall led to more rooms in the back, a staircase to more upstairs. "You alone?" Pearl asked as she limped toward a chair.

Simmons nodded. "What happened?"

"We had to jump out of a moving wagon," Nora said. "Before we wanted to."

Simmons looked over his shoulder at Nora. "You're Irish."

"I have no disease if that's what ye're thinking," Nora said.

He squatted to look at Pearl's swollen ankle. "Can you move it?"

Pearl sucked air through her teeth as she pointed her toes down and up.

Simmons ran his fingers over the ankle. "Nothing broken, just a bad sprain," he finally said. "Needs ice. Come on."

He led them down the hall to a room tucked into the back of the house. A table long enough to seat eight was pushed against a wall. Two buckets were underneath it and a pillow lay atop one end. In the corner stood a cabinet packed with brown glass bottles and metal canisters with handwritten labels. The doctor helped Nora lower Pearl onto a cot.

Gesturing at the door, he said to Nora, "There's a box outside covered in sawdust. Get a few chunks of ice."

When he'd wrapped, iced, and propped Pearl's foot he said, "You can't stay long. You're running from something. Might get me arrested." He raked both hands through tight, rolling waves of dark hair.

The girls exchanged a look. This was the first roof they'd been under in two weeks. Most of the trip from Georgetown they had walked in the frigid dark. The one wagon ride they had risked turned out to be a short one, the driver having not been fooled that they were boys and expecting favors for his kindness. Nora saw that coming with the looks he was giving them from his seat. She grabbed Pearl's hand and pulled her out the back. Pearl landed badly but ran somehow. When they walked into this house, the fire in the front room had nearly brought them to tears.

Nora sat down at Pearl's feet as if the doctor had invited her to visit for a spell.

"We're awful hungry," Pearl said.

He brought them beans and leathery ham, which put some life into their faces. While they chewed, he leaned against the table, arms crossed. "How'd you find me? I have no sign out there," he said.

"Asked around," Pearl said.

Nora nodded, though Pearl had known exactly where this doctor who would treat black people was.

He winced. "So, you've let people know that the authorities can find you here."

Pearl shoved more beans into her mouth.

Nora looked the doctor over. He seemed harmless enough with that soft jowl and cheeks as cobbled as the streets. The flat accent was odd — it didn't rise and fall in the soft-edged brogue of the Carolina male. "Where're you from?" she asked.

He took his time answering. "Massachusetts," he said.

"Why're ye in Charleston?"

One eyebrow shot up. "The Yellow Fever epidemic. Another reason for you two to get out of town."

Nora shook her head. "We'll not be leaving Charleston any time soon."

He gave her a look. "Why not?"

"I have to find my — " Pearl said.

"We have to earn some money," Nora said quickly. "Strong backs we have."

He gestured toward the streets. "But you can't work out in the open. Someone's searching for you, right?"

Pearl looked at the ceiling. "You got an empty room up there? We could make our own straw mattresses. Wash your clothes, tidy up this place? We'd stay out of sight."

Simmons gave a snort. "Excuse me?"

"I'm thinking ye'd like a hot meal every night," Nora said.

Another snort.

"Just for a while, sir. We don't have — " Nora looked at her hands.

"Anywhere else to go," he said.

The girls let silence hang now that pity was in the air.

Simmons took his watch out of his pocket and checked it as if he didn't already know it would soon be dark, when the City Guard would haul to jail anyone, man or woman, black or white, who broke the law by being on the streets after curfew. "Who're you running from?" he asked.

"A plantation," Pearl said.

"Whose?"

"Near Georgetown."

"Yes, but which plantation? Who are the owners?"

"Terrible people, they are," Nora said. "Sir."

Simmons leveled a scorched look at her. "You're not answering my questions."

"'Tis better if ye can say ye didn't know," Nora said.

"You haven't killed anybody have you? Haven't stolen anything?"

Pearl stared at the ceiling and mouthed *Lawd.*

Nora said, "No, sir, no one killed. The mistress, she beat us." That part was true.

Simmons went back to crossed arms and studied them — young, spindly, and members of two groups who were commonly abused in Charleston. Worse, they were female. In the growing gloom, they looked even more vulnerable than the children they pretended to be. There was nothing in the house worth stealing. "So, one of you can cook?" he asked.

Pearl came up on her elbows. "Yes, sir."

"And I can wash and mend," Nora said. Another half-truth.

"God help me. Two runaways." Simmons pulled a handkerchief out of a shirt pocket and dabbed his forehead. Someone's dried blood stained one of his cuffs.

Again, the girls recognized a good time to stay quiet.

Simmons straightened out of his slouch. "Well, just until her ankle's better. Three days, no more," he said. "I'm out all day in a hospital a few blocks away. Don't answer the door while I'm gone. There's an empty room upstairs, bare as an eggshell. Not so much as a chair."

"Perfect," Pearl said.

"You must not answer the door if someone knocks, day or night."

Nora wondered why he'd repeated that. The last thing she wanted to do was answer the door.

"This place is nothing official, not a clinic. The hospital, I work long hours there. During the day, you might hear someone knock, but — "

"Don't answer the door," Nora said with growing uneasiness.

"I just want to be here when a patient is in my house," Simmons said.

Nora looked at her hands again. *So he trusts us.*

"I won't pay you. I want hot suppers waiting for me."

So he's going to give us money for shopping.

"Three days at the most."

"We know," Nora said. "Thank you, sir."

That night, they lay on quilts in the first-floor room while the glorious fire throbbed in their aching bones. Simmons had laid more logs before going upstairs. While Pearl flipped side to side trying to get comfortable with one ankle on a pillow, Nora got up to poke around various drawers. In the back room, she helped herself to the doctor's paper, quill, and ink bottle.

December 6, 1849

Dear Clare,

I have run away from the plantation. I was a fool is all I will say and I have no one but meself to blame for what has become of me. By now Mrs. Manning has probably opened your last Letter and will be writing to your Mistress to ask for help finding me. I can't tell ye where I am until I find a safe way to send word. Do not come to Charleston. I hope you'll get this Letter soon so ye'll stop trying.

I need to earn money so I can take a Ship back to you, but I have to stay off the streets. I don't know how long this will take. By the time ye get this Letter, Christmas will be nigh. May yer Mistress find it in her heart to at least give ye a sweet biscuit and a day off.

Love,

Nora

Nora folded the paper and lay down beside Pearl.

"First thing tomorrow, he'll turn us in," Pearl said as she rolled toward her.

"And why would he do that?"

"Reward money. Notice in the paper 'bout us will be there soon. Handbills in the shops and offices. You watch."

"Ye think Tobias has told what he saw?"

"They know we gone, don't they?"

Stung, Nora went quiet for a moment. "The doctor won't tell. He has kind eyes," she said.

"You a fool when it comes to men."

Nora gave Pearl a look that would sear a side of beef. "What else would ye have us do, ye with that ankle that's running nowhere any time soon? Ye saying we should leave tomorrow?"

Pearl clasped her arms above her head. "We got to make money fast as we can," she said.

"Jaysus, Mary, and Joseph, ye think I don't know that? I need to buy me ticket out of here."

Pearl reached under her hips and pulled "M. Campbell's Self-Instructor in the Art of Hair Work" out of her precious seed sack.

"Ye brought that? Mother of God not hair work."

"Makes my skin crawl too," Pearl said with a shudder. "But we good at it."

Nora considered this. Even Mrs. Manning had said so.

"We need to order supplies and get some hair." Pearl's gaze shifted from Nora's eyes to her hair that flowed across her shoulders. "White people's hair."

Nora's hands flew to her head, but she couldn't say no, just as she couldn't ask where they'd get the money to buy supplies, how they'd sell their art, and how long it would all take to put cash in their hands. Pearl, the ball and chain, had brought the book and an idea with her. Nora wouldn't extinguish their only hope with questions like that.

The fire popped and hissed in its cove, throwing washes of amber against the ceiling and walls. The girls turned their faces toward the warmth. Dark roads and constant danger didn't own them tonight. There was a roof over their heads, a door, a lock.

"Jaysus, I hope Clare's all right," Nora said.

"I wish I could write to Mama like you just did to your sister," Pearl said. "I wish I could tell her where I been all this time, that I growed up well enough, that I will make money so I can buy her and free her. Even if I could write her a letter, though, she couldn't read it." Tears rolled down her cheeks. "What if she ain' at that plantation anymore? What if she ain' alive?"

"She's alive." Nora reached for her hand.

"I remember her arms, so big and soft 'roun' me. The way she laugh, the way she sing when she work. Behind the cabin, we grew sweet potatoes I think it was, and cabbage. She show me how to cook it with onions and meat in a big pot. I burn myse'f stirrin' one time. Mama kiss my hand and put some kind of plant on it for healin'. But there's one thing that I can't remember. It give me worriment."

Nora squeezed Pearl's hand for she knew what was coming: the impossible loss of images that should've been branded on the brain, as permanent as scars. Her father, her mother, her little sisters and brother—their faces were only outlines now, sometimes with eyes, but fading. Clare too, she suddenly realized.

"Her face. Seem like all I can remember is it shaped roun' like a bowl and her eyes, they always smilin' when they on me. But that's all."

"Ye'll see it soon enough, Pearl." Nora reached over to wipe the tears off her friend's cheek. "Ye'll find her."

"There's a man here in town. He's going to help me."

Nora got up on her elbows. "A man. Ye never mentioned a man before. Who—"

"Soon as I can walk, I got to get to him. He's going to help us get away. Me and Mama."

"Wait. What about me? Will he help me get out of here?"

"I don't know. We never talked about that."

"Who—"

"Let me see can I find him, Nora."

"Ye trust him?"

"Trust him? I love him."

Chapter Thirteen

In the morning, they heard the doctor on the stairs, then at the back door, then in the hall coming their way. He arrived in the doorway, arms full of firewood, and stared at the shivering runaways curled up on their mats in front of his cold fireplace. Without a word, he went to the hearth and laid the next fire — pine straw, twigs, and logs atop last night's residue. His bellows sent ash flying into the girls' faces. They didn't turn away, so anxious they were to see the next fire begin. The pine straw caught. He opened the kitchen cupboards and beckoned Nora over to show her the sack of coffee and a jar of tomatoes. They were welcome to them, he said. There was nothing else in the cupboards. Nora wondered how they were supposed to make supper but she didn't ask him for money for the market. She looked at the side of his head while she waited for him to say something about that. He had wet combed his wavy hair back, but one section had sprung apart at a cowlick. He gave her the side eye and bolted for the front door.

"Ain' you going to wait for coffee?" Pearl asked. "Nora, make some coffee."

Nora crossed the room to join him at the doorway. "We won't open this door no matter what," she said. Finally, he made eye contact. In his eyes she thought she saw regret, as if dawn had fully illuminated the risk he'd taken in the night before. She didn't see betrayal, though, so as he closed the door, she hoped she was right that he wasn't now on his way to the City Guard office.

Pearl commented on the impressive collection of ladles, utensils, lids, kettles, and cast-iron skillets piled beside the hearth, a sign that a serious cook had once lived here. "And look at that," she said, pointing to the silver-framed miniature painting on the mantel, no bigger than a clenched fist, of a young woman in a flowing gown, such a delicate thing among the crude hearth tools and rough pine mantel. Why had he placed it there, Nora wondered, instead of in his room, and of course, who was she?

Nora nosed around in every room, being careful to put things back exactly where they'd been. On his bedroom bureau, she found a sterling silver hairbrush and clothes brush, and now that she knew sterling from tin, understood that he wasn't a poor man despite the bleak furnishings in this place. Or, at least, he'd had a gentleman's money at some point. She put her nose to his shaving soap cake, finding it cedar-ish and extravagant. He'd made his bed, had smoothed the blanket to creaseless perfection. Downstairs in the treatment room at the back of the house, there were bandages and medical tools, a book about surgery, instruments of various lengths, the cot, the table with the buckets underneath. A roach skittered across the floor and disappeared into a gap between the floorboards. She found clean rags, towels, soap, and a basin.

When the kettle water was aboil, Nora brought the basin to Pearl on her cot. They bathed all the skin they could reach, worked under the filthy cuffs and collars of the clothes they'd stolen from a wash line. Afterward, they drank coffee, snuck looks out the curtained windows at the street of modest homes, slept, sniffed the peculiar-colored tomatoes packed in some sort of murky fluid, ate them anyway, and slept some more in their luxuriant safety.

That evening, the doctor walked in with a grease-stained paper bag, two dresses, and two wool scarves. "Something for you," he said as he handed the clothing to Nora who had met him at the door. "From the women religious at the Charleston Home for Children."

"Clean clothes!" Nora said. "Now we can take a real bath!"

"Let me see," Pearl said, limping over to reach for them.

"What's a Home for Children?" Nora asked.

"An orphanage," Simmons said.

"Orphanage," Nora said. "Ye mean a place where people take orphans in?"

"Yes, the women religious, the nuns." Simmons pulled a ham out of the paper bag.

"Never heard of strangers taking care of orphans before," Nora said.

Simmons put the ham on the table. "I assume you've found the plates?"

He ate at the kitchen table, they ate in front of the fire, all three sneaking looks at one another. Pearl asked the doctor did he like chicken and how should she cook it tomorrow, roasted or fried? Simmons dug in his pocket, laid several bills on the table and said, "Roasted."

The next day, Nora ventured out with Pearl's market list, Simmons's four dollars, and the letter to Clare, not that she had any idea how to mail it. Pearl had wanted to go with her, saying she had to get across town to her man, but when she couldn't walk to the door on her own, she waved Nora on. Frigid winds off the harbor a few blocks away scoured the streets, forcing Nora to put her head down as she scurried along. With her clean dress and her cheeks hidden under the coils of her scarf, no one looked twice at her. With Pearl's hand-drawn map, she easily found the Market Hall and Sheds. Vultures fought over the meat scraps that the butchers had flung into the street. The sellers were kind to her, didn't screw up their mouths when they heard her accent, so she asked the girl who bagged her potatoes how to mail a letter. The girl told her how to find the post office and as Nora approached the building, she realized it was inside the customs house where she had sat and cried on that first day in Charleston, homesick and scared, oblivious to Isaiah walking up with his white gloves and his gentle smile. Today, before the tears could start, she ran inside to barter with the clerk—a head of cabbage for some stamps. He dropped her letter into the mail sack and promised it would go out first thing in the morning.

She brought home chickens, bacon, rice, corn meal, turnips, onions, and tea. Pearl sat in a kitchen chair, foot propped on the other chair, and ordered Nora around, having learned more than she had ever appreciated at Bess's elbow in the Manning kitchens. Bacon bits to season the vegetables. Rice into the pan, add enough water as high as your first knuckle, not a bit more, put the lid on, hang the pan on the fire.

Two evenings of hot suppers for the exhausted doctor went by. The three of them still ate in silence—he at the table in the kitchen, the girls in front of the fire—but the sounds of pleasure that he made over his plate gave them hope.

On the third evening, he came home with child-sized boots, hairbrushes, and undergarments wrapped discreetly in paper. Pearl caressed the shiny boots, the first she'd ever received that reeked of boot blacking, not the stinky feet of previous wearers. She and Nora sputtered with thanks and glory be's. Simmons said that he'd looked through newspaper on the way home and found no ad for two runaways. The girls cut their eyes at each other and didn't ask whether there was an ad for three runaways.

After dinner, the dinner for which the girls had no appetite with tomorrow's eviction hanging in the air, Simmons joined them at the fireplace. He looked up at the portrait framed in silver and said something to the pink-cheeked woman in the flowing gown so quietly that the girls couldn't make out a word of it. They waited for the bad news they reckoned he'd come over to deliver. He began talking about his day at the Marine Hospital, a federal facility built for merchant seamen and other transients attracted to the port city. He told of broken arms, ship's fever, lice, and typhus as if Nora hadn't seen plenty of that on the coffin ship, but she welcomed this one-sided conversation, for there was no mention of eviction so far and no probing into their runaway story. When he paused, Nora jumped in with questions about his childhood to keep him going.

Simmons gave her a sideways glance. "I told you. Massachusetts."

"Parents? Brothers and sisters?" Pearl asked with a smile.

"Ah, my parents. Cold as a January night in Boston," he said. "My mother, she wanted me to continue the family legacies and there were many. For me she wanted prestige, honor, a well-rounded education grounded in the arts. Early on she insisted on piano lessons. At age seven, mind you. I hated them. Turned out I have neither rhythm nor ear. Finally, after five years, she gave up on me."

With that, the doctor said goodnight and went upstairs. Odd as that exit was, Nora and Pearl smiled at each other over what he had not said.

The next evening beside the fire, he picked up where he'd left off with the lice and typhus. All of her life, Nora had listened to story weavers, but she'd never seen one create so many pictures with his hands.

Simmons was running his hand across a patient's chest and shoulders. "So, the poor fellow came in with muscle pain and chills."

"Ship's fever," Nora said.

The doctor shook his head. "No rash though."

"Ah," Nora said.

Simmons put his hand, knuckle side down, on the forehead. "Within an hour, here comes the fever. Abdomen pain too. I had no idea what was ailing him, but—" Simmons threw up his hands and smiled—"a week later he was fine."

Nora studied his animated face. About thirty-five years old, she guessed, ears too big, a splatter of dark moles across acne-ravaged cheeks. A man could overcome such a face if personality drew one in. Did it draw her in? Well, he was earnest and hopeful, not deflated by abuse as most men—black and Irish—were in her experience. Sensitive, too, judging from how much he cared about his sick sailors. Why was he so kind? Why would he risk his life to rush into Charleston's epidemic? Could such generosity and unselfishness truly live in people?

Simmons moved on to digging a bullet out of some poor fellow's leg. His finger probed a bloody hole and found it. He plunged an extractor into the wound and pulled out the bullet, holding it up for the girls to see. "Got lucky and found that bullet right off," he said. "You can do a lot of damage just trying to find them."

Pearl, squirming in the chair beside Nora, made a face.

Nora kept staring at him. Why didn't a man his age have a wife? His looks, yes, they were uninviting, but he had a respectable profession, a tenderness, an intelligent mind, eyes that followed what you were saying if you were inclined to speak up. In her limited experience, Nora had observed that if a man didn't want to be a bachelor, there was always a woman within range who would happily help him shed that status.

Cupping one hand in the other, the doctor sat back in his chair to savor the attention of this good audience. After a while, he picked up the fire poker and poked. "Sometimes sepsis sets in, though. Likely that's their end. We do what we can," he said.

* * *

When perfect weather for launching their plan arrived four days later, it was time.

"Shoo, nobody will be out in this mess but us," Pearl said as she looked out the window at the rare December snow coming down.

"Just what we need," Nora said.

With scarves puddled up to their cheeks, they stepped outside. Nora followed Pearl at a safe distance — too dangerous to be seen together — toward King Street, the city's main merchant avenue. Every corner they turned bought the possibility of a broadside plastered on a brick wall announcing a reward for their capture, but they saw none. They turned onto King Street's icy sidewalks, which weren't as deserted as they'd hoped. A few bundled figures came and went from the stores, eyes on the slippery ground at least. At the first side street, Pearl turned. Here the storefronts were seedier, sadder, no longer promising London and Paris goods inside. Nora followed her past a narrow tobacco shop, a barber, then a storefront with a purple-framed window — a tad shabby — and when Pearl passed it, she signaled that that was it. Nora peered in the window jammed with ladies' hats, gloves, mantillas, and hair combs — a jumble so crowded it shouted desperation. *This owner*, Pearl had said, *she always been sucking on the hind tit, so she needs us. She won't ask a lot of questions.*

Nora said hello to the white-haired woman behind the counter. The woman looked over at the brogue and told Nora to stop right there. A froth of silver curls laced the edge of her muslin day-cap. The forces of prejudice and contempt seemed to be permanently marshalled on the wrinkled face.

The woman said, "Need something?"

Nora began her pitch. The woman sewed a band of ruffles onto a hat brim while she listened.

"Skilled at mourning remembrances made of hair I am," Nora said. "So skilled in fact that me mistress has given permission to sell me art around town." Nora promised brooches, braided bracelets, pendants, and the larger framed items as well—a wreath of family hair, perhaps? A cemetery scene with mausoleum and weeping willows? As soon as she got her supplies, she'd bring samples by. She'd give the milliner ten percent of whatever sold in her shop. Nora hadn't known what percent was, but she'd heard it at the market and the nice girl who sold vegetables showed her with ten potatoes how it worked.

The shop owner put her sewing down and raised her blue eyes to Nora's. "You Irish. You're vulgar, violent, lazy, clannish, and shiftless." She said this in a matter-of-fact way, as if stating the price of buttons.

"'Tis true of some," she said with an edge she couldn't stifle. "But not me. I'm dependable and I'm honest. I need the money."

The blue eyes considered this.

Nora plowed on. "These pieces will sell quickly. So popular they are right now. Sure and it's a good profit ye'll make."

The woman laced her fingers together on top of the counter. Greed had ignited in the blue eyes. Finally, she spoke. If the samples were satisfactory, she'd display them on her walls. If anything was ordered, she expected twenty percent of the sale. Nora panicked. With her heart in her throat, she said fifteen. The blue eyes calculated. Finally, the woman agreed.

"But you must do the deliveries," she said. "I'll not be traipsing all over Charleston to deliver."

Nora tried to shake the milliner's hand, but she just fluttered her fingers goodbye.

Nora crossed the street to sweep Pearl into a jig. As she reached for her, Pearl grabbed her hand and began pulling, not jigging.

"Come on," she said, drawing Nora toward an alley.

"But we need to go to the post office," Nora said, pulling the other way. "To order the supplies." She patted the four dollars in her skirt pocket, loaned by the softening Simmons.

"Who says you get to make all the rules? Who made you the missus?" Pearl put her hands on her hips. "You know how close the post office is to the Manning house?"

Nora shook her head. If on some level she'd thought of Pearl as Clare, the partner with whom things were just agreed upon without discussion because they had the same kind of brain, now she realized otherwise. "I'm sorry," she said. "I didn't know."

"Just a couple of blocks away, that's how close. The neighbors and they slaves might be out, might see me."

Nora didn't think so, not in this weather, but she wasn't going to argue. "All right. Wait here."

"Hurry. I got to talk to my man."

"I will."

"It's cold."

"All right, all right."

Nora soon returned to Pearl shivering in the shadows of a building. They took off down the sidewalk—Pearl fifteen steps ahead again—and the neighborhood became even seamier: a funeral home, a one-hall church, a livery stable where black men looked up from repairing harnesses. The girls walked past unpainted homes two rooms wide and two rooms deep. After a block of what appeared to be abandoned houses, Nora saw a black woman come out a front door to chase a dog off the porch with a broom.

Pearl waved Nora into the wooden shed next door, open on one side.

"Jack?" Pearl called.

Nora looked around the shed. An anvil sat on a rough pine table near a brick oven golden with dying coals. A bellows, hammers, and tongs hung on a wall.

"He ain' here," a voice said.

The old woman with the broom walked up, eyeing Nora and Pearl. A plaid shawl dripped off her meaty shoulders.

"He comin' back soon?" Pearl asked.

"I ain' his mama," the woman said.

"Could you give him a message? Tell him—"

Nora put her hand on Pearl's arm to stop her. The woman was looking them up and down way too closely. Even this woman might jump at the chance of reward money. Nora and Pearl were an odd pair. Unforgettable. Suspicious looking.

As they hurried away, Nora had a mouthful of questions about this Jack whom Pearl said was the ticket out of town. Pearl's and her mother's. The mother who may or may not be found, may or may not be alive.

Three blocks later, Pearl began limping. Nora thought they'd surely head straight home, but Pearl veered in the opposite direction. They passed the taverns, warehouses, and freight offices that meant they were nearing the waterfront. Pearl stopped in front of a one-story brick building set back from the street by a plot of bare ground dusted with snow.

When Nora caught up, Pearl said, "This be where I was sold." She pointed at two benches in the yard.

Nora stared at the building, too stunned to worry about being seen next to Pearl.

"The white man who carried me off the plantation told me to sit on one of those benches and he went inside. After a while, he come out with papers in his hands and another buckrah put me in a wagon that took me to the Manning house."

Nora put her arm around Pearl's shoulder.

"I been by here many times thinking somebody in there can look up where she is. I want to go in there, give my mother's name, ask where she is."

But ye can't, Nora thought. She looked up and down the street and, finding it empty, crept up to the darkened office — Pearl wouldn't take a step closer — and read the sign next to the door: "Lewis, Robertson, and Thurston. Factors." Through the window she saw two desks, cabinets, and shelves sagging with leather-bound registers. Those records held Pearl's name, but not necessarily her mother's. The factors might know how to track her down. But a slave trader was the last person they were going to talk to.

Chapter Fourteen

Frantic pounding on the doctor's front door woke the girls in the middle of the night. They sprang off their mattresses to stuff what little they owned into bags, pulled on skirts and boots, and ran downstairs for the back door. As Nora landed on the last step, she grabbed Pearl's arm.

"Wait. We can't go without saying good-bye," Nora said.

"He'll be coming out of his room any minute. We'll wave on our way out the back. Move!"

The pounding stopped. Someone pleaded for help. A man.

"'That isn't the City Guard. What should we do?" Nora whispered.

"Not answer that door like he told us."

"But someone's in trouble. He could be dying out there."

"The doctor will come in a minute. Come on!"

But Nora wouldn't move. The pleading outside dissolved into weeping.

"Aw, shit," Pearl said, running back upstairs.

Nora tiptoed to the door and heard pitiful pawing. She lit a candle and opened the door. The man fell face across the threshold, his bloody hands landing left and right as if crucified. Nora pulled his legs inside to get the door closed. He began clawing his way across the floor.

"Hold on, mister, the doctor's coming." Nora bent down to touch his shoulder.

As the man rolled over, his black hair fell away from his face. Nora lowered her candle to it and at the sight of those features she reared back as if scalded. *Impossible. It can't be.* But there they were: the square jaw and sturdy brow of the man whom she had so many times hoped was imprisoned, or enslaved, or decapitated by the devil and eaten from the neck down while his wicked heart still beat in his chest.

Patrick. It was Patrick.

He opened his eyes and jerked at the sight of her. His boots began digging grooves in the floor to get away.

Footsteps were coming fast and light down the stairs. Nora rushed to meet Pearl halfway. "Pearl, stop. He mustn't see you," Nora whispered.

"Who?"

"Patrick. Jaysus, it's *Patrick.*"

Pearl clamped her hand over her mouth.

"Go back upstairs," Nora said. "'Tis bad enough he knows where one of us is."

"Well, he's gonna die, sounds like."

"And what if he doesn't?"

Simmons flew past the girls.

Pearl hurried upstairs.

Nora ran after the doctor. "He was already on the porch, at the door, making such a racket, I—"

"Bring the candle closer." Simmons ripped open Patrick's coat and ran his hands over the shirt where a crimson ring the size of a fist was blooming wider by the second. Simmons tore the shirt open. Blood oozed from a coin-sized hole in the belly. With a nod at Nora to get the bandages at the back of the house, Simmons pressed his hand on the hole. "You got a gun on you?" he asked.

"No, no, sir," Patrick said.

"Shot somebody? Tell me the truth or I'll send you back out that door." With his free hand, Simmons rummaged through Patrick's pants pockets.

"No, I swear," Patrick gasped.

"Robbed someone?"

Patrick threw an arm over his eyes. "No, no I tell ye. Don't let me die," he cried. "I didn't do nothin'."

Nora came back with cloth bandages.

"Just this one gunshot wound?" Simmons asked.

"Yes, maybe. Don't know. He squeezed a couple of shots out."

Simmons rolled Patrick onto his side, pulled the shirt up to look for an exit wound, rolled him back, scanned his legs and arms. He placed a bandage on the belly wound. "Nora, press this. I've got to get the tools to dig this bullet out and thread a needle with suture. It'll take me a minute. Keep the pressure on or he could bleed to death. Surprised he hasn't already, poor devil."

Simmons hurried down the hall.

Tears tracked through the grime on Patrick's cheeks. He lifted a begging hand at her as he said, "I—"

"Shut up," Nora said, pressing the bandage with one hand

and holding the candle with the other. "Poor devil my arse. What're ye doing in Charleston? I thought ye'd be several states away by now."

"I was. What're *ye* doing here? The Mannings — aren't they looking for us? Do ye know anything about that?"

"Shut up."

He ground his palms into his eye sockets.

"Why'd ye come back?" Nora asked. "No, don't tell me. A girl. Another fool."

"I couldn't get work anywhere, not in Georgia, not North Carolina. The free blacks with a trade, they beat me up town after town. I had to come back here to work in the shipyard. The pay, 'tis just a spit in the wind, but it's something."

"What about the money from the jewelry?"

Patrick looked away.

"Idiot," she said. In the candlelight, she could see a row of crusty sores on his lips, the lips she had once found so irresistible. An old bruise yellowed around one eye, still swollen. A front tooth was chipped. What had he done tonight to earn this bullet in his belly? Nothing would surprise her. She hoped it was the girl he'd wronged aiming straight and true. Nora's brain was afire and soggy at the same time, and she wanted her hands to be free so she could pound the other eye black and blue, but she had to press the bandage down.

Or did she?

The idea swept over her, repulsive yet seductive. No one would ever know. Just the lifting of one innocent finger, then two, then five and his life would flow away here on this floor and no one would ever know that she'd just sat there and watched it happen. It wouldn't take long for him to finish bleeding out.

The doctor would be back soon. *Now or never.*

She looked into his eyes. There was no light there, only the glaze of liquor and shadows of fear because, she could tell, he was reading her mind.

"I won't tell anyone ye're here," he said.

Liar, she thought. *Ye think me stupid? Well, of course ye do, and ye're right to. Such an óinseach I was, such a trusting fool and now look. Ye've put me in the worst danger of me life.*

Ye said I was pretty.

"Nora, I'm—" he said.

"Shut up."

Oh, he was such a thief. Robbed she was. There had been no declarations of love precisely, but there had been promises. With his betrayal, all the wonder and joy, security, money, protection, and happiness she'd pictured with him had collapsed into cinders. She had every right to lift her fingers one by one.

Hurry up before ye lose your nerve.

But she couldn't. Religion was a laughable concept to her, the fires of hell no threat she feared, but letting someone die? She felt certain that she couldn't shoulder that for the rest of her days.

"I'll get ye some money," Patrick said.

She leaned closer into those panicked eyes. "Say ye're sorry. 'Tis all I want from ye."

Patrick nodded furiously. "I'm sorry. So sorry."

She wanted to say *all right,* but it wasn't all right.

Simmons rushed back in with forceps, needle, and oil lamp. "How's he doing?" he asked. "Never mind. Get the Donnelly."

She went to the kitchen and lifted a bottle of Donnelly Rye Whiskey off the shelf. The bottle was only half full but that would be enough to do the job. Being Irish, she'd seen and even appreciated liquor's power to deaden pain—there were so many kinds of pain when you were Irish—but tonight she despised that power. And then her eye landed on a water bottle that she had filled to its neck just that afternoon at the pump. Without hesitating, she poured most of the whiskey in the sink and refilled the bottle halfway with water.

Back at Simmons's side, she offered Patrick the whiskey bottle. He struggled up to his elbows to take the bottle, upended it, grimaced, and gave her a knowing look. She allowed the edges of her mouth to make the slightest curl. None of this exchange escaped Simmons's sharp eye as he waited for the patient to finish drinking.

When Patrick had handed the bottle back to Nora, Simmons said, "Hold him down. Here we go."

* * *

In the morning, the patient had left nothing but smears of dried blood on the wadded sheets.

Simmons demanded the whole truth from the girls, and they delivered. Crying from the first word, they spilled their tales of betrayal, abuse, Captain Wells, Clare, Rebecca Manning, Patrick, the yearning for freedom, the stealing, more betrayal, and running. When it was all out, they wiped their noses and cheeks raw and looked at Simmons, sitting in his fireside chair, fingertips pressed together in a steeple.

"So, you lied to me," he said. "You did steal."

"Well—," Nora said.

"But that no count man stole from her," Pearl said.

Nora watched Simmons's face. The eyes were so cold.

"Why on earth did you two come back to Charleston?" Simmons asked.

Pearl cast a conspiratorial look at Nora.

"There's more?" Simmons shouted. "Out with it."

"She's got to find her mother," Nora said.

"There's an office near the market," Pearl said. "Ledgers inside say who sold me and from where, so maybe they say where she is."

"Torn from her mother's arms at nine years old," Nora said.

"I see." Simmons leaned back in his chair. "And you think you'll go in there, asking questions?"

"No, sir." Pearl pulled on her fingers. "Not me. But somebody. Somebody white. I don't know that part yet."

"Let's say someone actually tells you where she is. Then what?"

"I'm goin' to buy her."

"With the money from this hair art you've spoken of."

"Yes, sir."

Simmons dropped his chin to his chest and studied the floor for a while.

His silence was torture. Nora wanted to say, "But we're honest girls." Didn't he see that she hadn't let Patrick die last night when she could've? Didn't that say something about the goodness in her? Hadn't she and Pearl kept their end of the cooking and cleaning bargain and weren't his sterling silver brushes still on his bureau upstairs? Each second that he didn't erupt with *get out* was a good one and she would happily let him mull all morning, but when she looked over at Pearl to signal to be quiet, she saw that she was too late.

"If you're thinkin' to kick us out," Pearl said, "will you at least go to the factor's office and find out where my mother is?"

Simmons raised his hands, palms out. "Two runaways. I knew better. Knew it." He jerked his coat off the hook beside the door and left.

An hour went by, then two. At three o'clock, the girls began cooking what they intended to be the best dinner of the doctor's life. As the church bells tolled six times, the street door banged again. The piazza floorboards creaked under his boots. Simmons passed by the window on his way back in.

The front door opened. "Don't ever lie to me again," he said.

Chapter Fifteen

The acne-tortured postal clerk, bored and lonely, lit up when Nora walked into the post office. He took his time searching the shelves for her package while complaining about the price of boots, as if a woman would be charmed by that subject and the back of a man's head. Nora, who actually preferred the back of this particular head, mumbled a few uh-huhs while he poked around. She saw that this mail system thing was made up of slots and mailboxes — it appeared that those belonged to individuals — and then there were the general delivery shelves.

"Ah, here it is," he said, pulling a box down from general delivery. "Dr. Frederick Simmons. You going to pick up his mail regularly?" He looked at Nora hopefully.

Nora waved for him to hand over the package.

The clerk looked closely at the return label: M. Campbell's, Self-Instructions in Hair Artistry, New York, New York. He pushed the box toward her. "Hair artistry. That mourning jewelry stuff? Fine thing when a doctor makes money off of dead people."

"Not all of them are dead," Nora said on her way out the door.

That evening, Simmons came in soaked by the rainstorm.

Nora helped him peel off his coat. His shirt was stained with brown and yellow smears. Tension pulled at his mouth and eyes — the residue, she supposed, of a difficult day. Barely settled in a chair, he was trying to untie soggy bootlaces with fingers too tired to do right when Pearl came rushing at him.

"Did you go to the factor's office?" she asked. "What did they say? Where is she? How is she?"

Nora gave her a blistering look. Simmons had never said he'd to go the factor's office, and meanwhile, they were still on shaky ground with him. Pearl knew as well as Nora that they needed this roof above all else, and Nora thought they'd agreed not to do anything to anger him again and certainly not ask him for anything, but Pearl clearly had lost control.

Simmons pumped his flattened palms at her.

Pearl went back to putting plates and glasses on the table.

"I'm going upstairs to change," he said. As he approached the stairs, he saw Nora's unopened package on the first step. He came back, waving it. "My name is on this," he said.

Nora straightened from stirring the gravy at the fireplace.

His voice rose. "You had your mail delivered in my name to the post office? I never said you could do that."

Nora tried to answer. "What's wrong with — "

"Why would you do that?" he asked, getting louder.

"Because she can't use her name," Pearl said.

"But ye knew we were ordering supplies," Nora said. "How else — "

Simmons threw the box into a corner and stormed upstairs. He stomped around in his room, set the bed springs to creaking, slammed the door, went back to the bed springs. Nora poured him a glass of Donnelly and one for herself.

Pearl stirred the beans that didn't need stirring. His boots hit the floor, then the stairs, and he came back into the room.

"That's it," he said, leveling a finger at the girls. "You opened the front door when I told you not to. You lied to me. You are, in fact, thieves. You didn't tell me about this. I can't trust you. You have to go," he said.

Nora stepped toward him. "What? We thought ye knew — "

"You've put me at great risk," Simmons said.

"Of what?"

"You have no idea."

"'Tis for certain!" Nora said.

"You two have to find somewhere else to live. Be gone in a week."

"What? That's almost Christmas Eve, for the lovea Jaysus," Nora said.

Simmons went for his coat. "One week. Find someplace else," he said on his way out. The bells of St. Philip's tolled the curfew for everyone to be off the streets. Needles of rain blew across the cobblestones.

"We got nowhere else," Nora called into the storm. "Ye can't mean it."

He answered with nothing but shoulders hunched against the rain that was hardening into sleet.

Nora dropped into a chair. Why was he afraid of the post office? She'd been buying things all over town with his money and his name. He'd never warned her not to. The man didn't get mail?

Pearl ran her hands up and down her apron. "He'll calm down like he did before."

Nora picked up the whiskey meant for Simmons and downed it. "Surely he'll come back and say he didn't mean it. What's the matter with him? Christmas Eve!"

Pearl picked up the package — their salvation and now their damnation. "We got to get to work," she said. "After supper. We goin' to cut every inch of that black hair of yours."

When the doctor returned, he walked past the aroma of dinner and the cooks' looks of remorse. Upstairs, he set the bed springs to squeaking again. Pearl piled a plate high with his dinner and left it at his door.

*   *   *

Nora placed five samples on the milliner's counter, stepped away, and held her breath. The old woman picked up a brooch with three black blades arranged into a fleur-de-lis and accented with gold wire and false pearls. She turned it over for closer inspection and did the same with the other items — two lockets, a braided cuff bracelet, and the basket of flowers mounted on a muslin-covered pine shingle that had kept the girls up until five that morning. "Why are all of these in black hair?" she asked.

Nora removed her scarf. Butchered locks corkscrewed from her head like piglet tails. "'Twas all I had," she said.

The milliner lifted one finger to her colorless lips to cover a smile. "Very well. I'll display them. We'll see if they sell." She wrote an agreement for two signatures. The third partner waiting down the street held no legal status and in any case was invisible to the milliner.

When Nora joined Pearl, they headed west on Boundary Street, a wide boulevard that sliced across the peninsula from the Ashley River on the west to the Cooper River on the east. Pearl led Nora through an area of institutions and columned homes, a part of town Nora had never seen. They turned south on Pitt Street into a more crowded neighborhood of clapboard row homes perched sideways to the curb, like Simmons's home. Under a porch, chickens clumped together, feathers fluffed against the cold. The girls' legs had gone soft from too many days and nights at their worktable. Nora's were cramping. They took a left on Beaufain Street, then a right on Franklin, and Nora saw that this neighborhood was more of the same: rows of identical houses with darkened windows that seemed to mock her and this stupid spying idea. *No one home with answers for you,* the black windows said. The piazzas too, with their empty chairs rocking in the biting wind called to mind nothing but ghosts.

Just as she started to call to Pearl to say forget it, that they weren't going to find out anything here, same as they'd found out nothing about Simmons by going through his bureau drawers, Pearl pointed to a two-story building with a sign: Marine Hospital. A pair of archways stood like ground-to-second-floor bookends. Piazzas on both floors ran along the front and two sides. Identical windows flanked the plain front door. A man wrapped head to foot in blankets sat in a rocking chair. Unable to wave, he nodded a bandaged head at the girls. Pearl had assured Nora that the hospital existed, but she insisted on seeing it. She tried to picture Simmons inside at the work he talked about every night or used to before the silent suppers had returned. A woman emerged from the front door to help the patient out of his chair. The girls stared at her with thoughts of asking her about Simmons, but they walked away.

With Pearl in the lead again, they burrowed deeper into the neighborhood. On Queen Street, the sound of children playing grew louder as the girls approached a three-story building bordered on all sides by a brick wall. In the wall's center, three steps led to a landing that admitted visitors to the yard. A crucifix crowned the iron arch over the landing. The sign on the wall read "Charleston Home for Children, Sisters of Charity. Catholic Diocese of Charleston." Pearl breezed by without a look, but Nora walked up the steps to the landing to see the yard. A swarm of red-cheeked girls of various ages played games and chanted rhymes. Nora recognized one, a ditty her own little neighbors had tried to sing as they wrung the breath out of their hollow chests chasing one another across the fields.

Mrs. Mason broke a basin

How much will it be?

Half a crown, leave it down

Out goes she.

Irish children then. Could she call them lucky to be orphans? They were clean, their shining hair tied up with blue ribbons, their dresses immaculate. They were rosy-cheeked, well-fed. They were able to sing and run at the same time.

Nora hurried to catch up with Pearl, now almost an entire block away. They turned left, right, left, and soon Nora realized that she'd been here before. There was the funeral home, the one-room church, the livery stable. Again, Pearl led her to the wooden shed open on one side, but this time Nora heard the ringing of hammer on anvil and a man singing.

Before Pearl stepped into the yard, she unwrapped the scarf around her cheeks and smoothed her hair.

A young black man with arms thick as tree limbs slammed a ball-peen hammer into a wagon wheel. A fire roared in the brick oven behind him. He turned toward the sound of boots on grit and broke into a smile. "Well, looky here," he said. "An angel just flew in." He wiped his hands on a rag and reached for her.

"Jackson, Jackson," Pearl cried, gathering her skirts to run to him.

He swept her into hug that plucked her off the ground. As he started to kiss her, he saw Nora a few feet away. His hug dissolved.

Pearl patted his arms. "That's Nora, my friend. Nora, this is Jack."

Nora felt a flush of pleasure at being called Pearl's friend. She took a step closer, raised a hand hello.

Jack flicked a nod her way. "What's wrong?" he asked of Pearl. "You never in town in December."

Pearl told him everything.

"Y'all runaways?" Jack waved the girls deeper into the shed, shooting an especially alarmed look at Nora, the thief.

"They don't seem to be looking for us," Nora said.

"Uh huh," he said.

"We can leave town together now, Jack," Pearl said. "Like we said."

So, Nora thought, *Pearl has a partner and a plan. Thank God. She'll be all right when I leave for New York.*

"She comin' too?" Jack tilted his head in Nora's direction.

"No," Pearl said. "She's got her own way out."

"Where you stayin'?"

"Well, we got a problem wit' that. Might need to stay here."

Jack ran his hand over his face. "Shooo, angel."

"And Mama got to come wit' us."

"Whoa, whoa, gal. You never said nothin' before about her comin'." Jack held flattened palms up. "You tellin' me you found her?"

"We will."

"We?" Jack asked. He looked over at Nora again.

"I need you to go to the factor's office on Cumberland Street and ask about her. You bein' a free man, I thought you—"

"Gal, them buckrahs won't help me. They'll be askin' why I be diggin' 'roun' 'bout this ol' woman, they'll get suspicious, they'll throw me out, maybe call the guard on me. I got to keep my head down."

"I'm going to buy her."

Jack's eyes widened. "Buy her! You a slave and a runaway. You cain' buy her."

"But you can. I'll give you the money."

"Where you goin' to get that kind of money? You steal some jewelry too?"

"We'll be earnin' honest money soon," Pearl said in a huff.

"Well, even if they tell me where she is and even if her mas' is willin' to sell her, they'll take your money but I cain' set her free. There's a new law. Nobody, black or white, can buy slaves and free 'em."

Pearl grabbed his arm. "You wrong."

"Angel, with the law after you now, you got to get out of here fast. That's fuh true."

"No, no, no. We're goin' to get Mama and then go like we said. Together," Pearl said firmly.

"Shhh!" Jack pulled Pearl closer to the fire. Nora crept in too. "It gone get worse," he whispered. "People sayin' that high buckrahs are writin' laws to take away our freedom."

"Make ye a slave again?" Nora asked in astonishment.

Jack plowed on as if Nora wasn't there. "Slave prices are high. Planters sellin' their slaves to cotton growers out west, so black workers free and slave hard to come by," he said. "People kidnapping us to sell us. Things are bad, Pearl. Y'all need to just keep on runnin'."

"Not without you," Pearl said. "And Mama."

Jack gestured at the three walls of his shop. "I'm makin' good money here. Got to make some more first."

"Me too." She grabbed his hand, limp as a half sack of rice despite her clutching.

"How you goin' to make money?" he asked.

"We got an art we goin' to sell. When I have enough, I'll buy Mama. And then we'll go. You, me, and Mama."

"'Tis true," Nora put in. "We'll make money."

Jack glanced over at Nora. She couldn't see his eyes, backlit as he was by the fire, but she could read the resistance in his stance that Pearl could not. Would not.

"Yeah, sure," Jack said.

"So, we can stay here in your house if we have to?"

"I guess." Jack went back to his hammer and wheel.

On their way home, Nora asked, "Where will ye and Jack go?"

"We talked about lots of places. Philadelphia, New York, Boston."

"How?"

"He said he'd work that out. Walking, stealing horses, I don't know."

"New York." Nora said this without joy or hope or any knowledge of the place, but it was all she knew of America.

New York was the heaven everyone on the boat had held onto for six weeks. Philadelphia and Boston were just sounds rolling of the tongue, empty of life, like the dead leaves that skittered across the windy streets.

Chapter Sixteen

The wick that Simmons had lit in their lives had burned down to sputters. As their final hours in his home flew by, Pearl and Nora worked through the night before Christmas Eve to finish three orders. Worry weighted the air of their small room, already heavy with the fruity fumes of gum arabic, until one of the girls would open the window for relief, then after a few minutes of freezing, the other would close it. As Pearl wove someone's auburn hair into petite curls for a brooch, she talked of the few Christmases at Millberry with her mother that she could remember — days of dancing and singing, tasks suspended, firecrackers set off by the master's sons and nephews. Later, at Oakwood, there had been the same sort of singing and dancing over three days but also Mrs. Manning's sugar, coffee, and whiskey, which she exchanged for the slaves' eggs and chickens, though everyone knew she didn't really need any more eggs and chickens. In January, she bestowed shoes that rubbed sores because she never bothered to measure feet.

Whether Simmons felt remorse, they couldn't tell. He kept up a stony demeanor and said little, not even a word about Christmas. The day after, they'd be out. Jack had offered them a night in his barn, maybe two. While they still had this bedroom, they worked as fast as they could.

On the afternoon of Christmas Eve, they heard the front door open, heavy footsteps, and the thud of hard things hitting the floor. The girls came downstairs and found the doctor stacking logs on the fireplace grate.

"It's Christmas Eve," he said with a shrug. "We should have a proper meal."

They looked at the brown paper packages on the table that meant he intended for them to make that proper meal, the kind that would take them away from their work for hours. He was going to hold them to their bargain right up to the end.

The girls opened the packages: mutton, potatoes, eggs, cabbage, hominy. Nora pulled out the pots and banged them around harder than necessary. Pearl washed and seasoned the mutton and vegetables as fast as she could. The doctor lit a fire, lifted a glass of wine to the miniature painting on the mantel, and settled into his hearthside chair. Nora saw that toast and looked away, certain now that she'd never hear the story of the pink-cheeked woman.

While they ate, Christmas carols rang from steeples throughout the city. Nora and Pearl picked at their food as Simmons devoured his. He poured wine into their pewter cups that they tried to push away.

"It's Christmas," he said. "Come on."

They took sips. Their faces went warm, their shoulders relaxed. Simmons poured another round. They cleared the table as soon as he took his last bite, and tried to go upstairs, but Simmons waved them back to their chairs at the fireplace. Nora sat on one side of him, Pearl on the other.

"The nuns," he said as he reached for his leather bag near his feet. "They sent gifts."

The gifts were identical: two pairs of tobacco-colored cotton stockings, two blue hair ribbons, two rosaries. Hot tears flooded Nora's eyes. She had never received Christmas gifts, and if she had, if Da and Mam could've managed it, they would've done exactly this — given her and Clare the same gifts.

"'Tis so kind of the sisters," Nora said. She lifted the ribbon, so silky it barely registered to her touch. She shot a look at Pearl that said, "What would the sisters say if they knew he's kicking us out on Christmas Day because of some fool package in the mail?" That question burned in her throat like a hot coal, and she wanted to spit it into this coziness he thought he was creating, but the wine hadn't loosened her tongue enough for that. Nora had decided that Simmons, with his education, his status, and his sex, didn't understand the realities of the girls' lives. She had refused to look at him for the last few days, not that he'd noticed, him with the male blinders on.

"You tell them you puttin' us out on the street tomorrow?" Pearl asked.

Nora took a big gulp of her wine.

His face was as flat as a slab of granite. He took off his boots and presented his white toes to the fire. Musings born of the wine began then — philosophical comments about life, justice, love.

Nora couldn't stand it. *All of this talk, 'tis as airy as the bloody clouds,* she thought, *when me life is down here in the dog shit in the street.* But then a thought occurred to her. Maybe Christmas was loosening his resolve? Maybe she should calm down and wait to see where he was going, for his mood seemed to be turning like a slow tide. He was steering, she felt, though toward what she couldn't tell.

Pearl got out of her chair. "We got to get back to work," she said.

Simmons held his hand out to stop her, then held the other toward Nora, who saw for certain now that he meant to sweep them into something. He picked up the bottle beside his chair, offered the girls another pour, and this time they held their cups out. The wine flowed in amber streams lit by the dancing fire. Nora pretended to drink.

"This is Madeira," he said without prelude. "The signers of America's Declaration of Independence toasted the signing with Madeira."

"What's that?" Nora asked. "Declaration of — "

"It was the American colonists' declaration of rebellion against England's tyranny," Simmons said.

"God bless 'em then." Nora raised her cup in solidarity.

Pearl, still on the edge of the chair to leave, looked past Simmons at Nora and saw her mouthing *wait*.

"Benjamin Franklin. It was his idea, the Madeira," Simmons said, refilling his cup.

"Ah," Nora said. "And who's he?"

"He was one of the signers of the Declaration. Almost a hundred years ago."

All three tucked their cups to their chests and stared at the flames.

"And so was my grandfather, Benjamin Rush," Simmons said.

Rush, thought Nora. "Your mother's father then," she said.

"No, no. My father's father. I was named for him."

Nora felt the current picking up. She looked over at Pearl, who was frowning now.

"He was a physician in Philadelphia. A member of the second Continental Congress. An abolitionist. They were friends, the two Bens. They founded the Pennsylvania Prison Society."

"Oh, no," Nora said. Christmas forgiveness had just evaporated.

He raised an index finger. "Not what you think. They argued for prison reform. They saw brutal conditions in the city's jail where men, women, and children starved and died. The Bens were compassionate. They wrote . . ." Simmons sat up straight and proclaimed to the fire, "The obligations of benevolence are not cancelled by the follies or crimes of our fellow creatures."

Nora didn't know the words benevolence, follies, and obligations, but she understood that our fellow creatures implied kindness. "Your grandfather wrote that?" she asked.

"A benevolence that the people of Maryland do not share," Simmons said. "Not toward me anyway."

"But you're from Massachusetts," Nora said.

"What's Maryland got to do with it?" Pearl asked from her side of the conversation.

"Long story," Simmons said.

Pearl's frown deepened. "You runnin' from the law, ain' you?"

He let that hang for a minute, then: "Murder was the charge. A woman."

The girls flicked worried glances at the stranger between them.

Simmons held up a hand. "I was working in Baltimore. That's in Maryland. I sometimes cared for the children in an orphanage. An orphan had just turned fourteen, so the orphanage sent her out into the world as orphanages do, to apprentice as a domestic. Big Baltimore mansion. Eleven months later, she came back to the orphanage, very pregnant. I'd seen that tragedy so many times, the predator master of the massive home, waiting and watching in his endless, darkened hallways for one of the household's girls. When this poor child went into labor the sisters sent a runner to me to report her convulsions. I knew what that meant, so I got there as fast as I could, hoping her body was ready to deliver and fast. She was so young, a kid from a Jewish ghetto, having trouble with the delivery. I took forceps out of my bag and began to examine her. Downstairs, there was a ruckus, then it came up the stairs — women's voices, arguing. A woman with a pistol burst into the room yelling that the girl — her housemaid — had seduced her husband. She rushed at the girl and me, spewing accusations. One of the sisters ran at her, the lunatic woman got off a shot but missed, so I went for the gun. We fell, another round went off, her head hit the marble hearth of the fireplace. The crack of her skull — all of us heard it above the laboring girl's screams. The woman went limp. Head injury like that, I knew she was gone."

"Not murder then," Nora said.

"The husband didn't see it that way, and he had influence. The authorities came looking for me."

"Wait — the baby, the mother?" Nora asked.

Simmons shook his head. "The infant was fine. The mother died shortly after. She had never seduced anyone. She was the victim."

Nora closed her eyes.

"So you came here to hide," Pearl said slowly, as if trying to decide whether to believe this tale.

Simmons tilted his head toward the streets. "The sisters sent me here to one of their most distant convents to hide for a while. I forged credentials with a new name, found work at a hospital desperate for help. So many sick and dying here nobody asked a lot of questions."

Nora had a lot of questions — she still didn't see why his false name on a parcel at the post office was a problem — but she didn't want to knock him off course, a pardon possibly being around the bend.

A log disintegrated into red chunks. Outside, the bells of St. Philip's and St. Michael's, the sovereign Episcopal steeples in town, sent out their carillons of twelve bells followed by "Silent Night."

"Despite what you think, I do understand the vulnerabilities of your sex," Simmons said. "When you came to my door that night, I knew I shouldn't let you in. I had my own safety to worry about. But I understood what you faced out there." He settled back into his chair with satisfaction. "I have no family that will claim me, no sweetheart waiting for me — what? With a face like this?" He smiled and looked only at Nora, this time clearly searching for reassurance. "All I have is you two."

And there it was. Forgiveness.

Nora and Pearl leaned forward past his chest to widen their eyes at each other.

"That business about you using my name on your package? I didn't want the clerk to start asking about the new doctor he'd never heard of. Charleston's a small town."

"He didn't," Nora said.

"When I need to receive mail, I have it sent to Sister Boniface, Mother Superior at the orphanage, so the sisters pick it up at the post office. You gave away my false name and my real address. You didn't know. Tonight, I asked Sister Boniface if you could receive mail through the orphanage too, and she said yes."

Nora sat up straight. "What did ye say?"

"They'll accept your mail."

Nora shot out of her chair. "Saints be praised. Sister Boniface be praised. Now Clare can write to me — thank you, thank you! Jaysus, Mary, and Joseph! 'Tis a glorious Christmas gift from the sisters, Dr. Simmons!"

"And from me," Simmons said, raising his glass to himself.

Nora ran around the room shouting glorious glorious while Pearl sat quietly. She watched him turn away from Nora's dancing to speak to her.

"Pearl, like my grandfather, I'm a patriot. I love this country, but the principles of freedom for which the revolutionaries fought aren't granted to all people in America. My grandfather was an abolitionist and a slaveholder, the hypocrite. First thing on Monday, I'll talk to the factor about your mother, see what I can find out."

And then Pearl was on her feet too.

* * *

December 25, 1849

Dear Clare,

Good news. At last, I have an address to give you. Address your Letters to Sister Boniface, Charleston Home for Children at the Charleston post office. She'll pass them on to me.

Oh, me dear sister, now we can plan together. Pearl and I are earning a good wage as hair jewelry artists. Soon as I can, I'll buy a ticket to New York. Have ye received my Letters telling ye to stay there? Are ye still employed by the same mistress?

I hope ye had a good Christmas and that I'll be opening a Letter from ye soon. To speed ye posting it, here's a stamp I'm sending.

Love,

Nora

Chapter Seventeen

Frederick Simmons left the offices of Lewis, Robertson, and Thurston with a smile creasing his pockmarked cheeks. The man who had risen from his desk a few minutes earlier to greet him was friendly enough. Mr. Lewis said he'd see what he could find out about a Rose at Millberry, but why did Simmons want to buy such an old woman, he wanted to know. He looked slantways at the doctor. "You're from the North, aren't you? You're not thinking to free her, are you?" he asked. "Against the law, you know."

Simmons explained that his servant, Rose's daughter, fretted so about the long-lost mother that she would scarcely wash a dish. The fretting was driving him mad, he had lots of dirty dishes piling up, he had enough money, so why not bring the mother into his household?

"But she's old. Could be fifty or so." Mr. Lewis raised his nose, still sniffing around Simmons's story. "You won't get a lick of work out of her. Nobody brings aging, useless slaves into Charleston, Dr. Simmons. People send them out to the plantations to live out their days. She won't so much as shell a bean pod for you, I'm telling you, sir."

"Ah, but I'll get more work out of her daughter. How much do you think she'll cost?"

"Woman that age — probably about six hundred dollars."

"Offer three hundred. I'll be back here in a week," Simmons said.

The office was on the edge of four blocks that held forty businesses that brokered slaves or managed matters for plantation owners. If while he lived in the North, Simmons had been aware that Charleston was the epicenter of the buying and selling of enslaved Africans in the United States, he'd never seen the actual businesses nor talked to the actual brokers. Now he walked past the brokerages, stunned by their staggering number. Thousands upon thousands of African lives had been sold behind those doors. He hadn't chosen Charleston for his life and he wished the nuns hadn't. If only he had known about the wealth and the greed.

Rice, of all things, was at the root of it all.

Simmons had heard the hospital workers talking about how the rice business generated the local luxuries. He read the newspaper. Rice planters were the wealthiest of the wealthy. There was more money per capita in Charleston than in New York or Philadelphia. Rice stored well, shipped well, sold well all over the world, or rather used to. Now rice prices were falling as Asian planters produced a cheaper rice. Simmons sensed panic in the salty air, which threatened southern patriarchy, as did the demands of abolitionists throughout the nation. South Carolina had always been their uniquely heinous target and now he could see why. Forty brokerages in four blocks testified to the number of slaves exchanging hands. South Carolina rice plantations required ten times the labor of Virginia's tobacco plantations or Georgia's cotton fields, a huge investment. No wonder the rice planters were digging in.

Simmons came upon an archway that marked the entrance to a brick tunnel lined with waist-high iron rings, the kind to which one might tether a horse. The sign above the archway read, "Auction" and Simmons realized he was looking at a place where human beings were chained while buyers strolled and evaluated before bidding. The wide stones in the middle of the passage were worn smooth by more than a hundred years of hard boots, while the stones at the sides where bare feet had waited were rough. Simmons hurried away.

* * *

On the other side of town, Pearl knocked on the door of a one-story row house. A curtain moved, she waved, and Jack opened the door. She gave him a peck on the cheek as she breezed in. "Angel's here," she said.

Jack squinted at her as he closed the door. "Somethin' happen?" he asked. "You all wiggly."

"Well, I love you too," she said with a playful swat. "The doctor, he say we don't have to leave his house." Pearl led him to the wood stove in the corner and took off her scarf. They pulled chairs into the stove's warmth and sat down.

Relief washed over Jack's face. "Thank Gawd. If my neighbors was to see y'all here — "

"And he went to the factor today to see if he can find out about Mama. Meantime, me and Nora, we can stay and work and make money. How much you think Mama goin' to cost?"

"Couple hundred I reckon, but — "

She reached for his hand. "When I get her — "

"That doctor going to buy her with your money? He said that?"

"Not 'xactly, but when he does, where are we goin'? Boston?

Philadelphia? How we goin' to travel?"

Jack shifted in his chair. "What about your friend? She still leavin' on her own?"

"She goin' to get on a boat to New York soon as she has the money."

"A runaway on a passenger boat like that?"

"I'm tellin' you, Jackson, they ain' lookin' for us. Now, what about you and me? What's our plan? How're we goin' to get to the North? Where we goin'? You got people who'll help us on the way?"

Jack stared at the floor. "Yea. Through South Carolina, North Carolina, Virginia, on up to Boston."

She squeezed his hand. "I want to wake up next to you every day in Boston. No more of this rootin' 'roun' and pushin' into each other in a hurry on Sunday and then me leavin' to get back to the missus."

"We need more money, Angel."

"Shooo, we fillin' orders more every day. You watch how much money I get and how fast."

* * *

The purple-windowed millinery shop was packed with customers. Word had gotten around. Ladies came in twos and threes to see what everyone was talking about. They studied the samples on the walls—the framed angels and wreaths under glass, the watch fobs, snuff boxes, bracelets, and a family tree, all of it made of hair. Murmurs of admiration for the quality and creativity floated over to the milliner at the counter, ears afire. She couldn't shove the customers' orders into Nora's hands fast enough. Meanwhile, Nora had also placed samples in another shop and soon she was delivering orders to homes all over the city. At the customers' requests, Nora delivered to the front door, not the back, as if the memorial deserved a proper arrival to the household. If the lady of the house wanted to talk about the person who had been memorialized, Nora had to stay and listen, but she was nervous, being a criminal. She shifted foot to foot, hands clasped behind her back, waiting for the woman to take a breath so she could say she had to run along. Often, she saw tension in the papery, pampered faces. Some of the ladies stole anxious looks at the servants all around as if checking on what they were doing behind her. There were always so many. In one house, Nora counted six black women coming and going, and those were just the ones she could see. The missuses of Charleston were outnumbered.

With each day that passed with no newspaper ads or hand-bills announcing three runaways from Oakwood Plantation, Nora began to relax during her travels. She looked for Patrick on the streets. She couldn't help it. Was he back in the shipyard? Had he recovered from his wound? Who was he loving?

After deliveries, Nora hurried back to the shops to get paid, then home to stare at the dollar bills with Pearl. They had twenty of them, their first very own money, actual cash, fuel of their dreams. It was Pearl who had the idea to hide the money in an envelope glued to the backside of a framed work sample that hung in their room. She announced that they wouldn't touch it until they'd raised whatever was the price of an old slave woman on Millberry Place Plantation. At this, Nora fell silent. She needed only ten dollars for the packet ticket to New York and her half was already there, but she couldn't take her share and just leave Pearl. *Just another week or two,* she thought. *Stay another week and help Pearl get closer to her three hundred, four hundred or five or whatever it will be. Clare and I, we're scared but safe. We have time, and Pearl doesn't.*

The girls continued working late into the nights, long after the doctor had gone to bed. With spring coming, they wouldn't be able to hide behind their scarves much longer. Drunk with fatigue, they talked hopefully of the Mannings never trying to find them. In the mornings, they both shook their heads at that fool notion. Rebecca Manning liked her things—jewelry and servants especially—and she'd want them back.

Clare's lot, at least, was getting better.

January 5, 1850

Dear Nora,

I was so worried, not hearing from ye since September when ye told me to stay here in New York. Then yesterday, I get yer Letter telling me ye ran away! I hope that Sister Boniface gets this Letter to ye. I worry about ye having to hide. So the Mannings are coming after ye, are they?

I have changed jobs since I received yer last Letter. Me new mistress is so Loud and full of blarney. She writes what she calls essays and tries to get them published in the Newspaper here. Her name is Esther Klein. Her house is so big. 'Tis in the city. Takes up half the block. There are six of us Irish girls working to clean and wash and serve. All but me live in the house. She lets those that want to go to Sunday Mass go, though she won't give us the holy days off. She never calls me low Irish. The food, 'tis so glorious and the cook orders the same good food for us as she does for Mr. and Mrs. Klein. Even roast beef. Abraham Klein is his name, fond of his Roasts and puddings, but we don't see much of him. No children. So, Mrs. Klein spends her days painting flowers and fruit, writing her essays, and having luncheons for other loud ladies. I hear their talk of what they call social Justice in the South. 'Twould have been nice if someone had spoken up for us when our landlords made our lives hell.

I saw an Irish greenhorn the other night on a street corner. I thought it was Martin O'Malley from home, but when I went closer to see better through me tears, I seen it wasn't him. Since I can't see yer face, seeing his would have done me a World of good, but it wasn't Martin.

I can't wait for yer next Letter. I wish the Mail didn't take ten days down there and ten days back.

Love,

Clare

Chapter Eighteen

One afternoon, as Nora scooped ashes out of the fireplace of the front room, she thought about the ten days she'd spent with Captain Wells—his depravity, the profanity, the whiskey-soaked boasting of the crimes he'd committed, and that smell, always that smell that preceded his arrival. When she did get on a ship out of Charleston by Jaysus, it would be nothing like his stinking ship. It would be a steam ship, all white and gleaming, and she'd be in clean, crisp sheets every night. Long ago, she'd had so much hope about America. Now her dreams had boiled down to a quiet room in New York with Clare, a job in a respectable house where no one beat anyone, some roast beef now and then. Reunited with Clare, she could pick up her dream again in this new world, wiser, tougher.

A thought hit Nora so hard she backed out from her deep digging in the fireplace to sit on her heels. What if Clare found a sweetheart before Nora could get back? A stable hand at the grand house, say, or the man who delivered from the bakery? Where would that leave Nora? It was possible a fella might take a shine to Clare. *Oh, but Clare, don't ye be believin' him,* she thought. *Watch out for what he's asking of ye.* There were good men in the world, though. Of course there were. Clare might stumble across the one in New York. Even lasses with horsey faces find sweethearts.

Don't they?

Nora went to the mirror and tried to look at her face objectively, as a fella would. She didn't have the delicate features that so many women in this town had — the rosebud mouth, the submissive little chin at the bottom of a sweet oval face. No, she had Da's boxy jaw and those two front teeth with the gap she'd come to hate. What man would ever look twice at such a face?

Patrick did. Is he still in town? She closed her eyes. *Stop it.*

She heard footsteps on the piazza, the scrape of the doorknob turning. It was mid-afternoon, too early for the doctor to come home, so this was probably Pearl, but Pearl was supposed to be on the other side of town.

Frederick Simmons walked in, packages in hand.

"Oh!" Nora said as she got to her feet. "What's wrong?"

Simmons laughed. "Nothing's wrong," he said. "I decided I've earned an afternoon off. I brought home some supplies for the clinic." He put the packages on the table and shot her a quick smile. "Where's Pearl?"

"Errands." Nora went back to working inside the fireplace. She'd never heard him laugh so heartily. It was a nice laugh, rich and genuine. The kind that made you smile. When she finished dumping char and grit into her bucket, she headed for the back door with the bucket.

"Need some help with that?" Simmons asked as he followed her, bundles under one arm. Without waiting for an answer, he hurried ahead to open the door, followed her outside, and watched her empty the bucket into a bin.

"Ye need something?" she asked on her way back inside.

Simmons closed the door and opened one of the bags. "Help me put these away?" He handed her a box of bandages.

A box. Ye need help with one box? Nora put it on the shelf and turned back for more.

He handed her another. "So, that letter from your sister. Is she faring well in New York? Everything all right?"

"Aye, she's a lucky one, she is. Has a new job with a lady who sounds fair and kind."

"You've never told me about your life before America."

"Ach." Nora placed the box beside the first.

"Other sisters? Brothers?" he asked, handing her the third box.

"Three. All dead," she said, putting it on the shelf.

Simmons winced at his blunder. "Oh. I'm so sorry."

"Mam too and probably … " Her voice trailed off. "Da."

"I'm sorry. I shouldn't have — "

"'Tis all right. I'm grateful to ye for asking." Fighting tears, Nora looked at his second bag for more. "Ye know, sometimes I despise the place of me birth. Sometimes I'm glad to be rid of it, a feeling me mother would've taken a stick to me for, God rest her imperfect soul, and so would her mother before her and the mothers in all those hills who birthed and raised us. They would've beaten me for saying it."

Simmons took his time tearing away the strings on the second package. He unwrapped a white enameled bowl and tweezers. "My mother? There was no would've about it. She did beat me, well my fingers she did, at the piano, as if that was going to make them do right. She was brimming with the Rush family's legacy, its accomplishments and humanitarian ideals, but she was dry-bone empty on the humane treatment of imperfect children." He handed the bowl and tweezers to Nora, who had turned her unguarded face toward him, just as he'd hoped. In her softening eyes, he saw concern for his seven-year-old self. "My mother wanted me to go to my famous grandfather's medical school in Edinburgh and so, of course, I did," he said.

"And ye graduated. I can't imagine doing such a thing."

"Mother said my hands were useless."

"But they save people."

Simmons's sagging face brightened. "That's been my wish," he said.

"If ye had a piano ye grew up in a fine house, I'm guessing," she said.

Simmons nodded. "And you?" He winced again. "Oh, wait, I didn't mean—"

"Oh, we liked our cottage with the dirt floor well enough. Mam and Da made a good go of it on our plot I suppose, raising the five of us to be kind and hard-working if not God-fearing. They scoffed at the teachings of the priests, themselves too fond of the pint. But the priests offered to teach us how to read and write English, and so if they slipped in the Holy Trinity occasionally Mam and Da tolerated it. Far as I can see, though, despite what the priests said about a just and forgiving God, he plays pretty rough."

Simmons nodded.

"Looks like we've emptied yer bags." Nora picked up her bucket and headed for the front of the house.

"So, you're the older twin," he said as he followed.

Nora went back to the fireplace and chased after the last of the cinders. "Aye. Five minutes."

"I wonder if a little bit of you now is enjoying being a separate person?" Simmons asked.

Nora sat on her heels and looked up at him with surprise. She'd been feeling exactly that way over the last few weeks. No longer half of the Murphy twins. Just Nora. Nora who'd helped a slave escape, survived a creek ride in a snub-nosed bateau to Georgetown and the wagons to Charleston, learned a trade and how to figure percentages with potatoes, and how to negotiate with uppity shop owners. And then the guilt would begin coiling around her heart. What kind of person would feel that way about her twin? "I miss her, of course," she said quickly.

"Of course," Simmons said with a sympathetic look.

"What made ye think of that?" Nora asked.

"Just listening to you talk the other evening about your hair art. You're different, not the woman who came to my door weeks ago."

She went back to sweeping up the last of the ashes.

"You and Pearl, you'll be leaving soon," he said.

"Soon as we can."

"Back to New York?"

"Aye." She turned around to look at him. "Lots of questions today. How about ye? How much longer will ye stay here?"

"That's a very good one," Simmons said.

Chapter Nineteen

"Three hundred dollars," Simmons shouted as he came in the door on an evening in the middle of January. "That's what your mother's owner wants for her."

Pearl dropped a spoon into the pot of soup she was stirring and rushed at him. "She's alive? Still there? She's all right? Three hundred? That's nothing. When can we go get her?" she cried.

Nora flapped her apron with excitement.

"Hold on, hold on, let me get my coat off," Simmons said. "She's still at Millberry Place, in the Barnwell District. Upstate. The owner, his widow actually, reports that she's surly and lame and she's happy to get rid of her."

"Lame?" Pearl's face fell. "What did they do to her?"

"Don't think about that right now," Nora said, patting Pearl's arm. "Maybe nothing. Old people go lame sometimes."

"How far's Millberry?" Pearl asked.

"About a hundred miles away. When you have the money, I'll go get her, either at the plantation or at the factor's office," Simmons said. "Depends on the owner's preference, I gather. I've never done this before."

"Three hundred dollars then," Pearl said. "That's our goal."

Nora studied her partner and friend. The night before, Nora had counted one hundred fifty dollars in the envelope, the most money she'd seen in her life, and though half of it was hers, she wouldn't touch it. Except for two dollars. Tomorrow she needed two dollars and she wasn't going to mention to Pearl that she'd be tapping into their stash behind the frame.

*   *   *

The last pew in St. Mary of the Annunciation Catholic Church was nearly full. Nora slipped into a space next to a woman and child. The waxy pallor on the faces all around and coatless shoulders told Nora she'd found the Irish crowd. Had she not spent so much time working and hiding she liked to think that she would've been a familiar face to them. On her travels to and from the market, she'd heard the Irish music coming from the shanties, a sound that tore at her soul, but she dared not go near so much disease. The woman and child next to her weren't coughing, didn't have the tinge of Yellow Jack, so Nora relaxed. She scanned the crowd for one particular colleen. Black lace or hats covered every woman's head, making it hard to see profiles. Nora pulled the brim of her hat forward to hide hers.

At the front of the church sat the merchant class, mostly Italians, in good coats and hats. Nora looked around at the immaculate building less than ten years old, the first church she'd ever entered and what a glorious cavern it was, with the brilliant white balconies along the second floor and the colored glass windows ignited by the sun. On the ceiling, there was a painting of a woman draped in blue sitting on a bed of clouds. Cherubs pink and fat sat at her feet, smiling up in adoration. Nora figured that the woman was Mary — it said St. Mary's Church outside after all — and according to what the priests had taught, she'd earned all of that adoration, long-suffering mother that she was. A ring of angels above Mary's head smiled down on her.

The tinkling of bells at the altar brought everyone to their feet. As lace and hats shifted, Nora spotted who she was looking for three pews ahead — good old tough and practical Margaret, the bug-eyed bunkmate on the boat to Charleston. For the next hour, Nora went through the Catholic ritual — kneeling, standing, sitting, more kneeling — with growing frustration over all of that up and down and no understanding of what the priest was saying into the wall in front him. It wasn't even English. What was the point? The place was warm at least.

After the priest finally faced the assembled to bless them goodbye, the organist went at the organ with gusto. Nora picked up the words, English at last, being sung all around her. *My country 'tis of thee, sweet land of liberty. Let freedom ring.* Even the Irish were singing it. *Our Father's God to thee, author of liberty, to thee we sing.*

Maybe one day she'd believe that — America as a land of liberty.

Finally, the service ended, and people began leaving. Outside, Nora waited for Margaret and touched her arm as she went past. Margaret gasped. Nora was sad to see so little light in those eyes that had been so hopeful. Still no pink in the cheeks that should've been glowing from better food by now. Nora steered Margaret into hiding behind a tree.

Margaret was wild with questions. "Mother of God, where've ye been? Why haven't ye come to see me at the house? Why are we hiding?" Margaret finally took a breath and looked at Nora more closely. "'Pon my soul, what's gotten after your hair?"

Nora clawed at the ragged fringes springing away from her hat brim. "Well—"

"Yer sister — why isn't she with ye?" Margaret's eyes grew impossibly wider. "Surely she's arrived by now."

Nora explained her hair and all that had happened and

answered even more questions that kept coming at her like rocks from a gang of hooligans until she finally steered Margaret toward talking about *her* life, a story that took quite a while and though Nora did care and she was happy there was a husband now, she was nervous about being seen. Also, she was freezing. The two dollars that she'd taken from the envelope was burning in her pocket. Finally, Nora blurted that she needed a favor.

"Sure, if I'm able," Margaret said.

"The *Columbia* is scheduled to arrive in two or three days. January nineteenth or twentieth."

"That awful boat? What in the name of — "

"It'll be at Fitzsimmons Wharf. Will ye give this to the captain?" She put the two bills in the girl's hand. "I can't get near him. If he hears there's a reward, he'll snatch me up."

"A reward? But ye said — "

"I can't be sure there won't be ads. Look around the waterfront for handbills about me, will ye?"

"Aye, I will. But what's this money for?"

"I owe him. Remember?"

"That arsehole," Margaret shook her head. "Why bother paying him now?"

"I want him to forget about me. Pay him and tell him I left town a few days ago."

"How do I get back in touch with ye?"

Nora gave her the doctor's address.

Margaret put the money in her skirt. "God bless ye, Nora. I'll see ye in a few days."

Nora squeezed Margaret's hands and ran down the street.

* * *

Three days later, Nora opened the door to rapid knocking. Margaret rushed in like a hay field afire, as if she was the hunted one.

Pearl came running downstairs when she heard the panicked voice. Margaret gave a terse nod to her and went back to Nora. "'Twasn't there the first day nor the second, so I asked around about the *Columbia*," she said. "A man at one of the warehouses says that boat's in rotten shape. 'Tisn't sound, never on schedule. Says he wouldn't ship so much as a bale of hay on her. Captain Wells can't keep a nickel in his pocket for the gambling and drinking. Today though, when I went back, she'd arrived. Those same nasty deckhands slithering around the deck, then Wells."

"And?" Nora asked.

"I called out to him. He just glared at me. I didn't dare shout that I had money for him, so I made the coin-rubbing sign and he finally shuffled down the gangplank. Dear Lord, the unholy stink— it could choke a horse. I gave him yer money, said it was from ye, the wee Irish twin, to pay yer bill. You left town."

Pearl raised an eyebrow at the mention of Nora's money.

Margaret started talking faster. "His face lit up and he asked, 'Where is she?' I tried to back away, but he grabbed me wrist. 'Tell her I know she's running. Tell her I'm leaving tomorrow and if she pays me the reward amount, I'll hide her on this ship.' And then he gave me this." Margaret pulled a piece of paper from her skirt.

Nora unfolded it. Across the top—a black-ink, woodcut figure of a person running hard. Below it the headline: *Three runaways.*

Nora read aloud:

Two Irish servants indentured to Edward Manning, having run away from Oakland Plantation, Georgetown County, on November 22. Patrick O'Hagan, carpenter, twenty-five years old. Six feet tall. Black hair. May be in the Company of Nora Murphy, house servant who stole jewelry, short and slight in stature, nineteen years old, black hair, wide gap between front teeth. Also a female slave named Pearl, brown skin, very short, approximately nineteen years old. Whoever harbors one or all three will be prosecuted with the utmost vigor by Edward Manning. If seen, report to the office of Robert Huger, Factor, Cumberland Street, Charleston, for reward. Twenty dollars per runaway.

Nora turned to Pearl. "We have to get out of town," she said.

Pearl crossed her arms. "We ain' going anywhere 'til we have three hundred dollars."

Chapter Twenty

Frederick Simmons stood beside a dining room chair while he waited for his colleagues to get their wives seated. He was relieved that women were at the table, hopeful that the men's conversation that began in the host's library would not be resurrected. Surely his friends wouldn't scare their wives with their blunt observations that Charleston was becoming a powder keg. Well, not scare them exactly, for the women weren't deaf to the calls for secession and the tragedy that would bring, of course, but talk of seething Charleston wasn't polite dinner conversation.

The ladies eased their silk-draped bottoms into chairs and Simmons sat down. Spreading his napkin across his lap, he admired the most enticing food he'd seen since his Philadelphia days—roasted venison haunch, oysters, terrapin soup. Here was a comfortable table set with restrained amounts of silver and china, nothing pretentious in this home of an ordinary physician, his colleague Daniel McCarter. There were no enslaved people hovering in the background, hands clasped in front of their hips. Dr. McCarter had moved to Charleston from his ancestral home Virginia two years earlier, but he was firmly opposed to slavery. With the ladies' presence serving as a governor on the conversation, Simmons began to relax.

Mrs. McCarter — Dorothea — ladled the soup family style into bowls that she then passed. When everyone was served, she lowered her spoon to her soup and asked, "Well, Dr. Simmons, how do you find Charleston? You've been here how long now?"

"About a year, ma'am, and I've done little but deal with this epidemic," he said. "I don't have much of a social life." He savored the soup as it passed over his tongue.

"Those poor Irish," Mrs. McCarter said. "They seem to fall to the fever left and right."

"Yes, ma'am. They arrive in this country with little resistance to it."

The woman across the table from Simmons wagged a finger at him. "Dr. Simmons, you should venture out more often. Our architecture is some of the finest in the world," she said.

Simmons looked up from his next spoonful at Sarah Gadsden, whose accent and posture told him she was Charleston born and raised. "Well, I've seen the churches, of course, and the Exchange Building and that new Hibernian Hall on Meeting Street," he said. It was only because Nora had taken him to see it that he knew of the meeting hall for the Irish benevolent society.

"Keep a low profile here, Dr. Simmons. You have that northern air about you." This half-joke came from Sarah's husband, Dr. James Gadsden, a Medical College instructor who shepherded students around the hospital wards. He was a loose-jointed, ungainly fellow with too many cowlicks for one head.

"Oh, I do, I do," Simmons said, hoping he sounded jolly enough. But just as he feared, not even five minutes into dinner, Dr. Gadsden had dragged the powder keg into the dining room. Simmons tried to think of another subject to bring up — the horse races coming up in February perhaps — but he took too long deciding.

"Damn federal government," Dr. Gadsden said. "The federal hospital we work in is the most despised building in town. You know that don't you, Dr. Simmons? The government interfered with our planning it and did they ask any of us here to be part of that? No, they did not. Then they forced their Washington, D.C. architect down our throats."

Simmons dabbed his napkin to his lips.

Mrs. Gadsden patted her husband's hand. "Darling, that architect is a southern boy. He was born and raised right here in Charleston." A young but severe-looking woman, Sarah Gadsden had a face that was a badge of authority. Simmons could tell she liked to ensure accuracy in conversations, if not the world.

"Well, he should've stayed here instead of moving to the North," Dr. Gadsden said. "And then there's the government pressing its authority in our face by maintaining three federal forts in the harbor and building that new customs house over on East Bay so they can collect their import duties."

"It's abolition, not buildings, that's the bigger thorn I think," Mrs. McCarter said.

And here we go, Simmons thought.

"No question," Dr. Gadsden said. "The slaveholders are going to do us in. Big investments, those rice plantations. You can see why the planters won't back down."

"Plenty of people besides the planters own slaves," Dr. McCarter said.

"Mr. Allen who owns the bookstore on Meeting Street, he has five," Mrs. McCarter said.

"And he's from Massachusetts," Dr. McCarter said. He waved a spoon at Simmons. "Like you."

Simmons nodded and dipped again into his soup.

"Well, the planters are in a panic not only about their finances. It's all about their status, their patriarchy, including the obedience of wives and children. All of it's at risk if abolition succeeds," Dr. Gadsden said.

"Everyone's whispering that there will be another slave uprising," Mrs. McCarter said.

"They outnumber us three to one," Mrs. Gadsden said.

Simmons reached for the nearest bottle of wine and refilled his own glass, a gauche move that would've mortified his mother, but he felt confident that if she were here, she'd do the same.

"I heard that the planters' wives aren't sleeping well these days. They're afraid their servants are just biding their time before killing them as they sleep in their rice beds," Mrs. McCarter said.

Finally, all soup spoons and goblets being lifted to eager lips paused.

These wives are the scary ones, Simmons thought.

"Good thing we don't have servants, Mrs. McCarter," Dr. McCarter said with a smile.

"Don't joke," Dr. Gadsden said. "The rice and cotton empires are teetering. When the abolitionists push them over the edge, we'll all go, slave owners and not."

"Empires don't teeter, darling," Mrs. Gadsden said. "Vases on mantels during an earthquake teeter."

* * *

The carriage that Simmons had hired couldn't arrive at McCarter's door fast enough. After waving goodbye to the dinner companions who had robbed him of enjoying a meal that had held such promise, Simmons settled into his seat. A civil war was brewing, and as in all wars, only the lucky would survive it. Bravery and skill and wealth would have nothing to do with it. How much more time did they all have, he wondered — he, Nora, and Pearl. How much money had the girls earned? Not three hundred dollars yet, obviously. Of course, they'd split the profits, which meant Pearl had only half of whatever. He had tried not to pry into their affairs, but he couldn't help noticing a growing tension in Nora. Why didn't she buy a packet ticket and leave? All she needed was ten dollars for the fare.

He'd considered giving her some money so she could flee and leave all their profits to Pearl, but he knew Nora wouldn't accept it. And when he let his imagination go down a certain path that he loved to walk, he thought about going with her.

She didn't trust him completely; he could see that in her eyes. He'd withheld his own truth from her, so he understood. The previous night, he'd pulled her chair out from his dinner table for her. Would an Irish girl raised under a thatched roof understand that such a move blurred the line between employer and employee as intended? She accepted his courtesy and looked over her shoulder at him with softer eyes, so perhaps she did. So much feistiness in such a little colleen. He couldn't imagine the aura that two of Nora — her and Clare — would generate. Could he survive them? Could he survive Nora if the twins never reunited? *One thing at a time,* he told himself.

And then there was Pearl. He'd known from the minute he laid eyes on Nora and Pearl, that mismatched pair licking their plates clean, that they were as connected as ligament and bone. Was Nora delaying her departure so she could help Pearl earn the price of her mother? What other secrets did they share? The stolen jewelry, that didn't really offend him, for he knew some women had to do immoral things to survive. Nora's tale was the same tale told in Charleston's constantly flooded shanties full of women, black and white. The Marine Hospital took care of seamen and transient workers, all men, but he could scarcely walk the streets without seeing women who should've been in that hospital. Benevolent aid societies did what they could.

He told the carriage driver to let him out two blocks from home. The hour was late, but he needed to walk. The officers of the City Guard knew him from his walks home from the hospital long past the curfew bells of St. Michael's. Into the pools of light thrown by gaslight lamps Simmons strode, shaking the cigar smoke and the table conversation out of his coat. Sooner or later, the federal government would send an inspector to the Marine Hospital to review the physicians' credentials. He had his plan for leaving, the where and how of it. *When* was always the question. And recently, another question had entered the picture: with whom?

When he opened his front door, he saw a crumpled paper on the kitchen table. Opening it, he read Edward Manning's demand for his runaways.

Chapter Twenty-one

The Manning carriage rattled down East Bay Street with Isaiah and Tobias sitting ramrod straight on the driver's seat. Two blocks ahead, Pearl hurried home from the market, towel-padded at the hips and bosom to disguise. A scarf hid all but her eyes. The sidewalk was full of people on errands and deliveries.

As the carriage closed in on Pearl, Tobias recognized the sloped shoulders and the wiggle of the bottom. He sat up even straighter at the sight of the pretty red bird whom he'd hoped to catch for as long as he could remember. Isaiah recognized the wiggle too. When the carriage arrived alongside her, Isaiah pulled the horses to a crawl so slow that Pearl shot a look of alarm their way. The men nodded and looked away as if she were a stranger, but not before seeing the fear hardening in her eyes.

At home, she rushed into the bedroom where Nora was working and told her the Mannings were back in town.

Nora came out of her chair. "Ye sure it was Tobias and Isaiah? Jaysus, I told ye not to go outside today."

Pearl pulled off her coat. "It's all right. I been thinkin' 'bout how to get the missus off our tail. Now that she's back in town, I can do it."

"What are ye planning?" Nora asked in a tone that said she didn't really want to know.

Pearl took the money from behind the picture frame and counted it. "Two hundred," she said.

"Would ye stop counting the money?" Nora shouted. "We did that last night."

"I need a little to buy a few things for what I got to do."

"Like what?"

"You want me to get rid of the missus or not?"

"How much are ye taking?"

Pearl shook the bills at her. "Three dollars, all right? One more dollar than you took without a word to me!" She tucked the remaining bills back into the envelope. "What's the matter with you?"

"Jaysus, Mary, and Joseph. How can ye ask me that?"

"You got somethin' you need to say? Somethin' about the money?"

"Well—"

"You took some a while back, didn't you?"

"Pearl," Nora said slowly. "We haven't talked about this. Half of that is mine."

"You think I don' know that?" Pearl's brown eyes went resentment hard. "This is three dollars from my half, all right?"

"I know. I'm sorry. But I'm afraid." Nora sat back down, squeezed her hands between her knees.

Pearl put her hands on her hips. "You afraid that we'll run away without you?"

Nora shook her head. "What do ye mean? I don't expect ye to take me with ye."

"You and I both know that you ain' leavin' here on a regular boat with all them runaway handbills all over the wharves."

Nora crossed her arms against her stomach.

"Didn't Jack say he'd take you with us?" Pearl asked.

No, Pearl, he never said that Nora thought.

"Well, he will." Pearl picked up her coat and scarf. "Like I say, it's time to scare off the Mannings."

* * *

The next day, Pearl hid in a narrow street two blocks from the city's merchant district and watched Rebecca Manning's dressmaker hand boxes of gowns and tassled bags to Isaiah. Above the rooftops, gray clouds muscled into one another, so the two hurried to finish loading. Isaiah closed the carriage door, the woman closed her shop's, and when the carriage arrived where Pearl stood, she pulled off her scarf and stepped off the curb.

Isaiah sucked air through his teeth as she climbed into the seat beside him. She threw her arms around his neck and buried her face in the grizzled folds. When she let him go, he said, "Little gal, thank Gawd. I was so glad to see you the other day. We all 'fraid you was dead. But what you doin' in Charleston? They lookin' for you."

Thunder muttered in the distance. Two men down the street ducked into a building. Isaiah's horses snorted and pulled to get home. He steered them into an alley.

"You been here this whole time?" he asked.

She nodded.

"Wit' that girl?"

"Yes, with Nora, and we're making money, Isaiah. I'm going

to buy my mother. I found her still living at the plantation I left." She searched his eyes for shared joy but found only raw fear.

"You ain' been out there to that place have you?" he asked.

"No, I just found out where she is."

Isaiah studied the reins in his hands for a while. "I got to get on back."

"Not yet. Tell me—why did it take mas' and the missus so long to put out the reward flyers?"

"The missus, she took real sick with country fever. Then the mas' found out some fiel' hands stole some seed rice out the barn, so he went runnin' to Georgetown to catch 'em 'fore they could sell it. He was too late to stop that, so he was hot as fire when he dragged those men back to the driver for whipping. Then little William took sick. Missus went crazier than usual, said wit' all the troubles goin' on, someone put a root on the family. The mas' have his hands full with that woman."

"William all right?"

"Yeah, he come 'roun'. Everyt'ing settle down, so we come back to town for the parties."

"Isaiah, I need your help."

Isaiah shook his head. "No. Whatever you thinkin', this ol' man's answer is no."

"Will they go to church as usual this Sunday?"

He wiped dust off the reins.

"Isaiah?"

"Far as I know."

"You'll bring the carriage 'roun' to wait for them on Meeting Street as usual? They'll come out the front door?"

"Prob'ly."

"I need for you to oil the front gate there on the street."

"Lawd, Lawd."

"And tell Hettie to be sure to stand behind the mas' as he opens the front door for the missus."

"What for?"

"Hettie needs to be there to explain."

"Explain what?"

"Just tell her to be there. She'll know what to say when she sees it."

* * *

On Saturday night, a night robbed of light but for the meager pulse from the crescent moon, Pearl crept down Meeting Street, avoiding all the houses that she knew to have dogs that might bark. There were few City Guards here in wealthy districts such as this one south of Broad Street. The wealthier the neighborhood, the fewer the drunks and sailors on the streets and the fewer the thieves who preyed upon them. That left no one but Pearl for the moment on the darkened sidewalk as she inched along hugging brick garden walls. Nothing stirred, neither man nor beast, not even the papery palm fronds. She scanned the silent street for the slightest movement.

Something shot in front of her so fast Pearl tripped over her own feet and fell, one hand squelching her scream. The cat raced across to the other side of the street and disappeared into moon-silvered bushes. Pearl looked back the way she'd come to see if it was still clear for a retreat, but she was more than halfway. She picked herself up and pressed on.

She pushed the Manning wrought-iron gate open an inch to test it. Not a sound. Good old Isaiah. Holding her breath, she tiptoed up the steps of the front porch, left her message for the missus at the door threshold, and ran home.

The next morning, Rebecca Manning stood before the vestibule mirror tying the ribbons of her yellow spoon bonnet under her chin. Beside her, Edward brushed the lapels and shoulders of his frock coat one more time. Hettie stood a few feet away, hands clasped under her pendulous belly, alert as a mother hen, but for what, she didn't know. She looked for clues at the mirror, the floor, the windows, and Isaiah beside the carriage outside. Edward reached for the doorknob.

Isaiah tried to affect his usual smile as he watched the front door open. Moments before, he had searched the porch steps, the windows, the massive front door, and when he saw what lay on its threshold, his heart stopped. Back to the carriage his old hips and legs carried him with greater speed than they had for many years.

Rebecca stepped over the threshold, took two more steps and spun around, saying, "What was *that*?" She bent down for a look at the tiny bundle she had almost stepped on—a crispy snakeskin wrapped around a dried frog, which was wrapped around two rusty horseshoe nails. Beside it sat two pecans, old and pale, the brown bleached out of the shells long ago.

Hettie looked around Edward who had stopped dead in the doorway. "That's a conjuh," she cried. "Someone's tryin' to put a root on you. If you don't step over it, though, you be all right."

Rebecca gave Hettie a look that would kill weeds. "I just did, you idiot." She backed away from the threshold. "No, no, no."

"Why darling, it doesn't mean a thing," Edward said. He kicked the dried frog down the steps.

Rebecca clawed at her arms as the magic dug into her porcelain skin. Her trembling hand went to her throat. "I can't breathe. Edward, go get that thing. I can't have it here, on our land. Take it to the river. The pecans too. Throw them in the harbor," she cried.

"I never seen no pecans with a conjuh before," Hettie said.

"It's from Pearl, don't you see? They're from that seed sack of hers," Rebecca cried. She looked over at Isaiah, standing as straight as he could. "Isaiah, did you see her out here? You saw her, didn't you? It was Pearl. I know it was." Rebecca's screaming sent the birds scattering.

'No, ma'am. Didn't see nobody out 'yuh this mornin'." He put on an earnest show of looking up and down Meeting Street, mostly to hide his expression.

Rebecca collapsed to the porch floor. "Hettie, get me a chicken, a white one. If you kill a white chicken it'll kill the conjure," she cried. "Isn't that right?"

"Yes, ma'am," Hettie said. She declined to say that there was also a way to reverse the reversal.

Edward looked down the street too. "If Pearl's in town, we'll find her," he said.

"No, not now! Leave her be. We have to go back to Oakwood. We have to get out of here," Rebecca cried.

The next-door neighbor came to his porch, Sunday hat in hand, to squint at the commotion.

"Hettie," Edward said as he made collecting gestures above his wife's shoulders. "Help me get her inside."

Hettie took one arm and Edward the other to hoist Rebecca to her feet. She wobbled up for a moment and fell back into a heap of skirts. "The curse, look. It's already working," she cried. "My legs, paralyzed. Look!"

Hettie and Edward dragged her inside.

The next day, the newspaper ad clerk gave Edward a funny look when Edward told him what to write down. The clerk said he'd never heard of such a thing. What was the point of such an ad? As Edward paid him, he told him to just do it. Two days later, advertisements appeared in the Charleston and George-town newspapers.

Search abandoned for the November 22 runaways from Oakland Plantation. One male Irish carpenter, black hair, twenty-five years of age, and one Irish female house servant, Irish female, five feet tall, nineteen years old, gap between two front teeth. One female slave, also nineteen and five feet tall. No gap. If seen, do not molest.

– Edward Manning, Oakwood Plantation.

Chapter Twenty-two

Into the streets of the city that clung to its aspiration to be Paris and London no matter what, Nora now swept with fewer scarves. Like the flowers rising in Charleston's babied gardens, she offered her face to the sun. She walked past the customs house and returned the smiles of the happy people flowing through the doors. At the wharves, where crates of furniture from England and stylish carriages from Philadelphia came off ships, she stuck her head in offices to check the walls for the Mannings's flyers, all gone. In her customers' homes, she relaxed while waiting in the vestibule for payment, and sometimes, if party preparations were underway and the servants knew her, she tiptoed deeper into the house to peek at dining room tables set with dinner plates rimmed in gold and blue, glasses, silverware, candelabra. Elaborate silver stands held bottles of spirits of various colors—garnet, rose, and amber. On the mantel, camelia blossoms clustered in shallow bowls of twinkling crystal. Her favorites were the pink ones frosted with white flecks.

One rainy day, she walked into the millinery shop to pick up new orders. The owner drummed her fingers on the glass top counter while she watched people pass by her store. "Hmmm," she said.

Nora looked around the empty shop as she shook out her shawl. She handed over twenty dollars she'd collected for recent deliveries.

The woman pointed at the people on the street. "They're not coming in this door in the numbers they used to."

"Since when?"

"Couple weeks now, so it's not the weather."

"How many orders for me today?"

"Just one. I think people are tightening their belts."

"I don't know what that means," Nora said with an edge. If bad news was coming, she wanted to hear it in plain English. "Just out with it," she said.

"It means that people are cutting their spending, girl," the woman said. "Not the elite, for they have appearances to keep up and not enough good sense to be careful. But the next class down, the merchants, factors, and lawyers, they're attentive. They're cautious." The woman pushed a bag and an order form toward Nora. "Just this one order today. Mrs. Ravenel has ordered a family tree with flowers and such. Lots of Ravenels in these parts, you know." She lifted a box from under the counter and tapped a ragged fingernail on it. "Some of them shovel horse manure at the docks but not these Ravenels. This is Mrs. Ravenel with the eight bedrooms on South Battery Street." She pulled a booklet and several dollar bills from the box. "Twenty-five dollars for you today," she said, noting the disbursement in the booklet.

Nora walked out the door thinking about the city's elite and all the classes below. Charleston was a city of layers in which people struggled to better their lives, but always within the floors and ceilings of their place. Elite white, poor white, mulatto, free black, enslaved black. That's how the layers stacked up. The Irish were in a class of their own, the sub-human class that the milliner had described within thirty seconds of meeting Nora. They were between the free black people, who fought them for jobs, and the not-free black people, who couldn't fight for anything. As she walked down King Street, Nora had the sensation of being locked in a dark, airless cargo hold once again.

At the other shops that displayed Nora's samples, the news was the same: Fewer orders coming in. There was one order from one of Nora's regulars, Mrs. Alston, the shipping tycoon's wife on Charlotte Street. Nora covered her head against the light sprinkle and began walking home. She thought about the envelope behind the frame in the workroom. *Two hundred and seventy-five dollars.*

She pivoted and headed down Boundary Street toward the west side of the peninsula, less populated than the east side, dirtier and rougher, the side of town where the long arms of sawmills' piers collected lumber that had floated down the Ashley River. Storefronts of the vendors of lumber, bricks, lime, and naval stores ran in a line along the water. Blacksmiths worked behind this strip offering their skills to those in the building businesses. Coopers hammered away day and night. Ladies had no business being on the west side of town, which made it perfect for Nora at this moment. She was in no mood for a sidewalk conversation.

The gray clouds that had hunched over the city for hours were on the move now. A thunderclap sent people running for doorways. Nora strode through the cleared sidewalks, as restless as the sky.

Their income was drying up.

The wind off the river rushed down Boundary, blowing grit into her face. White caps began to toss on the Ashley River, but she kept on. One hundred thirty-seven dollars for Pearl, nowhere near what she needed, and one hundred thirty-seven for Nora, more than ten times what she needed. The dollars hadn't come easily. The girls' fingers were raw from the glue, their eyes constantly burned, their sleep-starved brains were like the gooey pluff mud that lined every Lowcountry waterway. They were partners, their money was theirs together, they had agreed not to touch it again without discussion, but Pearl's situation scared Nora. Simmons's attentions, paltry as they were, scared her too. She wanted to be absolutely alone at this moment. The storm and that nasty riverfront where no respectable woman would go would ensure that. Lightning flashed, sending the last of the horses and people scurrying for shelter. A child squalled on a distant piazza.

Nora arrived at the cement wall that kept the river at bay. The Ashley was a roiling chop speeding toward the harbor with a fast tide. In the sawmill's floating corrals, logs bobbed and banged like frantic cattle. Raindrops bit her face. She wanted to cry but the tears wouldn't come.

Only one thing stood in Pearl's way: twenty-five dollars. Pearl had a mother to redeem. Nora had thought they had more time to earn, but now, with slaves being sold away to other states for obscene profit and free blacks disappearing at the hands of desperate men, Nora feared they did not.

Torrents of rain swept down from the angry sky. Lightning flashed again, scorching the river and finally scaring Nora. Then the tears did come. They came because of her cursed life and for her defeats in trying to set it right. She cried for home — that hunger never really went away and now she knew it never would — and for exhaustion. She was so tired of being suspicious and suspected in this brutal country. But there were two things she was not. She was not alone, and she was not powerless, for she understood now that she could do one life-changing thing.

On this spring afternoon in Charleston, with the rain driving all the new daffodils and hyacinths into the ground, there was no brightness, but there was clarity, and it was this: Money. Pieces of government paper that would make an owned mother not owned.

Chapter Twenty-three

Pearl paced the sidewalk in front of Lewis, Robertson, and Thurston. Simmons was inside laying cash on a desk. She'd promised him she wouldn't forget to act like his housemaid when he came out with her mother, wouldn't make a scene. She'd fall all over her mother, of course, but couldn't thank the supposed master who'd just bought her. Truth was, Pearl didn't know what would come out of her mouth when her mother walked out that door, if the woman who came out was in fact her mother. First thing was to figure that out. Surely she'd know her mother, even with more wrinkles and maybe pounds. She'd know those eyes.

Pearl looked at the bench where her nine-year-old self had sat gulping back tears ten years ago. She thought about walking over to sit there now, to claim that bench as her free self, but she couldn't lift a foot to cross the yard.

The way Nora had given her the money was so quiet and undramatic, rather unusual considering this was Nora. She'd come into the bedroom soaking wet, handed Pearl the twenty-five dollars she'd just collected, walked to the picture frame and pulled out her share of all the money for Pearl too. Pearl didn't have to count it; they both knew the total now in Pearl's hands. They held each other for a long time, hearts pounding into each other's chests, then ran downstairs to shove the cash into the doctor's hands.

The factors' office door opened. Simmons stepped out, head turned toward the last of his conversation with a man in the interior shadows. He tucked some papers into his coat pocket and stepped into the sun that cast a feeble light on the surrounding buildings. Behind him, a frail woman carrying a cloth bundle poked her way forward with a stick.

Pearl searched the face of this woman scowling into the sunlight, especially the yellowed eyes that bristled with confusion, but even scrunched up as those eyes were, Pearl knew them. The mouth—she knew that too. Her heart leapt. Those were the lips that had told her stories and kissed her cheeks streaked with tears.

"Mama!" Pearl screamed as she ran toward the woman.

Simmons stepped out of the way.

Startled at the sound of that word, Rose looked with disbelief at the hysterical young woman rushing toward her. Recognition dawned on the wrinkled face. Dropping her bag, she held one hand out while barely keeping her grip on the wobbling stick.

Pearl grabbed her mother's shoulders, snatched her into a hug. "Mama, it's you. It's really you," she cried. "Oh, thank Gawd, thank Gawd."

Rose's astonished cries got buried in Pearl's chest, and Pearl's wails got buried in Rose's neck. Finally, the two had to part to breathe, but only for seconds as a new round of thanking and beholding started up.

A man in the office came to the window to stare.

"Enough, enough," Simmons said with believable arrogance. "Let's go you two." He pointed at the street.

With a dip of her shoulder, Rose picked up her bag and started forward on the good leg, then rocked sideways on the bad. As Pearl took the bag, she saw that her mother's arm was as wooden and gnarled as a wisteria vine and her smile was one-sided, just half a curl. She hadn't uttered a word yet. Alarm shot through Pearl, but she said, "We're goin' to talk and talk and never stop, Mama." Her hand cupped the old woman's elbow. "Come on, now. Wait till you hear what I got to tell you."

Rose grunted some sort of excited response and found new energy for her shuffle.

The walk to the sidewalk, then to the street corner took forever. Simmons led the way with an air of annoyance until the three of them were around the corner. "Pearl," he said tenderly, reaching out to stop her. "She's had seizures."

Rose looked up at Simmons's gentle hand on her daughter's shoulder.

Pearl gave her mother a one-arm hug. "It's all right, Mama. We're together now. This man is going to set you — "

"Not here," Simmons said under his breath. "Keep your voice down until we're home. Those bastards. If I'd known she was this lame, I'd have hired a ride for us. They could've told me."

Rose stabbed her stick into the sidewalk and began a determined forward march. Simmons hurried to get back in front where masters were supposed to walk. Mother and daughter followed, shoulder to shoulder, stealing looks at each other, one of them bursting with questions that her lips could not release.

When they reached the house, Simmons helped Rose up the three steps to the piazza. Nora threw open the front door in time to see the wiry woman struggling to step forward. Pearl waited behind her, bag in hand, beaming with joy. Simmons shot a worried look at Nora, which made her look more closely at Rose. Seeing the frozen shoulder and arm, she understood.

"Welcome, welcome," Nora said as she took Rose from Simmons.

Again Rose looked up in disbelief at a stranger moving her along with so much familiarity, so much kindness. She tried to twist around and speak to Pearl.

"I'm here," Pearl said. "I'm still here, Mama, and you're here. I can't believe it. Oh, y'all let's get inside so I can make a scene."

They got Rose settled in a chair. While Pearl knelt in front of her, the crying and patting went on for several minutes with Pearl saying, "I tol' you, I tol' you." Simmons and Nora stood in a corner crying and wiping their eyes and noses. Pearl launched into answering all the questions she saw in her mother's eyes — where she'd been for ten years, who'd raised her, the kind of people who bought her.

When she finally took a breath, Simmons said, "Tell her that all of that back there at the office, my arrogance toward you two, it was for show. I didn't buy her. You did."

Rose nodded her head that she already understood this. With her good hand, she cupped Pearl's face, sprayed with the freckle mask a mother would never forget. Her watery eyes took it all in — the fuller lips, the more defined cheekbones, the worldly eyes — all the changes that had taken her baby from girl to woman. Rose's lips puckered sideways and after a string of grunts, she managed to say, "Mah Pearl."

Now it was Pearl who couldn't speak. She kissed the hand that held her, the knees that pressed against her chest. Finally, she whispered, "I'll be right back," and seconds later she was laying the seed sack across Rose's lap.

Nora went to a drawer for fresh handkerchiefs.

The old woman dug one-handed for the dress she'd sewn a lifetime ago. For a long time, mother and daughter looked at every hole and stain. Rose fingered a small rip in the hem. "Cat," she said with a chuckle.

"I'm going to put our names on this with thread," Pearl said. "Mama, I can read."

Rose pressed her hands together in thanks to a higher power.

Nora began taking the cloths off platters on the table. After they ate, Rose's shoulders curled into a deep slump.

"I think she needs to lie down," Nora whispered to Pearl as they cleared the table.

Simmons helped Rose to the cot in the back of the house. Pearl squeezed in beside her and he closed the door.

Pearl held her for a long time, still not believing they were breathing the same air. She smelled her mother's skin, the same musky scent she remembered. After a while, she asked, "Mama, your leg and arm—did they hurt you?"

Rose shook her head. "Head pain," she managed to say. "Fell down."

"Fuh true? Don't hold nothin' back."

Rose nodded.

"All this time, I've been working on a rice plantation, sometimes here in Charleston in a big house. Kitchen work, housework. Showed 'em right off that I knew how to wash dishes, hang and fold laundry so they wouldn't put me in the fields."

Rose looked relieved.

"Then a while back, I run away with Nora that Irish girl there in the front room."

Alarm shot through Rose's eyes.

"Yea, I'm a runaway, but the Mannings, they've stopped looking for us."

Rose said, "Never."

"Well, for now they have I think, but we need to leave this town soon as we can."

Rose shook her head, pointed to the back door, struggled to push a word out of the quivering, gray lips. "Now."

"Mama, no. We can't go yet. I got to stay, make money, pay Nora what I owe her."

Rose ran a hand over her face.

"You jes' rest now," Pearl said. "I got a plan. My man, Jackson — he's such a good man, Mama — he's going to take us north. He's a free man, knows people who can help us make our way. I'll see him soon, let him know I've got you now. He's a good man, he's got a trade, said he'll take us."

Rose's nodding had slowed, her eyelids were sliding down. Pearl pulled her body closer, the memory finally made real in her arms. When the old woman's breathing became steady, Pearl pulled her arm out from under the gray-haired head and ran out the back door.

She raced across town to Jack's street, his house, his door, where her knocks went unanswered. The blacksmith shed was empty of tools. Pearl was standing there beside the forge gone cold, hands on hips, fighting what her eyes were telling her when the barrel-waisted neighbor appeared on the sandy patch of land outside.

"Heard you over 'yuh," she said warily.

"Where'd he go? Where is he?" Pearl hurried to her, grabbed her arms.

"Gone." The woman struggled out of Pearl's grip. "Yesterday, some white men was pokin' around over 'yuh askin' me where's the blacksmith? Day 'fore that, I heard, some white men dragged away the blacksmith on Water Street."

"What? What you say? What you mean? So, he's hiding somewhere?"

"This mornin' 'fore day clean, he knocked on my door, tol' me a girl would come lookin' for him and gave me somethin' to give her, but you got to tell me your name 'fore I say anything else." The woman looked up and down the street.

As she crumpled to the ground, Pearl said her name.

The woman's eyes, softer now, followed Pearl all the way down. "He loves you, he say, but he cain' stay. Took his tools and got in somebody's wagon. Tol' me to tell you he's sorry."

"Where'd he go? Am I 'sposed meet him somewhere?"

The woman shook her white head. "Chile, he didn't say nothin' like that, but he tol' me to give you this." From her skirt, she withdrew a roll of paper stained brown along the edges by many a working man's fingers.

They unrolled the document, big as a barrel head, on the ground.

The woman said, "I don' read, but I know what this is. He paid a lot of money for it fuh true, but he say he wanted you to have it."

Pearl stomped on the document until the woman pulled her off saying if Pearl didn't want that map, she sure did. Pearl picked it up, shook it at the sky and cried, "I know you're skeered, Jack, but so am I. You go on, you just go on to Boston. I'll be going too."

Chapter Twenty-four

Just before dawn, Nora gave up on sleep. *So many reasons to lose sleep in this godawful country,* she thought. She threw off the bedcovers and splashed her face at the washbasin to try to flush the dread of going downstairs away. The evening before, Nora and Rose had been powerless to calm the raging Pearl. No words, no stroking, not even two glasses of Donnelly calmed her down. Then Simmons came home, drained from his hospital day, and walked right into the teeth of the storm. Nora watched him lower himself into a chair slowly, as if a new burden had settled onto his shoulders, which of course, it had. Now he had three women under his roof with no end in sight.

Nora dried her face and wiped up the spills around the basin. She wasn't sure she had the strength to go back to Pearl and Rose. She pulled her chair up to the worktable, strewn with the supplies for two orders just begun, to think of what else she could possibly say to the broken-hearted Pearl. Her mother's infirmity had been a blow, a setback that Pearl pretended to dismiss, but now she moved like a caged, frantic bird. For their flight north, they wouldn't be climbing in and out of wagons, wouldn't be going down ladders into root cellars to hide. Jack would've helped with that. Not now. Pearl was bouncing from dazed to furious to outraged to bereft, then back to dazed. Until she recovered, she'd be as crippled as her mother.

A headache nagged at the base of Nora's skull. With three fingers she pushed on the muscles that she imagined were the roots of it. The household of runaways now numbered four, each of them bound by different sorts of chains.

Rose, at last a free woman, had the bad leg and arm. Pearl, not legally free, had two good legs but no money anymore and no connections for the journey north. Nora had no money. The doctor, ah the doctor. For him, the stick in the cartwheel spokes, as Mam would say, was destination. Where could he go and not end up in jail? Not Maryland, not Pennsylvania, wherever those places were, not even out West, whatever that meant. A few days earlier, he'd said that when war came, as it surely would, he'd be swept into a medical corps, North's or South's, where he'd be discovered, prosecuted for murder, possibly hanged. *Imagine that*, he'd said with bitterness. *A son of a son of a Son of Liberty, hanged for protecting an abused orphan from a jealous wife. Maybe the armies will need doctors too much to hang me, but I've seen too many imbecilic judicial decisions in Maryland to put any stock in that.*

Nora decided she needed coffee. She got dressed, took a deep breath, and went downstairs with no idea of what she'd say to Pearl other than they should get back to work. Pearl was circling the front room. She hadn't made the coffee. As Nora lit a fire for the kettle, she noticed that the miniature painting was gone.

Pearl stopped her circling—Rose was following with her hand quaking helplessly on the stick—to give Nora an apologetic hug. They held onto each other for the moment they both needed and then began setting up for breakfast.

The doctor came down next, wary, bleary-eyed and sniffing around for coffee. After everyone had a cup, they sat at the oak-plank table looking at its whorls. "You're not alone, Pearl. We'll figure something out," Simmons said.

Pearl burst into tears. Nora pushed three fingers back to the knot at the bottom of her skull. After a while, she put a second pot on the fire and stared into the flames.

Simmons walked over to stand beside her. "Shall we get some fresh air?" he asked quietly.

Nora suspected nothing good within that invitation. Back home, when someone in the household said that, it meant he or she had something to say away from all the ears in the cottage. It was never good news.

"All right. I'll get me shawl," she said wearily.

Pearl and her mother watched them go and then turned back grim-faced to the oak whorls.

Simmons and Nora walked in silence for a while, eyes on the sidewalk, while she waited for whatever he had to say. Right off, he'd switched from walking on her right side to walking on her left, something she'd seen other Charleston men do to put themselves between their women and the street, as if to shield them from runaway barrels or horses. With or without barrels and horses waiting around the corner, it was a protective gesture and it calmed her.

"All three of you — you, Pearl and her mother — need to get out of town," Simmons said.

Nora rubbed her mouth to avoid saying something nasty about stating the obvious.

"Let me lend you some money so — "

"I can't let ye do that."

" — so you can get back to Clare. You're the easy one, Nora. It's Pearl and her mother I don't know yet how to get out."

"Give them the money so they can buy forged freedom papers, bribe their way north."

"Pearl won't leave until she's paid you back."

Nora stopped. "How do ye know that?"

"She told me a while ago. She thought she had time to pay her debt to you. But now . . ."

"Aye. With Jack running like he did, she sees things are worse than she thought."

They walked in silence for a few minutes. Then Simmons spoke again. "For you too," he said.

"What are ye saying?"

"The Mannings. Sooner or later, they'll change their minds about looking for you. Pearl's the one who put the root on them. You, they're not scared of. Spring's coming. People will be out. You're delivering your orders to people's homes, their friends. This is a small town. That gap in your teeth, it makes you quite distinctive."

Nora walked away from the conversation.

Rushing to catch up, Simmons said, "You can pay me back for your ticket to New York."

"I can't be sure how long that would take."

"Think about it?"

Nora pulled her shawl tighter across her shoulders and turned right to circle back to the house.

Simmons didn't make the turn with her. "I have something else to say," he called after her.

Nora looked back. "'Tis so kind of ye Dr. Simmons, but I — "

"Would you like to come with me to the hospital this morning?"

"What, ye mean to watch ye work?" she asked, returning to his side.

"Yes. Would you like that? Get out of the house for a while? Would it scare you?"

"Scare me! After all that I've seen of blood and agony?" Her hand flew to her mouth. "I'm sorry. That was saucy."

"It's fine."

"What about the yellow fever there?"

"Much less of it now with the cold weather."

Nora looked in the direction of the house. "Pearl and I have two orders to fill—"

"Leave her alone for a while."

Nora kneaded the base of her skull and looked at Simmons. He was clasping his hands behind his back in the way that meant he was weighing his next words.

"Nora, I'm thinking you'd make a good aide in a hospital."

Her fingers flew to her collarbone. "Me?"

"You have nerves of iron. You never flinched while I dug the bullet out of that bloodied fellow who came to my door that night. Doctors need people like you beside them."

That bloodied fellow. Instantly, the memories flooded in like a swollen river breaching a dam. All of it was *right there*—the touch of Patrick's lips to hers, the scent of his skin, his hands pulling her hips into his to show her the proof of his lust. Guilt rushed in, pushing all that hot pleasantness aside, insisting on being heard. Here the doctor was complimenting her, telling her that she had worth, protecting her from barrels and horses, and she was thinking of Patrick's hands on her arse.

Certain that her red cheeks were betraying her, she looked

away. "Aye, I mean no, it didn't bother me, the gore. Me, though, a nurse?" she asked.

"You must be prepared to leave certain things behind. Propriety, clean skirts. Do you think you can do that?"

"I suppose, but why?"

"I'm thinking of your future, of your need to have a skill that'll enable you to support yourself."

"Ye mean I'd get paid for it?"

Simmons smiled. "Well, yes."

"Oh."

"Let's see what you think, shall we?" He held out a hand to indicate they should move on.

He took the same route Pearl had chosen weeks ago — down Beaufain, left on Franklin. The hospital's facade of five arches soon appeared and as they got closer, Nora saw several patients, blanketed and tucked into their chairs, sitting on the first-floor piazza. They nodded hello as Simmons and Nora walked up the porch stairs.

Inside, men and women carrying pans and blankets bustled up and down the central hall. A few waved at Simmons and sent curious looks at Nora, but everyone kept moving.

He hung their coats in a closet and withdrew a stethoscope and an apron. As she tied the apron strings, Simmons moved behind her to give her help she didn't need, but she let him anyway. He led her down the hall, gesturing at the tall-ceilinged rooms on the left and right. "Two rooms with thirty beds down here — congestive fever, smallpox, bowel complaints, ship's fever — and thirty beds upstairs — broken and crushed bones, surgical cases, and . . ." He put his hands in his coat pockets and gave her a sober look.

Nora braced for something truly disgusting, which, given what she'd seen, would have to clear a pretty high bar.

"Social diseases," Simmons said. "Judgment. You have to leave that behind too,"

"Oh, social diseases. I spent nearly two months with sailors, you forget. Dribblings, itchy balls. There's nothing I haven't heard about," she said.

In the first ward a long row of beds butted against the bank of windows. Men lay fully clothed on top of blankets or partially under, a few of them being attended to by men with rolled sleeves. One of those attending looked up from palpitating a man's belly, saw Simmons, and sent a respectful nod his way. Students stood near beds throughout the room, arms crossed, watching treatments being applied to limbs, torsos, and heads.

"Let's begin with Squid," Simmons said as he led Nora to an emaciated man with tattooed arms. "Lung fever."

The patient's eyes brightened at the sight of Simmons pulling up a chair to his bed. He nodded with great effort during the introduction. In his bloodshot eyes Nora saw respect for the doctor now putting a stethoscope to his chest.

"Chest sounds better today, Squid," Simmons said. He picked up a chart hanging on the side of the bed and scribbled something. "Do you think yesterday's mustard plaster helped?"

"Aye, I do and—" Squid dissolved into a coughing fit.

"Another one for you today then." Simmons wrote more on the chart and looked up. "Nora, please go over there—" he pointed at a corner cabinet "and ask someone to help you gather the things you'll need."

"Me?" Nora said. "I'm going to do a mustard plaster?"

"Go on now." Simmons smiled at her. "Go mix it. You can do it."

An aproned woman standing at the cabinet watched Nora approach. Fair-skinned, delicate-featured, and blessed with a healthy bust even the starched bib apron couldn't hide, she was giving Nora the same once-over that Nora was giving her. Barely into her twenties, Nora guessed. Alert green eyes registered surprise. Nora hoped it was just because of her short hair.

Nora stopped a few feet in front of her. "Could ye please show me what I need for a mustard plaster?"

The woman opened the cabinet's glass doors and began pulling out towels, a spoon, and a can of dry mustard. "I'm Jenny. And you are?"

"Nora."

Jenny clutched everything she'd fetched from the shelves. "No, I meant you're what …in relation to Dr. Simmons?" The girl's eyes bored into Nora's.

Nora took a moment to recover. *In relation to Dr. Simmons. That skins the bark off the tree, doesn't it? Why am I trying to control my voice? Why do I care? Why don't I just say house servant. 'Tis what I am, isn't it?* "Just lending a hand today," she said. "House servant."

"Oh," Jenny said, relaxing her stare. "I mean, Dr. Simmons, he's such a good catch, isn't he?" She watched Simmons wind his way through the ward to touch foreheads, check throats. "Look at him there—those knowledgeable hands. So smart about healing people. The patients trust him, the students adore him. All of us do." Jenny wiggled her shoulders and her arms still full of things. "You can't say he has much of a pull with that puss of his, and we all know about he can be so reserved and remote—the students call him Dr. Melancholy sometimes—but he's still a catch for other reasons, you know?"

"Aye. A man to be respected, that one," Nora said, reaching for the supplies.

But Jenny began unloading her arms onto the mid-cabinet ledge as if she had all the time in the world to talk. "A bachelor. They're few and far between, decent ones, know what I mean?" She put the can of mustard down, then the sack of flour. "Does he have a special lady friend? I mean, you'd know, being there in his home." Next came the bowl, spoon, flour sack towel, and washcloth.

"'Tis none of my business. If ye could spoon the flour — "

"Really?" Jenny looked at her as if she was as thick as axle grease. "Very well, don't tell me then. You run along. I'll mix this. Go tell Dr. Simmons I'll need him to come take a look to be sure I did it correctly." Jenny smiled as she spooned mustard into the bowl.

"What would ye be needing him for? 'Tis as simple as making biscuits, 'tisn't it? He said I'm to mix the plaster and you're to show me how."

Jenny narrowed her eyes. "Calm down, calm down. Four spoons of flour into this mustard then. Add some water."

Nora quickly spooned, poured, mixed, and picked up the flimsy flour sack towel. "This goes on the chest, then the plaster on the towel I'm guessing."

Jenny raised and dropped a shoulder. "If it's so simple, you figure it out."

Squid himself supervised the slathering of the yellow paste, having been blistered the day before by a student who'd slopped some on his collarbone and left it there. He told Nora to make sure the paste went on the towel, not his skin. "I'll be sweating like a whore in church in a few minutes," he said between coughs. "Mind you now, come back and check on me soon."

Nora trailed Simmons from malaria to camp itch to loose bowels. With each interaction, whether with medical students or other physicians or patients, faces brightened when he approached. She saw that the staff eagerly sought his opinion, and the patients his words of comfort, and sometimes comfort was all he could offer after certain examinations—a leathery man paralyzed on one side, another who was yellow with ship's fever spewing the black vomit that even she knew meant the end was near. With these patients, Simmons spent a little extra time.

A calm hung in the room that was as light as the dust motes floating through the sun rays. Every worker moved from bed to bed to bandage and clean, console and wipe with kindness. Humanity's miseries were endless, the body seemingly so cunning in producing new ones—Nora had certainly observed that in her nineteen years, but she'd never seen anyone outside family who cared. In here there was charity and order, not indifference, not chaos. Moaning, yes, but even that was attended to with cloths to the forehead and comforting hands on shoulders. And clean—the scent of lavender water emanated from every corner. Surely there was learning going on too, she thought, as a ring of physicians and students gathered around Simmons to discuss a wound. She stood to the side and listened. Knowledge grew here. Against the tide of mystery and misery, these men and women had driven a stake deep into the riverbank and held on to understand as much they could. Nora felt their resolve, sweet and addictive, pulling on her.

Simmons left the circle of men still discussing the wound and waved to Nora to join him back at Squid's bed.

Jenny moved around the room sneaking glances at Simmons and Nora.

Nora lifted Squid's towel off his chest. Its imprint bloomed in pink, not red, so she was just in time, Simmons said. Sweat rolled down Squid's ribs, as intended.

"Good job," Simmons said quietly.

"Aye," Squid managed to squeeze out before a new round of hacking took over.

"I'll check on you tomorrow, sir," Simmons said. "Keep your head propped so your lungs can clear. Drink a lot."

"Aye," Squid said.

"Water, I mean."

"Yeah," Squid said. "I was afraid that's what you meant."

"Nora here will get you cleaned up, and then she's done for the day."

Outside, Simmons turned left to begin their walk home, but Nora touched his coat sleeve. Could they stop by the orphanage, she wanted to know, to see if the nuns had any mail for her?

Chapter Twenty-five

While Nora waited for the doctor outside the orphanage, she pictured the same brightening of faces going on inside. His entrance into a room, she understood now, was like a spring rain sweeping across parched fields.

Simmons came out the front door skirted with four little girls jostling to hold his hands. As he slogged toward Nora, one of the girls ran to her, blue-ribboned pigtails flying.

"Are you the missus?" the girl called out.

Nora pushed the gate open to get a better look at her.

"Well?" The girl, no bigger than a pile of laundry, said.

"Such a cheeky one ye are," Nora said with a pull on a pigtail. "Smart too, I'm thinking."

The child froze, grey eyes considering the stranger's appearance. "What happened to your hair?" she asked.

"Don't know what you mean," Nora said as she brushed the wisps away from her face.

From the doorway, two nuns called for the children, who finally released the doctor and turned home, except for a girl who came back to get the pig-tailed one. The doctor, pink with embarrassment, was already gesturing to Nora to get on with their walk home. At first, Nora hid a smile to save him further embarrassment, but then she thought maybe he'd like it if she turned this moment into something shared — wasn't she embarrassed too? She lifted her face toward him, warm and reassuring, and held it there for him until he noticed. His face lit up in a way she'd never seen before. It was relieved, unguarded, joyous. He looked into her eyes for the length of time that two people know as too long to be meaningless. After much throat clearing, he pulled an envelope out of his coat pocket and handed it to Nora.

She squealed at the handwriting on the envelope. "Finally!" she shouted.

They sat on a garden wall while she read it aloud.

January 25, 1850

Dear Nora,

'Tis a miracle. When Mrs. Klein found out I have a Sister in Charleston, she was so happy. Her friends say one of them needs to go to Charleston to see the heart of America's slave trade, as they call it. Bullseye of the abolitionists' outrage, they call it.

Best of all, she wants to bring me with her. Dear Sister, I know ye've told me not to come, but what can I do? She wants to visit real plantations and since she don't know a soul there, she says ye can show her around. She plans to write about it all for a Newspaper.

We have tickets on the Anne B. Jones, a steamship, so the trip will take only three days. A real steamship, can ye believe it? It will arrive in Charleston on February 10. Mrs. Klein says she'll bring ye back when we return. She's that rich, to help someone she's never met. I haven't told her ye've run away from yer mistress, but I think she'll celebrate that, ye running away from the evil rice barons as she calls them.

If ye're afraid to meet us at the boat, send me yer street address by what Mrs. Klein calls a Telegraph. Mrs. Klein says it's this new thing for messages. The information is safe with her. Oh, dear Sister, we will be together again. I have so much to tell ye.

Love,

Clare

Nora shook the letter. "Coming here? In five days? No, no, Clare. I told ye not to come."

Simmons dropped his head into his hands.

"Visit a plantation all nosey like? Is she out of her mind?"

Simmons glanced at her.

"She'll make a stir, this one."

"A stir?" Simmons blurted. "That woman will be lucky to make it out of here alive. It's illegal here to argue against slavery. And there your twin will be, in the thick of it."

"There she'll be — "

"Looking just like you, having bricks thrown at her, described in the newspaper. You."

"Yes, I see. Oh, Jaysus."

"And keeping you in town while you should be hightailing it out."

"Clare says here the woman will take me back to New York."

"You believe that?"

"I don't know what to believe. Ach, Clare. I told ye not to come!"

Simmons stood and held out his hand to her. "We should get back to the house."

Nora took it and with the feel of his warmth, a calm washed over her. She got to her feet, planning to step forward into the long walk home but she felt his fingers wrap around hers with urgency, a protectiveness against dangers all too real now. There was nothing imaginary about what could be coming around Charleston street corners at her once Clare arrived. He pulled her closer.

"Dr. Simmons, I—"

"Frederick," Simmons said. "Please call me Frederick, at least while we're still here in Charleston. Later, call me Benjamin."

Later. She let him wrap his arms around her, this man who had never asked her for anything, only given.

* * *

Pearl didn't think her mother could climb the steep risers, but Rose was showing her otherwise. Pulling up the steps with her good leg, she dragged the useless one along behind. She wanted to see the hair work upstairs that had bought her freedom. Foot by foot, they made the slow trip, Pearl's hands on her mother's waist to support her. As she steered Rose toward the worktable, she felt the frail body stiffen at the sight of the hair nestled among the supplies.

"Do you want to turn around?" Pearl asked, hating how little she knew about her own mother's abilities. Rose moved forward again, her cane tapping gently on the pine floor. They sat down. Pearl explained it all—the supplies, the frames, the braiding device—and took the sample off the wall to show her the hiding place. She fanned the dollars in her hands and counted aloud what was there: twenty-two dollars. Instantly Rose uttered two words: *freedom papers.* Pearl shook her head, explaining that this money wasn't hers to spend.

After the trip back downstairs, Rose wanted to rest. Pearl pulled a quilt over the raw-boned shoulders and held her mother's hand until it stopped squeezing back.

Alone again in the front room, Pearl went back to circling. She knew she should get to work upstairs, but three hours had gone by since Nora and the doctor went out for fresh air. Just as she went to the window to part the curtains, she heard the street door open, boots scraping on the grit on the piazza. Pearl opened the door as Nora was turning the knob.

"Where've you been?" Pearl cried.

Nora raised her palm to stop her.

Pearl looked around her for Simmons. He was tucking a handkerchief into his coat pocket as he hurried down the street. "Something happen?" she asked.

"Clare has happened," Nora said, stepping around Pearl to get inside. "Where's yer mother?" Nora pulled out a chair at the kitchen table.

"Sleepin' in the back." Pearl sat down across from her and finally got a good look at Nora's panicked eyes. "Is Clare all right?" she asked.

Nora laid the letter on the table. "She's coming here, she says. In five days."

"Oh no."

"Her employer, she's coming too. An abolitionist, a reporter. She intends to have a look at Charleston and write about it." Nora gestured toward the street and Pearl knew she didn't mean the city's architecture.

"She going to raise a ruckus?"

"Sounds like it."

"Oh. Oh Lawd. Ain' things bad enough already?"

Nora rubbed her neck. The headache was back. "Pearl, Clare's me twin. She looks exactly like me. If she's with this woman when rocks get thrown, people will remember this face."

Understanding dawned on Pearl's face. "Well, you have to tell her to stay off the streets, stay with us here."

"There's more."

"Lawd."

"This mistress of hers, she told Clare she'll take me back to New York when they leave."

Pearl leaned back in her chair. "Oh."

Outside, a fishmonger's singsong call rose and fell as he passed the house.

"Oh," Pearl said again.

"I'm not leaving ye here," Nora dropped her voice, "with yer mother the way she is. Ye can't run without help."

"Yes, you are. You got a free boat home—"

"I'm not. We have to buy some freedom papers."

"Shoo, you're bull-headed." Pearl stood and dug into her pocket. "Haven't shown you this yet." She unrolled Jack's map across the table. "Jack left it for me." Pearl jabbed a finger into the bottom right corner. "Don't this say South Carolina right 'yuh? And that—" she ran her finger north to the next shape outlined in red, "—say North Carolina?"

"Yes."

"Look at all them towns we have to get through. And then there's Virginia."

"Not a free state either."

"I know." Pearl's finger kept going up the east coast. "Some people say they'll run to Pennsylvania. There are people there who take runaway slaves in, get them schooling and work."

"The Quakers, Dr. Simmons says."

"But he say, even up there, the slave catchers can snatch me if they can prove I'm a runaway. Dr. Simmons say here's where we'll be safe."

Pearl's index finger traveled north again, beyond the last state labeled in red — Maine — into an area the mapmaker hadn't bothered to identify other than to fling six letters across a vast territory. C-A-N-A-D-A.

"For the love of God, Pearl, that looks really far away."

Pearl sat down. "Uh huh."

"New York for now." Nora reached across the table for her hand. "We'll go together." She glanced at the door behind which Rose slept. "Somehow."

"She made it up those stairs right there. Wanted to see our workroom. Maybe she's stronger than we think."

Nora went to the coffee pot on the fire and poured two mugs. "Tell me," she said as she gave one to Pearl. "What's it like? To be with her?"

Pearl shook her head. "I keep staring at her face, to know it so I don't ever lose it again."

"Ye have her eyes, her nose."

"She's been crazy with worry, all these years."

"What happened to her arm and leg? Please say it's not from a beating — "

Pearl shook her head again, took a reckless sip that forced her to suck the coffee's heat through her teeth. "She say a pain come on like lightning in her head one day. She couldn't see for a while, couldn't feel her arms and legs. Some of the feeling came back, then her sight came back, but she was lame, couldn't speak right. Her words, when they come out her mouth, I see they take the wind out of her, but she keeps asking me to tell her again about the plantation, the missus, Bess, you. She keeps wanting me to write our names. Over and over, she's so proud I can read and write."

Nora smiled. "I can see that she can't believe ye're in front of her."

"Told her what you did to get her here."

Nora grabbed Pearl's hands. "We did it together."

"And now, your sister be here soon. She'll be different. You know that."

"Probably."

They downed the last drops and stared at the map with unseeing eyes.

"We should get to work," Pearl said.

"Aye. No matter what, we need money."

As they climbed the stairs, Pearl whispered, "Where did you and the doctor go all that time?"

When Nora answered with all the details—his concern for her future, the mustard plaster, her admiration for his skills, the orphan with her assumptions about them —none of it came as a surprise to Pearl.

Chapter Twenty-six

For centuries, the arrival times of sailing ships in Charleston were but a guess, never a specific week or even month. The mid-nineteenth century's new steamships, however, generally arrived on the expected day, and so a crowd of fifty people waited in front of the customs house with confidence. Across the street, people lolled on quilts under the live oaks. Baskets of food were opened from time to time by the hands that had prepared it. Every time a stream of passengers burst through the doors, everyone looked up. In twos and threes, people collected their baskets and their guests and walked away arm in arm. Carriages rattled down the streets, the horses' great cannonball hooves making their merry sound.

Nora and Simmons couldn't eat, couldn't loll. She'd brought the household mending to keep her hands busy, but after bloodying too many things because of her shaking needle, she put it all away. As the crowd thinned, Simmons asked a few of the arriving passengers if they'd seen the *Anne B. Jones* at the docks. No one had. Each time Simmons asked, a carriage driver walked over to hear the answers. Around four o'clock, a passenger said he'd seen a customs agent watching that steamship pull into a dock.

An hour later, another flush of people came through the doors. With her heart in her throat, Nora watched every body that emerged onto the second-floor landing. The elaborate hats on the ladies, the expensive cut of the men's coats—this was the steamship crowd for certain. They split left and right to descend the staircases into waiting arms. For a moment, the flow stopped entirely, and just as hysteria surged in Nora's chest, a woman with the largest hat yet came through and stopped at the rail to take in the sight of prosperous Broad Street. A look of rapture shone on Esther Klein's face. Next came a man gripping the long wooden legs of a box draped in black canvas. A bulging satchel swung from his shoulder, throwing him off-balance so much that he nearly fell into Esther. To get out of the way, she hurried down the steps. As the man struggled to follow her, a small hatless head came through the door and before it lifted to the sunlight, Nora began running.

Screaming in Irish, arms wheeling, she raced up the steps and grabbed Clare. In the middle of the landing, they buried their faces in each other's necks, then pulled apart to kiss cheeks, stroke hair, marvel at each other.

Clare grabbed her shoulders. "Saints be praised, look at yer hearty self," she cried. "A bit of flesh on yer bones. Getting' fat ye are."

"Thank ye, thank ye. Ye too." Nora patted the face that had filled out. "I can't believe me eyes."

"Nor can I. Here ye are, out in the open, so I'm thinkin' ye're safe now?"

"For now. Yes, I think."

Clare pointed at Nora's hair. "What—"

"Ach, my hair. I'll tell ye later."

Other passengers trying to come out the door frowned at the reunion blocking their way.

Nora kissed Clare's forehead. "I have so much to tell ye so come on." She pointed at Simmons on the street corner. "There's someone I want ye to meet."

Clare called down the steps to the enormous hat at the bottom. "Mrs. Klein," she said. "I'll meet ye at the carriage."

Esther's gloved hand flapped to acknowledge.

Simmons hurried over to take Clare's bag. His eyes went from her face to the one that he knew so well then back to Clare's. He made the usual polite inquiries about the trip and heard the familiar voice answer him. While they talked, Nora watched her sister. Clare's hands flew to her collarbone the way they always had when she was nervous. Her hair, thick and shiny, was styled in a way that struck Nora as rather elaborate for a servant. Severely parted in the middle to allow swoops over the ears and parted again mid-crown to be drawn into a bun in the back, well, it was the latest style. The navy-blue dress with lacy collar and pearly buttons was another surprise — so fashionable. And she smelled so good — lavender soap and freshly laundered cotton.

A loud yoo-hoo floated over from the street corner where Esther stood talking to the carriage driver. Clare waved back at her mistress, reached for Nora's hand, and stepped into the street.

"Mrs. Klein," Clare called with warmth. "Here she is."

Esther watched them approach. "Ah, Nora," she said.

As Nora shook her hand, she saw that Mrs. Klein's brown eyes were righteous and hasty. The woman held her mouth in a way that seemed ready to issue an indictment or a tribute, depending upon what her ears — long things ending in pendulous lobes — had taken in. Ringlets of gray hair hung in front of the lobes.

"My goodness, you are a mirror image of Clare. A pleasure, my dear," Esther said.

"Pleasure, ma'am," Nora said.

Clare's hands flew to her collarbone again.

Esther turned toward Simmons. "And you are?" she asked.

"Dr. Frederick Simmons." He put down Clare's bag and touched his finger to his hat brim. "Welcome to Charleston, ma'am."

"Thank you. Delighted to be here. Delighted." Looking him up and down, Esther again made no effort to hide her assessment.

"Dr. Simmons is my employer," Nora said.

"Ah." Esther pulled off her gloves. "Are you a native, sir? Do you know everyone and his pappy?"

"No, ma'am, not a native," Simmons said. "I'm from off, as they say around here."

"And this is … " Esther turned to summon the man with the equipment out of his slouch. "Mr. Hopkins. As you can see, he's a daguerreotypist."

Mr. Hopkins gave a timid wave.

"A what?" Nora asked.

"He makes daguerreotypes. Likenesses of people. 'Tis a new sort of thing," Clare said. "You haven't heard of it? You're joking."

Nora felt her neck go warm with annoyance, though Clare had said that so cheerfully.

Esther turned back to the twins. "Well, look at you two. My, you are truly the same. Except for your hair, Nora. Thank goodness I'll have that to tell you apart."

Nora pulled at the hair that had finally grown long enough to curl at the nape of her neck.

Clare looped an arm through hers. "Ye talk different," she said. "What's that accent?"

"I do not," Nora said.

Simmons pointed at the man who was tying a parcel to the back of the carriage. "I see your driver has your trunks loaded now," he said. "Which establishment, Mrs. Klein?"

"We are staying at The Charleston Hotel."

"I'd be happy to accompany you, to help your man there manage all of this."

"You're so kind." Esther picked up her skirts and headed for the carriage.

Nora felt her sister's arm slide out of their loop. "We?" Nora asked. "You're not going to stay with me at the house?"

Clare straightened, looked over at the carriage, and then back at Nora like a deer that had just emerged from the forest into a clearing — unsure, sniffing the air, cocked to run.

"Clare?" Nora said.

"Oh, well. I guess I could. Let me check with her," Clare said.

Her conversation at the carriage doors was brief. Clare came back with a lighter step, and the sisters began their walk along East Bay Street, arm in arm again. They talked over each other, their questions and answers flying back and forth in overlapping threads until it all became a tangle. Finally, Nora came to understand that the woman who had hauled Clare away from the pier on that awful day had taken her to a boardinghouse packed with Irish girls yanked from their destinations by Captain Wells. The woman hired them out for domestic work and pocketed their wages as payment for room and board, though there was no board. She told them to get their food in the houses they cleaned. In the boardinghouse, rats held their ground in the face of broom assaults. Winter winds whistled through the plaster chinks and window cracks. Water froze in the washbasins. All the girls hacked with wet coughs but still the woman sent them off every morning and let them back in at night, all of them with rattling lungs. A few had died in coughing fits. No one came looking for any of those girls from Ireland's tribes, no kin, no sweethearts. No one tended to the broken fingers Clare had brought back one evening after her first employer had slammed a ladle across them in a rage. She held her left hand up to show Nora two fingers twisted at angles like broken twigs. Wells had chosen wisely, she said bitterly. It was as if he knew from the looks of his passengers which girls knew not a soul in America. At this, Nora shot her sister a startled look.

"That's why he split us up," she said.

"Aye," Clare said. "The bastard."

"How'd ye get away from that first mistress?" Nora asked.

"I couldn't work with broken fingers, so she let me go. The boardinghouse witch sent me to work at Mrs. Klein's house. She saw me broken fingers. I live at her house now."

Nora kissed the fingers and noticed a thin silver ring with a purple stone. "What's this?"

"Oh, 'tis nothing. Mrs. Klein likes to give things to people." She pulled the hand away. "Tell me. Were ye beaten too? Is that why ye ran away?"

Once again, Nora began at the beginning. When she got to Patrick, she paused. She didn't want to admit to being made a fool and a thief, but of course there was no way around that, for what she'd done for him had triggered everything that followed. She could be honest with Clare, the mirror of her soul, who knew every bad choice she'd ever made in nineteen years and loved her still. At one time in their lives, when they were wee and pure and surrounded by the tribe, their bad choices were baby bad choices, nothing of real consequence. But in America, there were only bad choices and worse choices, with adult-size consequences. If anyone could understand the crimes that desperate Nora had committed in America, it would be Clare, so Nora told her everything—what had led to what—and when she'd finished, she realized that hers was the tale that was much more complicated, bizarre, and dangerous.

And then there was Pearl's life.

Nora started with Pearl's being torn from her mother's arms at nine and ended with their recent reunion.

"'Tis quite a story," Clare said. She turned to admire the outfit of a young woman passing by. "Upon my soul, what a dress."

A story? Nora thought. *Pearl's pain, her risks, her destiny defined by the color of her skin—a story?* Nora reached for her sister's hand. "I don't think ye understand. She's always in danger simply because of the color of her skin. Sometimes mortal danger. To call it a story, well, that doesn't do it justice, don't ye see? Free or slave, it doesn't matter. She's always suspect. People here think the blacks are going to revolt and who knows—they might. Things here are heating up." *I told ye not to come.* "We all have to go. Pearl, her mother, me—" Nora stopped herself from saying Simmons. She'd explain the accusations against him later. "All of us in the house have to get out of town and soon."

Clare stopped under the shuddering fronds of a palm tree and looked around. Aproned women gossiped on street corners, men sold fish from their baskets, a wagon driver unloaded crates in front of a tavern. "Heating up? Doesn't look like it. Get out of town soon? We just got here."

"'Tis a dangerous place, Clare. I know ye can't stop Mrs. Klein from doing what she's going to do—"

"Aye."

"But ye mustn't be with her in public when she does it." *I don't want to argue with ye, not right now.*

A strained look settled across Clare's features. "Because?"

"Because the crowds she'll attract—she'll enflame people. Ye could get hurt, which means I could get hurt because people will remember yer face."

"Oh, Nora, please don't be cross with me. I'm sorry I called it a story. Hold my hand and let's keep walking. Such beautiful flowers in that yard over there. What are they? How much farther is the house?"

Nora threaded her fingers into Clare's. "Camelias," she said. "Around that corner."

Chapter Twenty-seven

Nora couldn't fall asleep until she heard Clare's steady breathing, that old familiar raspy in and out, proof that she was alive. Nora had invited her to share her straw mattress, but she understood when Clare chose the one Nora had made for her. They'd be twenty years old soon, well into womanhood and well down the different paths that the last six months had forced upon them. To be in the same room right now, it was enough.

When they had arrived at the house, Pearl and Rose greeted Clare at the front door like a long-lost cousin. They swept her inside where she was overwhelmed even more by the amount of food they'd prepared. Rose hobbled over to pat her cheeks and push out one word as she beheld her — *darlin'* — for she felt she knew her, of course. With that one gesture, Rose had conjured up the matriarchs of the twins' village who loved them not only because they shared the same blood of the generations but also because they saw goodness, if not beauty, in the Murphy girls. With Rose's warm, knobby fingers on her cheek, Clare melted like she used to in that faraway place and time. Nora, to keep from crying, laughed and said, "Welcome to this family, Clare."

Simmons walked in soon after, fresh from unloading Esther Klein at the hotel. He opened a new bottle of whiskey immediately and gave Nora a worried look. During supper, she could see restraint on his face whenever Clare sang the praises of Mrs. Klein and her philosophies. Nora tapped her sister's foot to tamp it down a bit, though Pearl and her mother couldn't get enough. After the table was cleared, everyone finally yielded to fatigue and sought the quiet of a fireside chair or mattress or—in the doctor's case—a walk in February's crisp air. He invited Nora to join him. She grabbed her coat and they hurried out the door.

"She fancies herself a reporter for *The Liberator*," he said, driving his hands into his pockets as they made their way down the sidewalk. "That's the nation's largest antislavery newspaper. She has no actual role at the paper, mind you, but she plans to get the editor's attention with what she brings back. The photographs, she feels, will sell themselves."

"So, it's fame she's after?" Nora asked.

"My guess? Mostly."

"She's not sincere then?"

"No, I think she probably is, but she's fire, aim, ready. We have to get her out of here."

* * *

The lobby of the Charleston Hotel thrummed with people coming and going when the twins walked in mid-morning. While Clare got in line to ask at the desk for Esther's room number, Nora picked up the *Charleston Mercury* to check the ads. Perhaps Edward Manning couldn't let it go after all, but no, there was no ad. A headline blared of progress being made in Washington, D.C. with the shaping of a new federal law, the Fugitive Slave Act of 1850, which would make it legal for slave owners to pursue their runaway slaves in the free states. Every federal judge and commissioner would be required to direct their resources to assist with captures. *One may interpret the passage of this law,* the writer reported, *as northern states' confirmation that fugitive slaves are property that may be legally reclaimed no matter the location.*

Nora laid the newspaper on the table as carefully as if it were a loaded gun. She didn't understand all of the words, but she knew *fugitive* and *free states.*

Esther ushered the girls into her room. Clare dropped her bag in front of a closet and asked her if she needed anything—perhaps some wrinkles pressed after the unpacking?—as if to prove to Nora that she really did need to be available at every moment, even overnight. This was a sticking point between them now.

Esther was at the window, announcing that the streets of Charleston—the sights that were to be the backdrop for her articles—awaited the three of them. She waved the girls over to look at the city dripping with injustice. Her gray hair was frizzy and wild, like a halo of the silvery moss that hung from the Carolina trees. The eyes above the wedge-like nose were on fire, as if searching for Charlestonian feet at which to lay blame. "Let's get out there," she said.

"Oh, ma'am. I can't go with you," Nora said.

Esther stepped away from the window to zero in on Nora. "You're not going to show me around?"

Nora gave an apologetic shrug. "Sorry. I have a lot of work to get back to."

"Those people at the desk downstairs, I'm thinking they could give us a map," Clare said, pointing at the door. A nervous laugh escaped her lips.

Nora cut her eyes over at Clare. She didn't know that laugh. It sounded apologetic. What was she apologizing for? Nora's resistance? Another new thing about Clare. Nora could feel the heat of Mrs. Klein's annoyance too, though, and she had to be careful with what she was about to say, there being a free ticket to New York on the line.

"But if you don't show me around, how can I see the plantations, talk to the enslaved people upon whose backs all this wealth has been built? That's why I'm here you know, to write about this pernicious institution for a newspaper or two. Essays and such," Esther said. "*The Liberator*, the *New York Times*, the *New York Evening Post*. I shall make Charleston a crucible."

Nora took a deep breath. "'Tis evil for certain, Mrs. Klein, but I don't—"

"I see there's a Calhoun Street, named for that radical senator of yours, blinded by his own arrogance. Seems a good place to start my public debates."

Nora's hand shot out. "Wait—"

"You worked on a plantation. How about we visit that one? What was the name of it, Clare? You told me the name, didn't you?"

Clare smiled. "Oakland, I believe it was." She flicked a cajoling glance at Nora.

"Mrs. Klein, I ran away from that place. We can't go there," Nora said with as much force as she dared.

"Ran away? What happened?" Esther looked Nora over as if the girl held the keys to more Charleston secrets than she could've hoped.

"How about visiting one of the churches that the planters attend?" Nora asked. *No invitation necessary. Open to the public. She'd have to be quiet.* "St. Michaels? First Scots Presbyterian?"

"I'd never set foot in a church. I am neither Gentile nor Jew, Mohammedan nor Theist. My religion is the human family,"

Esther said. "Besides, I wouldn't get to talk to anyone. I'd have to be quiet."

Clare began gesturing at the door to the hall. "Mr. Hopkins must be waiting for us. I'm thinking we should go meet him downstairs?" She took a step toward the door. "I think I saw him in the lobby? There are black people on every corner out there. Ye can talk to them." Clare reached for the doorknob. "Downstairs."

"So, if you're a runaway," Esther said, "I bet that means a slave ran with you? Surely you didn't manage the woods and unfamiliar roads by yourself."

Nora had been protecting Pearl for so long she almost said no right off. But as she looked into Esther's brown eyes boring into hers, she felt a shift in the air, something like the wind picking up before a storm. Esther waited, wide-eyed and hopeful. Deferential, even. *The upper hand,* Nora thought. *That's what has just come my way.* She lifted her chin a little as she took it. "Yes," she said. "I ran away with a slave."

Esther clapped her hands in rapid, delighted flutters. "And where is she now?"

"Would ye be willing to buy her a ticket on the boat we'll leave on?" she asked. Out of the corner of her eye, Nora saw Clare stiffen. Nora couldn't believe she'd just said it either. Mrs. Klein hadn't said anything to Nora about taking her back to New York. That was Clare.

Breaking into a smile that flattened her nose like butter going soft, Esther said, "Yes, oh yes, what a story that will be."

"And her mother," Nora said, wincing.

"Two of them? Two! Of course, of course. You're not joking, are you? I'll be saving two?"

Joking? Ye think I'm trying to be funny with their lives? Nora thought.

"What a photograph that'll make. Me and the two women on the ship's deck slipping the bonds of chattel right here in Charleston's harbor. Where can I meet them? When?"

"Soon. Let me talk to them. I have to go now."

Esther grabbed Nora's shoulders. "I knew you'd help me. Isn't she wonderful, Clare?"

Clare finally let go of the doorknob. "'Tis quite the adventure she's had, this one," Clare said. "Just like I told ye."

Adventure, Nora thought.

*   *   *

Nora walked home astonished at her brazen self. Finding Pearl at their worktable hunched over a pair of earrings, Nora announced at the top of her lungs what Mrs. Klein had just agreed to.

Pearl jumped up. "You did what? She said what? That can't be. She don't even know us. Why would she—New York? Good Lawd. Wait, wait, wait." She sat down. "What do we have to do?"

"Talk to her."

"'bout what?"

"Tell her about yer life. She wants to write about it."

"That's it?"

"Aye."

Pearl shook a finger at Nora. "That story can't be in no newspaper until we're safe."

"No, of course not."

Pearl flew to the bureau the girls had dragged home from a curb and opened the top drawer. She unrolled the map on the table, tracing the route from South Carolina up the eastern seaboard until her finger stopped at New York. "Mama can go, we've got her bill of sale. The doctor can give it to this woman, but . . ." Pearl turned her head toward the downstairs cot where her mother rested. "I can't get on no boat without freedom papers."

"Do ye know where to get them? What do they cost?"

"I'm workin' on that." Pearl removed the envelope from the sample on the wall. "We've got thirty," she said. "But this is yours. I owe you."

Nora sat down at the table. "Let's just finish these last orders."

Side by side, they snipped, curled, braided, glued, and talked of New York as if they knew the place. In New York they would be owned by no one. They would be business owners. They made up the names of streets and the shops that lined those streets where they'd sell their art and buy beribboned hats and dresses in lucky red. They bought chairs and tables and rose-colored drinking glasses for the rooms they would rent—Nora, Clare, Pearl, and Rose—and created neighbors who would keep Rose company while Pearl worked in the respectable home Mrs. Klein would find for her. Pearl would get a real education, the kind that would teach her about the world, so she could make a life shaped by her own choices. The first choice was going to be a last name.

Around midnight, as the candles were about to give out, three gentle knocks on their door told them that the doctor had had enough of their chatter, so they fell silent.

After a few minutes, Pearl whispered, "That little framed painting that was on the mantel?"

Nora put down the glue and leaned closer to capture every faint word. "Yes?"

"She was 'sposed to marry him. She broke it off when the papers were full of the murder."

Nora nodded slowly as she absorbed this sad sliver of insight. "How do ye know?"

"Mama asked him."

"She told ye he said all that?"

"She said, 'promised to him' and 'newspapers.' She knows he's runnin' like we are."

"Mothers," Nora said, finally smiling. "Always watching."

Pearl finished the last braid of a cuff bracelet, and while she waited for the glue to dry, she said, "We can't take all of this with us when we leave." Her nod at the table indicated the supplies and the braiding platform the size of a dinner plate. "We should give it to somebody who needs to make money."

Nora looked up from tying a knot. "Margaret?"

"Not the manual, though. We takin' that."

With a smile, Nora said, "Aye. Ye are still in charge of the manual."

In the morning, the visit went about as well as Nora could've hoped. When Esther's knock came after the breakfast that no one had eaten, Pearl opened the door, gracious but stiff as a broom. Clare and Hopkins followed Esther in, and while Hopkins set up his daguerreotype equipment in front of the fireplace, Nora made introductions and offered coffee. Simmons watched from the kitchen sink to signal his refusal to be in any photographs. After cups were full, Nora joined him there while Clare flitted around Hopkins' elbows. As far as Nora could see, all the man had to do was get the three wooden legs of his contraption spread out, so why was Clare getting in his way with all that flitting? When Hopkins snapped at Clare, Nora felt a jolt of satisfaction.

As Hopkins arranged his subjects in chairs, Esther noticed Rose struggling with her uncooperative leg. The interrogation about Rose's leg began, and while Esther tried to make sense of Rose's garbled answers, she patted Rose's knee. Rose tolerated this uninvited intimacy with her usual dignity. After the photographs, Esther's questions dug into Rose's and Pearl's lives on the plantations, their memories of the day Pearl was taken from Rose's arms, how they coped, what their work was like, where they slept, who were the other enslaved people, the masters, the punishments. It fell to Pearl to provide all answers. Esther asked to see the sack and its pecans. Pearl brought it out. Esther took a moment to absorb the tragedy of it and the strength of the two women connected to it, then she launched into more questions and more note taking, occasionally asking Pearl to repeat. Tiring of this after a while, Pearl finally asked: Was Mrs. Klein really going to get them out of Charleston on a boat to New York?

Esther answered that indeed she was.

"You're goin' to buy tickets for me, Mama, and Nora on a boat to New York?" Pearl asked again. "Fuh true?"

"Yes, happy to," Esther said. "I'll tell the authorities I'm taking you and Rose to my house in Rhode Island. I'll have Rose's bill of sale and your freedom papers."

"You have freedom papers," Pearl said slowly.

"Oh, of course." Esther waved a hand in the air. "I have a satchel full back at the hotel."

Simmons took his elbow off the sink.

"The Aiding and Abetting Society sent me with blank papers already signed by a judge. We'll just fill your name in." She leaned past Pearl to look at Simmons in the kitchen. "I told you I'm important," she said to him.

"We should buy tickets immediately," Simmons said.

"Don't be silly. I just got here. I haven't seen a plantation yet," Esther said.

"Ma'am, I'm thinking ye shouldn't," Nora said.

"And the newspaper hasn't printed my essay yet. And I haven't picketed any churches yet, the ones the planters attend," Esther said. "What's the hurry?"

Hopkins pulled a handkerchief out of a pocket and dabbed at his brow. "That's illegal down here, you know, ma'am."

"She just got here, Nora," Clare said.

Nora fought the urge to race over and strangle her sister. She knew she couldn't blame Clare for not understanding what it felt like to work for that hag Rebecca Manning, to run through midnight woods that teemed with fangs and claws, to hide hungry and battered in wagons, to feel a reward on your head, to give away one hundred fifty dollars that you'd earned minute by repulsive minute. Perhaps not even blame her for smelling like lavender and owning a fine traveling dress. But she could blame her for not siding with her. Clare was her sister. She should be standing beside her twin here at the sink, not over there with *her*. The distance between them, just a few yards of wide-plank floor, yawned as wide as a fresh grave.

Clare looked away from the fury that was all over her sister's face.

Simmons folded his hand around Nora's. "It's settled," he whispered. "A few more days—we'll make the best of it. We have no choice. This is it. You're going to New York."

"We'll leave when I'm good and ready," Esther declared. "I have a job to do, people to meet."

Chapter Twenty-eight

The Irish shanties had sprouted in a place guaranteed to foster misery. In the 1700's, Charleston's city fathers had filled in a creek to expand the town, but during heavy rains the water always returned to its ancient bed. If the rain came at high tide, the water pushed even higher into the eventual market and neighborhoods. It muscled into homes and stayed. Murky pools lingered in first-floor rooms for days. The ground below clotheslines became sponges of filth and sewage. Nora had avoided the neighborhood when Yellow Jack still held the city in its grip, but on this blue-sky, sun-glorious winter day when she had a package for Margaret, she felt that the shanties were as safe as they would ever be before she left town. She walked to Lingard Street with a box full of the hair art supplies and the hope that Margaret would want them. They still had time for Nora to teach her the craft.

Two blocks away from Lingard, she heard riotous clapping and a fiddler's sawing out "The Rocky Road to Dublin," a song she never thought she'd hear this side of the Atlantic. Usually, the folks in these slouched houses weren't healthy enough to raise a fiddle and dance up some dust.

The music got louder — the fiddle went crazy, then a whistle joined in — and so did the voices roaring the song. Nora turned back for home.

Simmons was paying the fishmonger at the piazza door when she blew past him into the house.

"Pearl! Rose!" Nora called into the front rooms.

They looked over from shelving plates and cups in the cupboards.

Simmons rushed in. "What's the matter?" he asked.

"Irish music! Margaret's neighbors! 'Tis a miracle. Get Rose's stick," Nora yelled.

Simmons threw the fish in a bowl, dumped ice from the alley bins on it, and helped Rose to the door. Pearl fetched her mother's walking stick and ran after Nora already back out on the street. Simmons carried Rose out the piazza door and, seeing Nora and Pearl walking too fast for the old woman, continued to carry her down the street. The fishmonger stared at the sight no one was going to believe when he got home, the white man carrying an old black woman down the street.

Two blocks later, Simmons was puffing like a dray horse, so he set Rose down, much to her relief. Pearl put her mother's stick in her hands and nodded at Nora to lead the way. They'd do their best to keep up, she said. Simmons took Nora's hand to try to urge her to slow down.

The group rounded a corner and headed down Lingard Street's rowhouses, then into a narrow alley that sliced through a block of them. On a patch of ground out back, three men faced three women, their boots flying with whiskeyed abandon. Beyond the dust they kicked up, a cluster of people — all of them young and reed-thin — clapped and hooted in time to the music of a fiddle, a tin whistle, and a pipe. At one end of the dancers' line, a couple joined hands and fueled the frenzy with even fancier dance steps, soon joined by the second couple, then the third.

People waved at the newcomers, one of whom — Nora — was already dancing. Margaret shot out of the crowd, all wheeling arms and loose legs, to grab her. Nora lowered the box of hair supplies into her arms and yelled what it was. Someone found a chair for Rose.

The fiddler sawed away as if the devil would snatch him if he stopped. His fellow musicians — the woman with the pipe-like instrument and a man with a whistle — were no less frenetic. Someone handed Simmons a pair of spoons. He flipped them bowl to bowl, threaded the handles between two knuckles, hoisted his foot on top of a tree stump, and began a clatter against his thigh so perfectly timed with the music that a few heads turned. Simmons smiled into his music, his hands working furiously between thigh and flat palm above. Up, down, three, four — harder on the three. Then he opened that palm and spread his fingers wide, ran the spoons over them washboard-like to make a rippling sound. After three verses of the pounding rhythm, he began singing the chorus, easy enough to pick up. "One, two, three, four, five, hung the hare and turn her down the rocky road," he bellowed. "And all the way to Dublin."

Nora joined him to finish it. "Whack-fol-la-de-da!"

When the song ended, Simmons looked up from his spoons. People pounded his back, handed him a jug for a swig. Nora and Pearl stood transfixed at what they'd just seen.

"Upon my soul, Dr. Simmons!" Pearl laughed.

"Where'd ye learn to do that?" Nora asked.

"The orphanage," Simmons said with a laugh. "The sisters. All from Ireland you know."

"And ye can sing! Glory, what a voice," Nora said.

Simmons gave a little bow.

Margaret arrived with a loaf of Irish brown bread and the scrawny fiddler who turned out to be the new husband. Saluting Simmons with the brown jug in his hand, he said, "Here's to ye, sir. May those who love us love us and those that don't love us, may the Lord turn their hearts toward us, and if he can't turn their hearts, may he turn their ankles so we know them by their gimp."

Throughout the crowd, jugs and cups rose skyward.

Margaret saluted Simmons with the loaf. "Well done, sir," she said. "Pleased to finally meet ye. Have a bit of Irish blood do ye?"

Simmons broke off a piece of the loaf and shoved it in his mouth to avoid saying that every drop in his veins was English.

Another young couple arrived with a jug and tin cups and another round of pouring began. Nora looked around for Rose and Pearl, both of whom were already at her elbow, tin cups held out.

"Sláinte!" every Irish tongue cried. Health!

"Nora plays the fiddle," Pearl announced.

The fiddler handed his instrument to Nora, and she launched a rowdy song, the second of the only two she knew. Dancers grabbed partners. Simmons picked up his spoons. People belted out the lyrics. Bobbing and weaving, Nora moved through the crowd. Pearl followed, skirts a-swishing. As she rounded the edges of the melee, Pearl spotted the fishmonger standing in the alley, hands clapping in time. She pulled him into the dancing.

When Nora finished, she circled back to Simmons. In that usually stony face, surprise had arrived. His eyes shone with admiration. "When were you going to tell me you can do that?" he asked.

She grabbed his head and pulled him into a fierce kiss. The crowd roared. When she let him go, his face was the color of apples.

As the daylight began to fade, a chill settled across the yard. People lit oil lamps to squeeze a few more minutes out of the party, but the momentum was slipping away. Above the soft laughter, someone's serious song could be heard.

"My country 'tis of thee, sweet land of liberty," a man sang.

Margaret joined him. "Of thee I sing," she sang.

Others jumped in and did their best with the lyrics they were still learning. Margaret led the way with every word. She waved at Nora to join in. Nora could only listen, not being one of the faithful at St. Mary's and therefore not knowing the words. She understood them clearly enough, especially by the time the entire crowd was singing about freedom ringing from every mountainside. She hoped it was true. For the Irish, this country, brutal and prejudiced as it was, held the promise of better. *Sweet land of liberty.*

Nora looked over at Pearl and Rose and the fishmonger standing at the edge of the crowd. For certain people born in this country, though, freedom did not yet ring.

Chapter Twenty-nine

Decorative plaster roping framed the massive front door of the Alston home on Charlotte Street. Nora lifted the brass knocker and let it fall against its plate. The roping was designed to mimic the hefty mooring lines used in the maritime industry, a sign to all that the owner's fortune had been made in sea shipping. She'd learned that and a lot more during her deliveries around town. Wrought-iron pineapples atop entrance gates meant wealth, for only the wealthy could afford to buy the fruit imported from Barbados. Blue porch ceilings kept the *haints* out, a nod to sea islanders' superstitions. Rice spoons as big as a fist, always silver and monogrammed, served rice every morning, noon, and night. Don't pronounce the *h* in the surname Huger and especially, God help you, not the *r*. Soft *g*, long *e*.

Bollocks, Nora thought while she waited. *I hope I never hear another Lowcountry name or see another blue porch ceiling for the rest of me days.*

She looked closely at the floor-to-ceiling windows that ran along the front of the house. These too were bordered by plaster roping just to drive home the wealth point she supposed, which was fine with her. Mrs. Alston had been an insatiable customer, an open pipe of money. And talk. She was a foyer talker like no other. Talked a tear, as Mam would say, as in grabbing the conversation and tearing down the road with it. Today's package was Mrs. Alston's last, not that she knew that yet. Nora closed her eyes with relief that all of this would soon be over.

The servant who let Nora in told her to wait while she fetched the missus. No party preparations going on today, so Nora stayed near the door. However, there was something rowdy going on in the drawing room. Sounded like several men were into the grog already, although sunset was hours away. While Yellow Jack slipped in and out of town, Charleston's men were avoiding the taverns.

A plush rug of reds and blues ran from Nora's boots to the bloated staircase at the end of the central hall. She wanted to take them off and feel that kind of luxury on her bare feet as she did on that first night in Charleston when she tiptoed down the Mannings's carpeted stairs to peer out a window at Pearl's candlelight in the kitchen house. All that she and Pearl had survived together—achieved together!—since then was dawning upon her now in these final days in Charleston. The hair work, creepy but lucrative, had enabled them to pull themselves up. Maybe there was something to this country after all. Maybe you could let hope flicker in your soul. Maybe sometimes your hard work did make things come true.

The banter in the drawing room grew louder. She made out a word—*risk*—but couldn't understand anything else. She listened for the missus's footsteps upstairs or on the staircase. Nothing. Nora took a step forward, then another, being careful not to crinkle the paper package under her arms, until she stood at the edge of the drawing room doorway, one foot cocked behind to run. As she leaned into the limit of her forward knee, something hit her. A smell. A rancid smell that lit up her brain like nothing else on earth. *No, it can't be.* That weird man-stink of old sweat, mildew, and tobacco unique to one man. *Surely not — that wharf rat in this fine house?* But then she heard the guttural voice and the arrogant bray. Oh, it was him for certain. Captain Wells for the lovea Jaysus. *Run,* half of her brain screamed. *Listen* screamed the other half.

"Can't be done these days," a man said. "Been illegal for too long."

"Too many patrols on that coast," another said.

"Sure it can," a third voice said.

Nora held her breath. That was Wells.

"Plenty of slavers have gone over there and made it back with a full hold," Wells said.

"Lots of ocean between here and Africa, Wells," someone said.

"Which is why they won't catch me," Wells said. "Given a fast ship."

There was a pause. Glass clinked on glass as another round was poured.

"All that black ivory, it would be worth a fortune," someone said.

"I'm your man," Wells said.

Arguments rattled through the group. Finally, a man shouted, "All right, all right, gentlemen. I wager a thousand dollars that Wells can't do it. What do you say to that, Mr. Alston? Take my bet?"

Nora stifled a gasp. *The reputable Mr. Alston?*

"A tall wager my friend," Alston replied.

"I want a hundred dollars a head," Wells said.

"You won't make it back with any of 'em alive," a man said.

"But if he does," someone said. "They'd fetch seven, eight hundred apiece."

"Wells, what about all the officials nosing around the American ports and harbors?" Alston asked.

"I know them that'll take bribes," Wells said. "Give me a schooner that can do twenty knots in open seas and I'll be back by the fourth of July. North Carolina. Outer banks. I know just the spot to put in."

"You're on," Alston said. "One thousand dollars that Captain Wells will get back here with at least three hundred people alive by July four."

"Women and children count?" someone said.

"Always. They're the ones who don't cause trouble," Wells said.

More questions bounced back and forth. Nora pictured the men leaning against their leather chairs, whiskeys in hand, growing even drunker on visions of obscene profit.

"If they're from Sierra Leone," someone said, "the planters'll pay a thousand dollars each for those that grew tidal rice there."

"Aye, I know, I know," Wells said. "You think I don't know the market in this town? What about a ship for me?"

"I have just the schooner for you," Alston said "Just brought her down from New York. We can fit her out with a temporary slave deck, stow the supplies behind false doors. She's fast. She'll outsail any class of boat in the African patrols."

Upstairs a door closed. Someone stepped on a creaky floorboard, sending Nora hurrying back to the front door. Mrs. Alston swept down the staircase, silk purse clutched in ten acquisitive little fingers. Nora held the package out to her, nearly fainting for the woman to stop talking, finally saying she was taking on a cold and had to go. By the time Nora got back to the street, she had no memory of Mrs. Alston's story, nor handing over the package, nor taking her money — none of it. Panic seized her heart like a hand slipping under the ocean's waves.

She picked a direction and ran on legs she didn't trust, not toward anything that her brain could isolate. Just *away.*

Soon she stood near the intersection that forced her to think. Calhoun Street would take her home where she couldn't breathe a word of this to Rose or Pearl. King Street led to the Marine Hospital, where Simmons would tell her to keep quiet. Meeting Street led to the hotel where she could detonate Mrs. Klein, which carried all sorts of risks. But Clare would be there. What would she say? Clare hated Wells as much as Nora did. She'd take her seriously. She'd help her figure out what to do.

Nora leaned over, hands on her knees, to catch her breath. Why did this have to happen *now?* Why now, just as she and Pearl had everything that they needed to be able to leave? That vile scheme — she couldn't leave without doing something to stop it.

Carriages lacquered in garish colors rumbled down Calhoun Street, their passengers visible only by gloved hands fluttering with conversation or hat brims crushed against the glass. Church bells rang the half hour in their usual soothing succession, one toll overlapping another in the harbor breeze. People strolled by as if nothing had just happened.

It was just talk. What could the officials do with that? They'd laugh at her. *Mr. Alston?* they'd say. *Mr. Claude Alston on Charlotte Street? Be off with you, girl. Go home and sober up.*

Aye, it was a big ocean, that Atlantic. No one would ever catch Wells. She should go home, lay a fire, pour some Donnelly and sit with it in a corner.

But Meeting Street was empty of carriages and people, an unobstructed path stretching out before her all the way to the Charleston Hotel.

She found them in the hotel's dining room at a table for two, all cozy and absorbed with their tea. As Nora swept in paying no heed to the objections of the maître d' on her heels, several diners looked up at the girl in such a state. Clare saw the panic in her face and got up to reach for her hands. Esther waved at a waiter to bring a chair. More heads turned. Finally, the chair arrived and the two women helped Nora into it, for she seemed to not know what to do with a chair. While the waiter hovered, Nora met their questions with a finger to her lips. Esther sent him away and Nora shared her discovery in terse whispers. As the name Captain Wells settled on Clare's teacup, she pushed it away.

"They've done nothing yet," Nora said. "So, I suppose you'll tell me it's just talk."

"Nonsense!" Esther tapped her index finger on the table. "You must report this at once to the authorities."

Exactly what I thought ye'd say, thought Nora, who couldn't decide whether she was glad or terrified to hear it.

"We must tell the United States Navy," Esther said. "They patrol the seas for slavers, they and the British navy." She grabbed Nora's hands. "Oh, my dear girl, what a story you've stumbled across. International slave trade has been illegal for forty-two years. Many devils are still trying, a few have been caught, only one has gone to jail. No one has hanged. Yet."

"Hanged," Nora said, tugging her hands out of Esther's grasp. The woman was connecting an awful lot of dots.

"'Tis just talk, though," Clare said. "What can the Navy to do with that?"

Esther ran her finger around the rim of her cup. "You have a point. They'd want to catch him red-handed."

"'Tis just talk, Nora," Clare said again.

Something about Clare's saying it a second time made Nora screw up her mouth at Clare. Then she turned back to Esther. "'Tis a big place is it, Africa?"

"Indeed it is, but you heard him say Sierra Leone, so that narrows things down a bit. What else did you hear?"

Nora put her hands on the table. "Fourth of July, he said. Said he'll be back by the fourth of July. Outer banks of North Carolina."

"Independence Day?" Esther asked "Are you serious? The irony!"

"What do ye mean?" Nora asked. "What's Independence Day?"

"First thing tomorrow morning, we'll go to the government offices," Esther said.

At this, the twins shared a look of panic. From infancy they'd been immersed in Ireland's songs of rebellion against invaders and rulers, otherwise known as the government. When Irish clans gathered around their fire circles, the storytellers told bloody tales of the King's soldiers sweeping through the fields to beat people, set their homes ablaze, take wives and daughters off to do with as they pleased. Down to their marrow Nora and Clare were so distrustful of officers, uniforms, epaulets, metal badges, helmets, gold buttons, anything official, anything in the shape of official, that they couldn't imagine asking the government to do anything about anything. In many dreams, the twins had boiled the bodies of British dragoons in oil and fed their bones to the dogs.

Clare grabbed Nora's hand and made the wide-eyed stare that all of their lives had meant *don't*. *Don't what?* Nora wondered. *Don't go to the offices? Don't say any more?* Already, Nora was seeing her mistake in coming here. Mrs. Klein would hammer that naval officer full force—Nora could picture him reeling back in his chair—until he got so bloody mad he'd throw them out not having heard a word. Then Mrs. Klein would have a tantrum on the street, secrecy be damned, that would draw people, make gossip, and worst of all, alert Mr. Alston. He and

Wells would then find another way, another city where they'd launch their scheme. Nora had to stop Wells in Charleston even if she didn't know how to yet. She couldn't let him succeed because of Pearl and Rose and Bess and Isaiah and even pompous Tobias, and for the unsuspecting people living free at the moment under the Sierra Leone sun. She couldn't let Wells and the boat get out of Charleston for so many reasons on this American shore and Africa's, and while she needed Mrs. Klein's knowledge, the woman was one risky partner.

Clare began squeezing Nora's hand hard enough to choke a goat, so Nora looked at her even more closely. She read the message clearly then. *Don't make trouble. Don't pull me into this.*

Mrs. Klein was still talking. "He'll try to ignore you. I won't let that happen."

"No, thank you," Nora said.

Esther tilted her head in disbelief. "What do you mean, *no thank you?*"

Clare laughed that apologetic laugh again and sent a look of anguish Nora's way. Her pleading eyes made Nora want to shake her. "Ye have forgotten have ye?" she said to Clare. "What it's like to be shoved into a hold dark as hell, no water or food for days, people shitting and dying all around, no way out?"

Clare slid her hand across the table toward her. To Nora, it looked like a slinking, begging dog. *When did ye change so much?* she thought. *When did ye become a boot licker?* Nora shot to her feet. "I'll go by meself," she said.

"By yourself?" Esther asked. "No, no, no. I'll not miss this."

If a few minutes earlier Nora had thought she wanted Mrs. Klein's help, now she was having none of it. She was no boot licker, nor worse—a puppet with no power of her own. Still, she had to be careful, there being that promised boat ticket to New York.

"You don't know how to handle such people," Esther said.

"Tell me how then."

Clare drew in a loud, quick breath.

Esther straightened and leaned in. "It's just that—"

"If ye don't let me go by myself, I won't go a'tall."

Clare covered her mouth with her hands.

Esther slowly brought her teacup to her lips and took a long sip. As she returned it to the saucer, she viewed Nora with new regard. "Very well, Nora. Would you like for me to tell you what to say?"

A question, not a command. "Yes," Nora said.

"Let's go over a few things," Esther said.

Chapter Thirty

The afternoon sunlight was slipping away when they brought the dockhand to the hospital. Ten inches of bloody gash ran down his leg. Simmons hurried to thread suture through a needle while he still had good light.

"The pulley rope broke," the dockhand said. "Snapped in two. Them horses took off, then them barrels come rolling off the wagon and broke all to hell." He sucked air through his teeth as he squeezed his wound closed. "Barrel hoop sliced into me before I could get away."

"Lucky one of the horses didn't trample you," Simmons said. He poured water over the gash, then wiped it dry. "Here we go. Hold still."

Two students watched Simmons get to work. They were forbidden to touch the patients, but he saw them itching to help, so he waved them down to pull together the ragged skin flaps ahead of his needle, rules be damned.

As he punctured and pulled, Simmons heard a new voice in the room. One bed row away, a man walked slowly down the aisle, hands behind his back, his gaze sweeping left and right. Dr. Daniel McCarter, Simmons's dinner host of weeks ago, followed, eyes on the beds ahead of that sweep, as if to check that nothing coming up was amiss. In a room full of white-aproned men and women, the stranger wore a suit coat and pants.

"Who's that?" Simmons asked the students.

"Some inspector from the bureau of hospitals or whatever they call it in Washington," one said.

"Something happen?" Simmons pulled another stitch tight.

"You'd know before I did, sir."

The visitor was turning his head toward Simmons.

"Get up, get up," Simmons hissed.

As if scalded, the students jumped up, partially shielding Simmons from the visitor's view. Simmons tried to steady his hands for the last inches of suturing. Here was the inspector he'd been expecting. Why *now*?

The inspector arrived at Simmons's elbow, forcing him to look up while McCarter introduced them. The man studied Simmons's face as if trying to place it. "Doctor Simmons, have we met? I believe I know you somehow," he said.

Simmons smiled, cocked his head as if he were trying to re-member the visitor too, then shook it. "Don't believe so. Never been to Washington." He turned his face back to the stitching.

"Ah well, never mind." With a sympathetic look to the pa-tient, the inspector moved on to the next bed.

Simmons looped the last suture and tied it off.

He found McCarter in his office upstairs, pulling files out of a cabinet. Their friendship had blossomed in this room, refuge from professional formalities in front of watchful underlings. Here, an exhausted doctor could be just an exhausted man washing down the demands of the day with good whiskey.

When they hung up their aprons smeared with body fluids, the carapaces were off.

Simmons approached his friend, trying to read his face in the light of the one candle that gave the office a gloom that felt like stealth and midnight wakes.

"So, who's our visitor?" he asked in the tone of someone seeking the time of day.

McCarter ran his hand over his face. "He's gone, thank God," he said. He placed a stack of files on a table and turned back to the cabinet for more.

"What's wrong? Something happen?"

"No, just an inspection. The annual."

Simmons looked at the filing cabinet, where a certain record that an inspector mustn't find odd seemed to call out for attention. "Gone for good?"

"Back in the morning to look into these staff credentials." McCarter pulled out another handful. "Licenses, education, that sort of thing."

Simmons held his face as still as he could. "You think he's looking for anything in particular?"

McCarter looked up. "Like what?"

Simmons took a deep breath and wondered which way this was going to go. He was about to offer McCarter his neck.

The furrow on McCarter's forehead deepened. "Frederick, what's going on? For months now you've been literally looking over your shoulder."

"Have I?"

"You got something to you need to tell me? Before tomorrow?"

Simmons took a step toward his friend. "Dan, I'm a good man. You know me."

"Yes, well, I think I do."

Simmons shook his head. "I'll be gone soon."

"Oh?"

Simmons stared at his own hands.

McCarter went to a wall cabinet and took out glasses and a bottle of whiskey. "Come on. Sit."

They headed for the chairs in the corner that they always headed for. Simmons lit another candle on the table between them.

McCarter poured two glasses. "What're you worried about? A forged medical degree? Your criminal record lurking in Washington's files?" A smile rose on his lips as he put them to the glass.

"Yes."

McCarter leaned back in his chair. Restless winds rinsed the last daylight from the sky. Downstairs, someone screamed out in agony. "What's going on?" he asked.

"Simmons isn't my real name."

"Oh really?" The smile on McCarter's lips was gone. "What is it then?"

It was a name that the man staring back at him was proud of. Rather, it was the name of his grandfather, Benjamin Franklin's collaborator, that he was proud of, the legendary name that had gotten Simmons attention at medical school in Edinburgh where his grandfather had been trained, and attention everywhere else in his life, allowing him to bask in reflected glory.

"Benjamin Rush," he said.

McCarter blinked hard. "What? Good Lord. Benjamin Rush?" McCarter said. "You related to *the* Benjamin Rush?"

"Grandfather," Simmons said quietly, lowering his glass to the table. The whiskey shivered in swirls of amber and gold in the candlelight.

"Why the false name?"

"Back in Baltimore, a woman died. She had pointed a gun at me and a defenseless girl in labor. She said the girl had seduced her husband. A guileless, fifteen-year-old servant had seduced her husband? I pushed the woman with the gun away. She fell on a hearth. Fractured cranium."

McCarter closed his eyes with relief. "But that was self-defense — "

"'Course it was. But you know how these things can go, Dan. There's an angry husband."

"So, you're hiding."

Downstairs, cries of agony and fear exploded again. Boots raced across the floor.

McCarter swirled the last amber swig around the bottom of his glass and downed it. "Look, any discrepancies the inspector might find back in Washington, it'll take a while," he said.

"Maybe not. He thinks he knows my face."

"Frederick, all of us should leave Charleston, truth be told. Already, the North is doing everything it can to weaken the South. Our chloroform, our medications — "

"Manufactured up North."

"Yeah, mostly. When the war comes, they'll choke us off."

"Where will you go?"

"Back home to Virginia. Get my wife settled with her family, sign on with a Virginia regiment. What about you?"

Simmons stared into his glass. "Dan, I need a favor."

"The best I can do is two hundred dollars."

"No, no. When I get where I'm going, I'll need you to vouch for me."

McCarter nodded solemnly. "Of course, but don't tell me where you're going. Good luck, my friend. You'd better leave town soon and on a moonless night." McCarter stood to shake Simmons's hand. "Taking the Irish girl with you?"

"Still working on that." Simmons grasped his friend's rough hands in farewell.

Passing through the first ward, then the second on his way to the front door, Simmons looked around at the work he loved. Faces lit up as he went by, the brightest belonging to the bosomy Jenny who had no idea how barren was the ground upon which her beams had been falling for a year. Her mother was cooking bream for dinner. She'd told her to invite the doctor over. He passed by so fast. She raised her hand good night, but he didn't notice. Tomorrow then, she thought.

He hung his apron on the empty hook that everyone had always left alone as his, put on his coat, and went out the door. All daylight had bled out of the sky.

Two blocks away, he recognized her from the back, the short legs hurrying in the direction of home. Simmons rushed ahead to grab Nora's arm. She spun around as if fangs had just sunk in.

"Frederick," she said. "Oh, thank God."

"What are you doing out here? I thought you had only one delivery and would've been home long ago." Without waiting for an answer, he took her hand and pulled. "Come on."

"I had to go to the hotel —"

"Had to?"

"It's Wells, Captain Wells. He's here. 'Tis a horror what he's up to."

"Are you or Clare in danger?"

"Well, no, but—"

"Then it's none of our concern. Come on, we have to—"

She jerked her hand away. "Ach! Listen to me, would ye?" She waved him into the doorway of a shuttered storefront and told him everything.

He shook his head. "No, no. Let it go, Nora. We don't have time for this."

"Reporting it is all I'll do."

"What if . . . you could get pulled into . . . wait—all you have is a conversation overheard? You have nothing."

Nora's green eyes went hard. "I have a duty, is what I have."

"Look, Nora, I have to keep my head down now."

"'Tis your own head. Keep it wherever ye want." Crossing her arms, she glared at him.

Simmons grabbed her shoulders. "An inspector looked me over at the hospital today, a federal inspector, long and hard. Said he thinks he knows me. The murder scandal was all over the Washington and Baltimore papers because of my family name. Descendant of the honorable Benjamin Rush kills woman and flees, they said. Descriptions of me, even a drawing. When he gets back to Washington, he's going to compare my forged Charleston records with federal registries. He won't find a Frederick Simmons of Charleston, so he'll wonder about that. He's going to put it all together soon."

"So ye have a little time until he does," Nora said.

"But his mind is already turning. You should've seen the way he looked at me. We have to convince Mrs. Klein to leave soon. Buy tickets on the next packet north."

"To New York."

"Well, for me, on to Canada."

Nora's eyes softened. "Canada?"

"I'm not safe in this country."

"Mother of God—why can't ye just explain yerself to the police?

"You of all people should know how that can go."

"But—"

"I want you to come with me, Nora," he said in a gentler voice.

"Ye mean, to help ye with yer doctoring?"

Simmons took her hands in his. "No, that's not what I mean." He pulled her closer, looked into her eyes to be sure what he wanted to do would be all right, and when he felt her body relax, he kissed her. Then he said, "I want you to be my wife."

Nora blinked hard. "Right now? Ye're asking me that right now for the lovea Jaysus?"

"Well, these are desperate times."

"Because ye have to run for Canada?"

"Yes, well, no, that's not what . . ." Regret pulled at the edges of his eyes.

"Oh, no," Nora said, backing away. "'This isn't how I pictured this moment." She pressed her palms into her temples.

"I may not be a romantic man, but I'm an honorable one."

"Aye, that's true." Nora laid her hand on his arm.

"Well?"

"Wife? Canada? I don't know about wife."

Simmons threw up his hands. "What! We'll have a respectable situation or none a'tall."

For once in her life, Nora said nothing.

"Nora?" Simmons rubbed her arms in a cajoling way.

She surrendered by smiling but held up her pointer finger. "We mustn't tell anyone, not right now," she said.

"Is that a yes?"

Nora shook her head. "I can't tell Pearl, not with what I'm about to ask of her tonight."

Simmons stiffened. "What are you going to—"

"Yes. Me answer is yes," she said.

After another kiss, he offered his arm for the walk home and she accepted it with two hands and the gift of her silence, seeing no good reason to start an argument in the one luminous moment she'd found since arriving in America, although as they strolled, she was trying on the word. *Wife.*

Chapter Thirty-one

Nora and Pearl walked past the waterfront's sailmakers, outfitters, shippers, and purveyors and turned toward a pier. Among the hodgepodge of vessels, the Navy warship stood out with its gleaming black sides and pristine sails tied down in uniform bundles. America's flag flew from the stern. Arriving at the midsection of the *U.S.S. Allegheny*, the girls waved at the man on deck who had watched them approach. When Nora said she wanted to talk to the captain, the sailor laughed.

"What do you two want?" he asked.

"'Tis a private matter," Nora said.

"Oh yeah? How private?" The sailor looked Nora's body up and down with deeper interest.

She moved closer. "Someone is about to break the law," she whispered.

Pearl twisted her apron as she looked over her shoulder for anything that didn't look right, sound right. She hadn't wanted to come, had tried to say she couldn't imagine what she could add, but Nora insisted that the Navy wouldn't listen to an Irish girl alone, nor a black girl alone, but the two of them together, well, wouldn't that make them wonder why two of their kind would stick their necks out with such a story? *Besides,* Nora had said, *I can't do this without ye.*

A man in a silver-buttoned blue coat arrived at the rail and told the sailor to get rid of the girls. Nora yelled at the new face that she had to speak with the captain. Esther had told her to simply say the same thing over and over until she got better answers. A young black man with a mop—he wore the Navy's blue shirt but neither silver buttons nor wool coat—joined the men at the handrail to see about the yelling. Another voice called out from somewhere on the deck—Nora and Pearl stood on their tiptoes to see—and a man in a double-breasted black coat arrived. All the other men stepped aside for him. Two rows of silver buttons ran down the front that strained to contain the belly. Embroidered silver anchors on the shoulders, stripes around the cuffs, black captain's hat with a medallion—all the insignia that Nora hated.

"What's going on out here?" he asked. The jaw, covered by a trim white beard, jutted accusingly at the civilians, an odd pair likely up to no good.

"Sir," Nora said, stepping even closer.

"Don't touch my ship," the captain bellowed.

"I need to report something. Something being planned. 'Tis against the law."

"Well, take it to the City Guard," he said. Some of the annoyance had drained out of his voice, but it was still loud.

Nora squared her shoulders. "No, sir. 'Tis a crime of piracy on the seas."

The whiskered face broke into a smile. "Piracy is it?" He doubted that this Irish sparrow knew that that word meant a specific kind of crime to an American naval officer these days.

"Are ye the right man to tell? Are ye in charge of the United States Navy?" Nora asked.

The sailors fought with their faces to not smile.

"Open the damn gangway," the captain said to the man in the coat without silver anchors. A few seconds later, the captain stood toe to toe with the girls. "I'm Lieutenant Cowan. What's this about?"

"I was in a house here in town making a delivery," Nora whispered, "and I heard a conversation in the drawing room. The man who owns the house, he's in shipping, ye see. The men, they were wagering whether the sea captain in there with them … "

Cowan squinted and let out a long sigh.

" … whether that captain could make it to Africa, steal some people there, and bring them back here to sell," Nora said.

"Huh," Cowan said. So she did know what the word piracy implied. He glanced at Pearl, who held a stony expression.

Nora said, "The captain said—"

"Were you in the room?"

"No, sir, in the hall I was but—"

"Well then how do you know it was the captain speaking?"

"Because I know him. I spent ten days on his packet."

"I see."

"Robert Wells his name is, and he's taken the bet that he'll go to Africa and be back in North Carolina with slaves by July fourth," Nora said.

"Huh," Cowan said again. "Four months from now, so that part's believable."

"Believe it all, sir," Nora said, trying to ignore the slight.

"Do you suppose they were drinking?"

Nora realized that she hadn't seen the drinking and knew what the next rebuff would be, so she stayed quiet.

"Perhaps just the grog talking?" Cowan asked.

"No, sir. Ye don't know Wells." Nora ran her hands down her skirt. "He's desperate, he's vile, that one, he's—"

"Sounds personal."

Nora had no rehearsed answer to this bit of truth.

"Miss, without any evidence, what do you expect me to do?"

Nora was ready for that one. "Surely the Navy won't just let him and his crew steal people from their families, stow them in filth and darkness, and cross the ocean before ye can act," she said.

Cowan fired back. "There are five, just five mind you, United States Navy warships patrolling three thousand miles of African coastline at the moment. And you want me to send word up my chain of command that one of them should go looking for this Wells before he's actually done anything?"

Pearl came to life. "There's the British Navy, sir. They have eighteen warships. Tell the British," she said.

Cowan's eyebrows went up. "Who have you two been talking to?"

"Sierra Leone. He's going to Sierra Leone," Nora said.

"Oh, well, that certainly makes all the difference." Cowan gave a snort that triggered his digging in a pocket for a handkerchief. "Look," he said, "the Africa Squadron, it's the backwater of the Navy. Those commanders? It's the end of their careers. Nothing happens over there. Besides, what you've overheard, it's just rich men talking. I'm not touching this." Cowan turned his shoulders and their insignia away.

"But—"

"Dismissed," Cowan said, and he bounded back up the gangplank.

The girls returned to the waterfront with their hands jammed in their skirts, deflated but not surprised. Nora seethed with every Irish mother's words: *Never start a fight, but if there is one, make sure ye finish it.* A skin-prickling fury came over her — the quick-to-flame Murphy ire.

"Just rich men talking," Nora said.

"Let's get out of here," Pearl said.

The girls heard footsteps coming hard and fast. They turned to find the black sailor who'd held the mop. He seemed to be a proper sailor. His blue shirt was a sailor's with its flap across the back of his shoulders that opened at the throat. The pants were blue as well, twin rows of buttons at the top, wide bells at the bottoms. One arm ended at the wrist — he was missing a hand — above which he'd rolled the sleeve.

"Excuse me," he said, stopping a respectful distance away. "Need to tell y'all something." He waved them toward the shadow of a stack of cotton bales.

"Name's Guthrie, ma'am and ma'am." His head dipped to each of them. "Petty Officer William Guthrie. Ship steward." He raised his stunted arm. "Well, used to be before the accident."

"Nora Murphy," Nora said. "Sorry to hear that."

"Pearl," Pearl said.

"Back there, what Lieutenant Cowan told you, it ain' true. A patrol ship can seize a ship based on suspicious supplies on board," Guthrie said. "And there are plenty of Navy captains who'd like nothing better than to catch a slaver."

"Suspicious supplies," Nora said. "Such as?"

"Fittings and pre-cut lumber for the temporary slave decks

going in when the boat gets to Africa, or hundreds of wooden spoons, or big cooking pots and hogsheads of water. Rum, gunpowder, cutlasses, muskets, and other goods for trade."

"Well, why didn't he say so?" Pearl asked.

"It's a needle in a haystack finding that boat before it leaves America, much less on the return. Cowan's a lazy old salt, six months to retirement."

"But it's here. Mr. Alston said he's just brought the boat down from New York," Nora said.

Guthrie nodded. "Then that captain will outfit her here. He's only got four months, you said, to get over there and back. He'll hide her in one of these three rivers around here while they hammer in the iron fittings, load her with food and supplies. Do you know these rivers and creeks?"

Nora held up her hands, palms out. "Not me. I don't get in little boats."

"You?" Guthrie leaned toward Pearl. "Surely you know people who fish the creeks?"

"Might." Pearl shot a worried look at Nora. This was getting complicated.

"Ladies, you two is somethin' else having the gumption to bring this story to Cowan. Poor luck that he's the dumbest salty dog ever in uniform. The Africa Squadron ain' no backwater no more. The Navy sent Perry himself over there couple years ago to clean it up."

Nora squinted at Guthrie. "Who?"

"Commodore Matthew Perry. He's important — you don't know who he is? They sent him over there to catch slavers, cripple the South, and win international praise all at the same time." Guthrie raised both arms.

For the first time, Nora allowed herself a smile. That's exactly what Mrs. Klein had said would be the winning argument. Getting international praise. All that acclaim.

"So, yes ma'am, Cowan would be a hero if he'd get off his, um—" Guthrie said.

"Arse," Nora said.

"Yes, ma'am, sure would. Seizing a slaver before it even leaves Charleston would make him a hero. Dumber than dirt, that man."

"Seize it 'cause of spoons and iron fittings?" Pearl asked. "You can send a man to jail with just that?"

"It's been done. Look, y'all round up some fishermen who'll find the ship, lay her at Cowan's feet, he'll have to arrest the man. Meanwhile, ask around the forges to see if someone's been ordering ankle irons? Braces? Go to the lumberyards. Find out if someone's buying pine and having it cut in twelve-, ten-, and eight-foot lengths and where it went."

Nora looked down the street at the Ashley River, then looked in the opposite direction at the Cooper. Hundreds of creeks and even another river fed into these rivers, and twice a day many of them, swollen by the tide, were deep enough to accommodate a big ship.

Frederick was right. This could hold them up.

Guthrie dropped his voice. "Ma'am, I come from Alabama slaves who made it to New Jersey. I want to see this slaver captain hang. You find me some men who fish 'roun' here. They see a new boat upriver, they hear hammering? I'll go with them soon as I can to look her over, see if she's the right kind of ship."

"We have to hurry. We're leaving town soon," Nora said.

"That captain you hate, he'll be in a hurry too. It's up to you." Guthrie walked back to his ship.

Walking home, the girls were deep in conversation and didn't see Esther and Clare waiting on a street corner until Esther stepped in front of them. She made collecting motions at them to get them off to the side. How did it go? she wanted to know behind a tree. How could she help? Pearl shot a look at Nora, pinned against the tree by the force of Esther's demands. The captain, Nora explained, needs more.

"'Tis for certain," Clare blurted. "I told you."

Nora ignored that. "And we know what he needs," she said. "Fittings for slave decks and suspicious supplies."

"We need to find them," Pearl said.

"You must let me do something," Esther said.

"You know how to fish in a jon boat?" Pearl said.

"Well, no."

"We'll be askin' around," Pearl said. "No offense, Mrs. Klein, but this ain' somethin' a Yankee needs to be doin' in Charleston."

Esther fingered the pearls on her neck as she weighed the veracity of that unsatisfactory observation. After a while, with people on the street sending glances toward their tight huddle and Pearl studying the toes of her own boots, Esther picked up her skirts and walked away. Clare hurried to follow the swishing skirts. Esther Klein had no intention of letting anyone see concession on her face.

Chapter Thirty-two

Once again, Nora walked into the mayhem of the grittier side of town, this time with purpose. Logs that had floated down the Ashley River bobbed in holding ponds beside the lumberyard. The screams of its saws tore through the air. Hammers rang out in blacksmith shops and cooperages. Hogs banged around frantically in slaughter stalls, as if knowing that this was the last place on Earth they'd be standing. As cultured as Charleston was in the center of the narrow peninsula, this area along its edge—just a few city blocks away—was primitive.

Holding her skirts above the mud, she crossed the lumberyard and opened its office door. The long counter where she expected a clerk was bare, except for piles of papers velveted with sawdust. Behind the counter, stacks of rough planks created aisles, and in the third aisle she found a man trying to coax a splinter out of his pinky finger. When she asked for Georgia pine, he led her to another tower of planks.

"This all ye got?" she asked.

"How much you need?" the man said, sticking his finger into his mouth.

"A lot I guess. Me husband? He sent me over here to see

what ye have and if it's not enough, I'm to ask when ye'll get more."

"Your husband sent you here?" The man gave her a look.

"A broken leg he has."

"Huh, well, tell him we've got about a hundred board feet."

"Sell a lot of pine do ye?"

The man shrugged.

"Just wondering how quickly it goes. Lots of people been buying it?"

"Look, ma'am, this is all I got after that fella come in here and bought two hundred board feet a few minutes ago. Come back when you know how much you want."

A few minutes ago. "Did he have it cut? Ye do cut it, don't ye? Me husband, he's got plans for some shelves — "

"Yeah, yeah, 'course we do. We can cut it any length you want, eight feet, ten feet, like we just did for that fella." The clerk wiped his hand on his pants and walked away.

Nora hurried outside to the nearest wagon, but it was empty and no one was around. Down at the river two men were loading boards onto a rice barge. She walked toward them, thinking through what she'd say. What if her nonsense about Georgia pine and shelves made them suspicious? Why would a stranger start up a conversation like that? Her mere presence in the lumberyard, much less on the dock talking to two men, would make them nervous if they were doing what she hoped. Then what? They'd shove off as quickly as possible to disappear around the nearest bend in the Ashley. But in her brief life, Nora had learned that sometimes you might not get an answer to the question you brought, but you might get something else just as good, maybe better. The point was to show up and talk. She smoothed her scarf, forced herself to walk slowly, and stepped onto the pier. *All right — just ask that fellow there if he's planning to buy the rest of the Georgia pine inside, since me husband needs it bad.*

The overloaded rice barge sat low in the water, so she wasn't surprised when the man onboard picked up a pole to push off. The man on the dock wiped his hands on his pants, waved, and turned back toward land, head down. His hair was thick and black, its high gloss ignited by the noon sun. He took two more steps and looked up as he sensed her presence. A ragged beard covered the lower half of his face, but she recognized the coffee-colored eyes, the lips.

Patrick.

"Nora!" he said. "What're you doing here?"

The air between them bristled with enough mixed emotions for three bad marriages, and she knew that she should turn around and leave without a word, but he might be the key. He knew where that Georgia pine was going. She willed her heart to stop crashing against her ribs so her lungs could work again, and then, she hoped, her brain. All of the blasting she'd planned to give him if and when she ever saw him again, all of the retorts to the blarney that would be coming out of that mouth — she couldn't pull up a word of it.

Patrick closed the distance between them. She saw that he had something to say and it wasn't going to be about boards. The unreadable face finally readable. Nora wondered what golden words were about to come out of that mouth she could still taste. Part of her knew they would be horse shit, and part of her knew that if he touched her, her knees would buckle.

He stopped inches away. "I've prayed for this moment," he said.

So, horse shit right off. Still, she looked into his eyes. This was the last time she'd ever see him. He had something to get out and she wanted to hear it. His face had filled out, his eyes were clearer.

"I'm sorry, Nora," he said. "I couldn't come back to your house to say it, so I'm glad you're here. I'm sorry for what I did to you, the innocent *caílin* just off the boat."

Nora narrowed her eyes. "Why are ye telling me this?"

"It's weighed on me. I've had time to think."

More horse shit. Be careful. "A criminal ye made me."

"Aye, I'll not deny it."

"Should've let ye bleed to death on the floor there."

"Aye, I wouldn't have blamed ye."

"Huh." *This is different.* Nora's spine softened. "So, you're working down here? Thought you'd leave town."

"Here and the shipyard. Can't find work anywhere else without getting beaten for taking free blacks' work." He leaned against a dock piling, as if settling in for a pint and a smoke with her. He crossed his arms.

She looked at his hands, sliced and scarred. A purple crescent rose from the nailbed of a thumb—the marks of a working man, so maybe that much was true. Her heartbeat was settling, her brain was clearing. She pointed at the loaded barge cutting through the river chop. "Where's he going with that?" she asked.

Patrick's arms slowly melted out of their fold. "Why do ye—"

"Was it cut into, say, six-, eight- and ten-foot lengths?"

His face changed, his eyes grew cold. And with that, she saw that he knew why she was asking.

"Ye should go home," he said.

"How can ye help men like that?"

"Don't judge me, Nora. They paid me well to measure the ship for it."

"Measure the—where is it?" She grabbed at his arm.

"What! What are ye up to?"

"Where's the ship?"

Patrick shook his head. "Stay away, Nora. They're a dangerous lot."

"'Tis for certain. Where are they going, Patrick? I'll not ask ye anything else, I swear. Ye owe me that."

Patrick raked his hands through his hair while he absorbed that claim on his repentant soul. Finally, he said, "I think the ship is up the Wando River. Not sure. They blindfolded me for the trip but based on how long it took us to get there and the sounds of the harbor traffic, I think it's in a creek off the Wando, behind an island high enough to grow trees, ten or so." His eyes got glassy with fear. "What are ye—"

"What else? What's it look like?"

He shook his head. "I couldn't believe it. It's a racing yacht, Nora. A luxury yacht that no one will suspect. Below deck, there's rosewood paneling, satinwood cupboards, gilded mirrors, cigars in ebony boxes ready for the sharing."

"Jaysus, never mind the inside. What's it look like outside?"

"About a hundred feet long, schooner-rigged. Long sharp bow. Why are ye bothering with this?" A new thought bloomed on his face. "Is there a reward?"

Ah, there he was, the old Patrick, blind to immorality but not profit, always looking to line his pockets. What kind of man was he, what kind of Irishman to not fight tyranny and inhumanity in all of its forms on all shores, for surely he knew what the planks were for. Why did she have to keep learning this lesson about him? For all of his glory above the neck, she saw now that the shoulders were narrow and the chest puny, as if his body was a vessel too small to nurture the growth of character over the years.

"No, there's no reward," she said as she picked up her skirts.

"Next time I see ye, we'll just nod, square now we are."

"Ye won't be seeing me," she said, turning away from the river and all the foolish romantic notions of a young and ignorant girl from County Galway.

* * *

Pearl watched the back of the Manning house through a hole in the fence for a whole day before she decided the family was still gone. Isaiah had groomed the horses in front of the stable but never harnessed them to the carriage. The big house windows remained shuttered. Tobias had come and gone to his lessons, fiddle in hand. Hettie had taken no food from the kitchen to the big house. The in-town servants were in place, and they were all she needed.

The next day, Pearl put a basket on her shoulder to hide her profile from neighbors' slaves' prying eyes and opened the alley gate. She peered in the window of the cookhouse and found Hettie and Isaiah inside. She opened the door.

Hettie dropped a bowl at the sight of her. "What on earth? What you thinkin'?" she cried. "You crazy to be 'yuh."

Isaiah jerked out of his nap on the bench.

"Hettie, Isaiah! I found Mama!" Pearl said. "She's here. She's free."

Hettie's hands fell to her pillowy bosom. "Lawd awmighty," she said.

Isaiah shook his head. "Gal, why ain' ya'll gone?" he asked.

Tobias rushed in from the yard. "Red bird!" he shouted.

"Hush, fool!" Hettie said. "Close that door."

"Hey there, Tobias," Pearl said calmly. "Need y'all's help. Listen."

She pulled a chair up to the table that was the heart of their community, but only Tobias joined her. The others stayed rooted to their spots, unwilling to harbor her but not ready to throw her out yet either. They exchanged unsteady glances. Finally, Tobias told them to sit down.

She needed fishermen in boats, Pearl explained, a lot of them, to search the Wando and its web of meandering streams.

"Search for what?" Isaiah asked.

"A big fancy ship in a creek, looks like it's hidin'. There might be hammerin' and loadin' goin' on."

"Why's it hidin'?" Hettie asked.

"Why they hammerin'?" Tobias asked.

She told them. The men jumped to their feet, hands waving away the mortal danger. Hettie covered her mouth.

"No danger to nobody," Pearl said to the astonished faces. "Report back what they see, that's all," Pearl said. "Nora will take it from there."

"That Irish girl!" Isaiah said. "She thinks she'll get that man arrested like you say?"

"She does," Pearl said.

"Her haid took away," Tobias said.

"She say she can get the government on 'em," Pearl said.

Disbelief rippled through the circle again and hands went up again to push the scheme back Pearl's way, sending her into a fury. She climbed on top of the table, which sent spoons and mugs bouncing off, said all people had to do was fish like they always do and crane their necks to look at other people's business like they always do, and get word to her, and if they didn't do that, more innocent people were going to die or worse—live enslaved for the rest of their lives.

"All right, all right, come on down now," Tobias said. He offered his hand to Pearl to help her down and held on as long as she let him. "I know people," he said. "I'll talk to 'em."

"We need a lot of people," Pearl said.

"I know," Tobias said. "You said. I'll roun' some up."

"I know people," Hettie said.

"Yea, awright, awright, me too," Isaiah said. "Seem like the Irish girl got all the risk."

"Sure does," Pearl said. "Y'all just got to find that boat."

Chapter Thirty-three

On the morning of February 17, 1850, the *Charleston Mercury* published its response to a request that the editors had received two days earlier. Throughout the city, Charlestonians at their desks and breakfast tables read the headline on page two, "Treachery in Our Midst," and the seething editorial below.

This newspaper has received an essay and a request from its author to publish it. This author, a visitor from New York, has brought with her all of the abolitionist movement's offensive rebuke, righteous indignation, and economic ignorance. She has called upon us to encourage debate by printing her viewpoint. We will not.

This Mrs. Abraham Klein of New York City has been in our city only a few days, yet she has managed to defile every hospitality extended to her, having rebuked our citizens on street corners, accosted church goers after services, and taken an old slave woman for a tour of King Street shops in a wheelchair. We have long suspected the Aiding and Abetting Society of sending its agents into the South to incite. Little do they know their arguments only make the cause of the Southern states more cohesive. As Senator John Calhoun has written: "Abolitionism strikes directly at our prosperity and our existence as a people. It is a question that admits neither concession nor compromise."

If Mrs. Klein does not leave our gracious city within three days, our response will be to burn her essay in front of our office on Broad Street on February 20 at five o'clock. We exhort all citizens to support the cause by attending.

On the evening of that day that began with citizens slamming their *Charleston Mercury* against breakfast tables and desks, three men rowed a jon boat along one of the creeks that fed into the Wando River. The men looked like all black men who pulled their suppers out of Lowcountry waterways — pants the color of pluff mud, shoulder blades poking out the backs of their thin homespun shirts, crumpled straw hats. In a different feeder stream farther upriver and in another downriver, other men — two per boat — rowed the waters they knew so well. Throughout the infinite marsh, ten pairs of men in fact, were threading their way through the wide creeks fishing not for fish.

But one boat held three men. It passed a bank of oysters, startling a marsh hen out of her spartina grass. While two rowed, the third man scanned the water with a spyglass in one hand, his only hand. Sounds drifted across the glassy surface of the slack tide water, mostly bird calls and the soft bubbling of the oysters as they opened and closed their shells to feed. From the north, a man's voice — urgent and directive — wafted in, nothing unusual in these waters full of fishermen, so the rowers kept their pace. Then a hammer began slamming — metal on metal — and another joined in. Tobias and his fellow oarsman rowed faster.

A bump of land rose in the middle of the river high enough to nurture a stand of scruffy trees. The jon boat stayed well away, hugging the edge of the marsh opposite the island as fishermen would. As the boat came abeam the island, its rowers saw the long bowsprit of a sailing vessel, then two masts, then the entire sleek form of an elegant ship. The hammering was louder now, definitely coming from the bowels of that ship. Seeing no one on deck yet, the one-armed fisherman raised his spyglass again.

"Hooo-weee," he whispered. "Never seen a ship like this. Long sharp bow, bowed-in amidships instead of the usual straight sides. A cutaway stern. She's built for speed, that's for sure." He tilted his glass up. "I'll be damned," he said, pointing at the top of the mainmast. The triangular New York Yacht Club pennant flew in the breeze. The fisherman put his glass down. "This is it, y'all."

Two men appeared on the yacht's afterdeck. Spotting the jon boat, they ran to the handrails and yelled at it to move on. The hammering below deck stopped. The fishermen rowed as fast as poor men who didn't want no trouble would, but they stole a few final long looks over their shoulders. They then saw the other boat, a smaller one beached on the island. Men were unloading it, carrying boxes on their shoulders as they headed for the schooner's gangplank. With the first high tide of tomorrow, the yacht would push away into the waterway's deepest channels and on to the Atlantic, her hold full of supplies, her false deck for the captives sealed, duplicate papers and false invoices stowed for presenting to any authorities inclined to board and search, and the salon stocked with the world's finest brandies. Her name was *Remy Martin*.

* * *

"We found her," Nora called to Lieutenant Cowan when he appeared at the lifelines of the *Allegheny*. Petty Officer Guthrie stood on the dock beside Nora. Dawn's light had been warming the waterfront thicket of masts, yardarms, spars, and rigging for less than half an hour.

Cowan pushed aside the gawking First Mate who had roused him from his bed. "What the hell?" Cowan bellowed as he looked down at them. "Guthrie, what are you doing with her?"

"They were loading the boat last night, sir," Guthrie said. "Hogsheads, barrels. She's a schooner built for speed."

"Guthrie, I gave you leave to visit a dying aunt or something. You were out there looking for that ship?"

"It's a racing yacht, sir."

"Then it's a racing yacht, Guthrie."

"But she's upriver, hiding behind an island in a creek, sir."

"She's had pre-cut lumber delivered," Nora said. "He heard hammering."

"Maybe the fittings going in," the First Mate said. "Sir."

Cowan looked over at the First Mate beside him. "Anybody ask for your thoughts?"

"An international hero ye'll be, Lieutenant Cowan," Nora said. Esther had told her to say that. "Show the British navy what the American navy can do." That part, too, for what American naval officer would want to be bested by the British navy?

The First Mate raised his eyebrows at the captain. "Sir?" he asked.

Cowan squinted at Guthrie. "Shit. Where's she anchored?"

"Up the Wando."

"You were out there last night? Really? How did they not see you?"

Guthrie shrugged. "They saw three fishing buddies out in a jon boat," he said.

The First Mate said, "Sir, all we have to do is sit at the mouth of the harbor and wait for the yacht to come down the river. She'll sail right past us on her way to sea. We'll signal that we want to board her."

"But we have no reason to do that," Cowan said. "Her captain will be furious. What if — "

"Sir!" The First Mate tried to hide his growing contempt.

"These days all ships are suspect. Our orders are clear. We have the right to board any vessel we want, most certainly one in Charleston's harbor."

"Tide's coming in sir," Guthrie called. "She'll be leaving soon as she can float."

"What happens when ye seize a ship? Put the captain in cuffs do ye?" Nora asked.

"I knew this was personal," Cowan said to her. "And don't be thinking you're getting on my ship to watch."

"Wouldn't think of it," Nora said. "Just wondering."

"Get Guthrie on board and let's go," Cowan said as he stomped away.

The gangplank thudded to the pier. Guthrie turned his back to his shipmates, slipped his spyglass to Nora, made a fist of victory, and ran up the gangplank.

* * *

The small armada of jon boats and rickety bateaux approached a sandy shore a few blocks north of the Cooper River's last wharf. An onshore crowd watched them come. The boaters had put in at their usual places upriver, spots where the marsh was thin enough to let people wade to their boats. At this place, the Cooper River became the harbor. North of it, the Wando fed into the Cooper. The men and women waiting ashore in morning's rosy light waved at the boats to hurry, for the tide had started to slow down two hours earlier. Time was running out to go see what dozens of fishermen had been searching for and two of them had found. Every neighbor, brother, cousin, uncle, enemy, and jilted lover turned out to get in a boat and go see that yacht and what was about to happen to it. In kitchen houses and stables throughout the city, the black Charlestonians who were not free waited to hear. In a few hours, soon as high tide let the yacht clear the mud, she'd make her run for the vast Atlantic. Soon the warming earth would be stirring up wind, filling her sails, giving her speed.

Simmons held Nora's hand as they hurried down the path of crushed oyster shells to join the crowd. Pearl had raced ahead, elbows out to hoist her skirts above the water. All of them were late. The argument at the hotel had wasted precious time.

Clare had refused to join Nora in the little boats. Standing in her nightdress in the hotel suite — Esther in hers as she came out of her bedroom — she listened to breathless Nora's news of finding the yacht and, more important, finding Wells.

"Come see him get his due, Clare," Nora cried, holding her hand out to her.

Esther rushed toward Nora. "Found them! Oh my! Oh my, Nora," she cried.

But Clare was backing away from the outstretched hand. *Why?* she wanted to know. *Why would I get in a fisherman's boat when water is death? The last thing in the world I want is to be within spitting distance of it.* She said she'd wait on the city docks with Mrs. Klein to see the Navy bring in the seized yacht. It was good to know Wells might be punished, but she didn't remember him, not really. Never saw his face that day that the sailors dragged her off his ship.

Nora stalked over to her sister and slapped her. "What do ye mean ye don't remember?" she cried. "Ye said in your letters that he'd stolen ye. Stolen I was, ye wrote. Ye slept on that freezing boardinghouse floor and nearly died with the coughing. Ye got yer fingers broken with a ladle because of him, got thrown out to the streets. What do ye mean ye don't remember?"

Clare fell to the floor on her own — the slap didn't have that much force — and raised her arm against another slap, making her look all the more the victim to Mrs. Klein, which enraged

Nora so much she grabbed a handful of her sister's hair.

Nora shook her by the roots.

Esther fanned her hands at Nora. "Nora dear, stop and think," she said. "It's not a good idea for her to go. If this yacht gets towed in, people will gather at the dock and many of them will be angry at what they're seeing. You and Clare together, well, you're noticeable, memorable." Genuine concern deepened the wrinkles around her eyes. "You two and Rose—all of us—must leave on the next steamer north. I'll make the arrangements as soon as I get dressed, but when we return to the waterfront tomorrow, no one should remember Clare or you or Pearl." She nodded gently. "I know you must go but try to stay out of sight on the wharves."

Nora let go of Clare's hair.

"Pearl most of all," Esther said. "Tell her to stay in the shadows on the waterfront."

On her race home, smoldering and confused and weeping, Nora struggled to make sense of the turmoil that had gripped her heart since Clare had arrived in Charleston. The Clare she knew was gone, ruined, now a bootlicker and a coward, and there was nothing Nora could do about it. How could she feel so protective and so murderous at the same time? How could she have slapped her only living relative like that? Nora thought of their cottage at home, that vanished cocoon on the other side of the world, gone for good but not the memories of the unlikely joy her parents had wrung out of their grinding poverty. In her mind, she placed the old Clare in that cottage of their childhood and closed the door. There the gift that had been their relationship would live. Against the expanse of the future, Clare needed to see her way to a new life and so did she. Nora decided she would not grieve the old life, shriveling by the day.

She would not be her own tormentor.

* * *

Pearl climbed into a boat and waved to Nora that there was room. Nora scanned the river so wide that the trees on the opposite side were mere smudges of green. The jon boats—ten or eleven—were small, narrower, and less stable than the bateau she'd survived six months ago. She watched uneasily as dozens of people clambered into the boats and set them to rocking and banging into one another. Mothers trusted their children to the outstretched hands that lifted them in. Women gathered their soaked skirts and wiggled onto plank seats as calmly as if they were settling into a carriage. The men in charge of rowing wasted no time taking off. Within minutes, the only people left on land were Nora and Simmons. One jon boat waited for them. Pearl waved at Nora again to come on.

Simmons touched Nora's elbow, barely a nudge, but Nora locked her knees. "I can't," she said. She focused on the water lapping at the tips of her boots, its threat no longer distant and conceptual like a painting, but near and real, licking at her toes. Drowning didn't require much. In the mere inches of water in front of her—she could see oyster shells on the river bottom—she could die. Someone had told her that.

Pearl climbed out of the boat and slogged back through the water, her short-muscled arms pumping with determination. She grabbed Nora's hands, startling her into looking up. "I know you're scared, but look at you, what all you've done since you rode the ocean twice," she said. "And look at me, what all I'm goin' to do when the water takes me north. Goin' to buy those rose-colored drinking glasses we talked about. Don't be afraid of this 'yuh water. Ain' the water delivered you safe so far?" Pearl gave her hands a tug. "Ain' it saved you?"

How did Pearl always do it? Nora wondered. How did she always find that wellspring of faith burbling in the bedrock of despair?

The sun crested the line of trees on the opposite shore and cast a golden light across the water that was rushing inland toward Wells. Soon, he would sail by this very spot thinking he was safe. A mile downriver, the *Allegheny* waited for him at the mouth of the harbor. The ragtag jon boat armada was on its way there, full of people who could sink like stones to the river bottom too but had put their fear aside to see justice swoop down.

"Those people," Pearl said, jerking her thumb behind her. "They think you're coming. I told 'em you'd come. They know what all you did."

Simmons touched her elbow again. "Easy enough at the end of a day to lament what one should've done," he said. "But it's morning, Nora."

Nora squeezed Pearl's hands and began running through the water, boots and all. When she got to the boat, Tobias held out a hand to help her in. Nora was actually glad to see the runty Tobias—smiling at her at last—but even happier to see that his rowing partner was a thick-armed bull of a man. Both men told her to sit and not stand to see or call out or anything like that. Pearl climbed in behind her, then Simmons.

They caught up with the humble jon boat fleet that was closing in on the *Allegheny*, which was under sail but barely moving while she waited in the middle of the harbor. Her crew members elbowed one another at the sight of the little boats coming toward them like a string of ducks. Lieutenant Cowan broke through his sailors to swing a commanding arm at the rowboats to stay out of his way.

As the little boats gathered along the edge of the marsh, the passengers fell quiet, even the children straining to see over shoulders. The men at the oars relaxed. The current had stopped surging inland. The creeks were as deep as they were going to be this morning.

The sun inched higher in the sky. Seagulls crisscrossed overhead, their familiar cries weaving some relief into the tension in the air. Hands lifted to foreheads for the watch upriver until arms tired. Finally, three white sails appeared in the distance, then a colorful, triangular pennant flying from the schooner's mainmast. Nora grabbed Pearl's hand.

On the *Allegheny*, the sailors took their stations. Lieutenant Cowan stood beside the wheel, spyglass lifted. One of the sailors ran a small flag up the mainmast.

Simmons pointed at the flag. "He's signaling Wells that he wants to come alongside to inspect," he said.

"How do ye know that?" Nora asked.

Simmons shrugged in the way that men do when they want to say *because I'm a man* but don't because they've learned that things go better for them when they respond with just the lift of a shoulder.

The *Remy Martin*'s sails were full as they harnessed the wind. Nora raised the spyglass to scan the yacht's deck. She spotted him immediately. He had a spyglass raised too. When he put it down, he looked back at the First Mate at the wheel and said something. The yacht pressed on.

Over on the *Allegheny*, Cowan stared with disbelief at the captain who ignored his flag to douse his sails. The *Remy Martin* had the luck of a good wind at her stern and she was coming fast. The open sea was less than a mile away.

"He's making a run for it," Simmons yelled.

Suddenly, Cowan was barking orders and the *Allegheny's* crew was scrambling to adjust her sails, turning her slightly to position her battery to fire.

The racing yacht bore down, all of her masts, spars, and sails straining with the tension of twelve knots of speed.

An explosion scorched the air. When Nora opened her eyes, she saw smoke billowing from one of the gunports of the *Allegheny*. The cannonball landed two hundred yards ahead of the *Remy*'s bow, as warning.

Still the *Remy* pressed on, sails hard and full. Nora imagined Wells gripping the wheel, judging distance and speed and the range of the Navy's guns.

Two more cannonballs flew across the water, each explosion met with roars from the *Allegheny* and the little gallery bobbing along the shoreline.

Finally, as the *Remy* was almost abeam the *Allegheny*, Cowan fired again, no longer to merely warn. A cannonball snapped the yacht's bowsprit in half. The next shot tore away the jib. Her crew scrambled to pull in all of her sails.

The *Allegheny* circled back, her red-faced men wild with amazement at their luck and the captain's newly found balls.

In the little boats, oars went back into the water to move toward the moment of justice.

From their decks, the two enraged captains yelled at each other, not that either could hear. Through the spyglass, Nora saw Wells waving his arms with disbelief, as though he was so very wronged. Cowan and two of his officers climbed down a ladder, got into a cutter, and boarded the yacht. Wells continued his outraged victim act as Cowan went below to inspect.

"What's going on?" one of the fishermen called out to Nora.

"The Navy captain is looking around below," Nora said. "This could take a while."

No one else asked any more questions. Everyone knew what he was looking for.

But it didn't take a while. Cowan emerged from the hatch hurling accusations at Wells, which he deflected with white hot accusations of his own.

"That the slaver hollering?" a man asked.

"Oh yes," Nora said with a smile. "Quivering with rage, he is."

Cowan's hands were flying, pointing at the hold, the Wando behind them, then at the sea. The two captains stood toe to toe. Nora's boat inched closer. She looked at Simmons and Tobias and Pearl, all of them wide-eyed at the scene coming into focus. Wells heard one of his crew cursing at the approaching flotilla that was a sea of black faces save two. Both captains looked down at them. Wells yelled at them to get the hell out of his business and turned back to defending himself.

Nora stood up and waved her arms. "Hey," she called.

Pearl pulled on Nora's dress to sit down. Nora swatted her hands away.

Though his chest still heaved from the battle and his brain was on fire at the Navy captain shouting in his face, Wells looked over at the call.

Nora patted her chest. "It's me, captain. Me ye have to thank for this. Ye said they wouldn't catch ye. Ha!"

"Nora, sit down for God's sake," Simmons said.

Pearl wrapped her arms around Nora's knees. Tobias wrapped his arms around Pearl. "I tol' you," Tobias cried. "Don't stan' up."

Wells squinted at her, blood in his eyes, still confused.

"It's me. The Irish girl who paid yer lousy bill of two dollars. Ye tore me twin away from me in New York. Nora Murphy. Remember?"

Recognition dawned on Wells's face, then rage. He spewed

threats at her until Cowan recaptured his attention with a shove toward the rope ladder on the side of the *Remy Martin*. The *Allegheny* crew began setting up tow lines between the ships.

The little armada erupted with whoops and cries. Women wept, men pounded on one another's backs, rowers waved their oars.

"Justice, justice. Unbelievable, Nora," Simmons said. "Well done." He tapped his finger to his forehead in salute.

"I can't believe it meself," Nora said, grabbing Pearl's hands, solid and warm.

"I can," Pearl said. "Now sit down."

* * *

For decades, a small beach near the Cooper River's wharves had offered an easy landing for small craft, a spot every fisherman knew well. When everyone had hauled the jon boats up its slope, they ran to the Navy's pier, arriving in time to see the *Allegheny* and *Remy* gliding in. All along the waterfront, dockworkers, drivers, and seamen gawked at the bizarre scene: Navy warship towing a crippled racing yacht, a well-dressed older woman on the Navy's pier pumping her fists skyward as she watched the Navy pull in, and the fellow beside her with his head under a black drape taking photographs of it all. On the deck of the *U.S.S. Allegheny*, cheering sailors lined the rails like fenceposts.

As the crew began tossing mooring lines to fellow sailors on the dock, Esther ran to the middle of the pier. Hopkins gathered his camera and took off after her.

"Yoo hoo," Esther called. "Where's the captain?"

A sailor looked up from looping a line around a cleat. "Not now, ma'am," he said.

"I want to talk to the captain." Esther craned her neck to search the deck. "More to the point, he's going to want to talk to me."

"Who're you?" the sailor asked, eyeing Hopkins and the camera.

"I'm a reporter for the *New York Evening Post*. Tell him I'm out here and I have a photographer."

Cowan had already spotted the camera, however, and soon he emerged from the chaos with his prize, the handcuffed and belligerent Captain Robert C. Wells.

"Captain Cowan sir! You're a hero," Esther called out. "My photographer would like to make your image."

Cowan's chest lifted, his smile broadened. He handed Wells off to an officer and joined Esther on the pier.

From the wharf's shadows, Nora, Pearl, Simmons, and fellow boaters watched the scene unfold. More wharf workers joined the gang of earlier arrivals who were still trying to believe what they were seeing. No strangers to creative illegal slave trade schemes, they nevertheless shook their heads over the spectacular racing yacht that had just been seized. Theories flew as to who told the Navy to search her. The men turned their attention to the clump of black people behind them who had the audacity to stand there and watch the yacht captain's humiliation.

That clump began to break apart. Parents turned their children's shoulders away to get little feet moving. A woman touched Nora's shoulder, then Pearl's. She whispered her thanks and blessings, said she'd tell her grandchildren — when she got some — about this day. As Nora reached for her hand, the woman was already out of reach, joining the last of the crowd stealing away. A few hands waved goodbye to Nora and Pearl, deliverers of something they thought they'd never see.

PART THREE

The **bobolink** (*Dolichonyx oryzivorus; translates as "rice bird"*) breeds in the summer in North America and southern Canada. It winters in Argentina, Bolivia, Brazil, and Paraguay. Bobolinks often build their small nests on the ground in dense grasses. Both parents usually tend to their young, sometimes with a third bobolink helping.

Chapter Thirty-four

When Esther Klein's carriage pulled up to the wharf, four black people in faded plaid skirts and baggy brown pants — two men and two women — stepped forward to meet it. She nodded at them to come along. Eyes cast down, they followed her and Clare to the dock owned by the steamship company that had issued Esther's tickets to New York. Her purse held freedom papers signed by New York judges months ago. The names that Esther had filled in were Pearl, Isaiah, Tobias, and Hettie. Her entourage walked down to the salon on the second deck and settled on benches, the servants sitting opposite Esther, to wait for the official to check tickets.

Meanwhile, a second carriage delivered Hopkins, Simmons, Nora, and Rose. Hopkins wore glasses and a too-large hat meant to disguise. He had surrendered his precious equipment to the steamship company only after Esther had bought a special case for it because even he had agreed he couldn't be seen with the camera. All it would take would be one official noticing the daguerreotypist in Mrs. Klein's party and wondering if she was the New York troublemaker everyone was talking about. If that happened, the papers for her servants would come under too much scrutiny.

Isaiah hadn't wanted to come, said he was too old to survive the mas's beating if he got caught. Hettie and Tobias had argued with him late into the night, saying all of them were leaving or none of them, and they were leaving. No children, no lovers—well, none that mattered—no property. All three had nothing to lose. The lady from New York, she had the freedom papers, Pearl had said, and Pearl was no fool. Said she'd seen them herself. In the end, Isaiah, out of trust in the tiny Pearl whom he'd watched grow up into a courageous woman, nodded his white head.

A few minutes later, Simmons, Hopkins, Rose, and Nora entered the salon. Affecting the air of employer, Simmons directed Nora to help the wobbly Rose to a bench. He remained standing and lit a pipe. Hopkins stepped a few feet away as if offended by the stranger's smoke.

An official came in and strolled in front of the row of black people sitting quietly, hands folded in laps, eyes straight ahead. The rumble of the boilers two decks below began to vibrate through boot soles.

"These four with you?" the official asked Esther. His finger made an arc in their direction.

"Yes. I just hired them," Esther said. "For my home in Newport."

"Hired. So, they're free?" He waved for the documents. "Need to have a look at their papers."

After handing him the papers, Esther said something about needing a handkerchief and she began an earnest search in her purse, because for once, Esther Klein wanted to hide her face from male eyes.

The official held the documents up to the light to confirm the judicial seal. "Four seems like a lot," he said. "You came all the way to Charleston to hire servants?"

The rumble underfoot grew. The floor began to shudder. A steam whistle pierced the air.

"It's a big house," Esther said.

Though Esther had said that cheerfully, the man's eyes bored holes into her. Suspicion clouded his expression. He looked around and spotted Hopkins, a strange-looking fellow who'd been sneaking looks his way. "He with you?"

"No."

"Why's he watching me?"

"Never saw the man before, sir." Esther dabbed the handkerchief under her pearls.

Hopkins closed his eyes as if to survive Simmons's smoke, but the official approached him anyway.

Another man in uniform came into the salon and, seeing his colleague showering Hopkins with questions, stepped closer to listen.

The boat rocked with the last burst of passengers swarming on board. The sound of their boots shuffling on the steps floated in. Esther and her servants shifted down the benches to make room. The new arrivals took their time choosing their seats, thus obscuring Esther's view of Hopkins, the quiet, obedient, innocuous, abandoned man who had suddenly become the linchpin of the entire scheme. No one but the officials could hear Hopkins's answers. Hettie offered up silent prayers. Tobias dabbed a rag at his sweaty forehead. The freedom papers were in order, Mrs. Klein had assured them, but this was Charleston. Anything could happen when white people in Charleston got suspicious.

When the newcomers finally took their seats, Esther could see the official coming toward her, papers in hand. With a nod, he gave them to her and left. Hopkins was leaning on a post, chest heaving. He tucked his ticket back into a pocket, pushed the glasses up to the bridge of his nose, and smiled to himself.

Heavy mooring lines thudded onto the upper deck. The whistle gave a long, loud blast. Nora looked over at Pearl. Was this really happening? Pearl returned Nora's barely controlled grin. When the boat shuddered forward, Nora almost cried out in relief. Simmons snapped his fingers at his employees, the two girls, to join him on deck.

The descending sun was laying a milky kind of light across the skyline, the last of Charleston they'd ever see. Church bells in a steeple tolled five times, then in another steeple, and in another in the familiar overlapping way. In a few hours, when the light had seeped completely away, the bells would toll the curfew. The four fugitives wouldn't be there to hear it. The house of runaways was empty for good.

* * *

On March 1, 1850, the *New York Evening Post* published the image of Lieutenant William T. Cowan, commander of the *U.S.S. Allegheny*, on the front page beside the article written by Mrs. Abraham Klein, special correspondent. The commander smiled broadly as he stood in front of the confiscated *Remy Martin* moments after capture in Charleston's harbor. Its owner, Mr. Claude Alston of Charleston, South Carolina, and its captain, Mr. Robert C. Wells, faced charges of violating the Piracy Act of 1820, a capital crime, and would be tried in the Circuit Court of the United States. If convicted, the two men faced hanging. The New York Yacht Club had expelled Mr. Alston.

While Esther Klein issued essays and trial reports from her desk in the four-story Italianate brownstone on twenty-first street, Clare attended to her every need. Having served as the portal to the best articles and essays her mistress would ever write, Clare was granted a special status in the household. She no longer had to bother with the mysteries of answering the front door and ironing linens. There were five other women and two men in the household to do that, Tobias, Isaiah, and Hettie among them. Clare spent her days serving tea, plumping pillows, and refilling Esther's inkwell. At her insistence, Clare improved her reading and writing, the gateways to better articulating the link between the fight for abolition and the fight for women's suffrage. Both frontiers would keep Esther and Clare busy for the rest of their lives.

Clare's letters to Nora continued to find her on her travels north until finally Nora and Dr. Benjamin Rush settled in Montreal. Their wedding in a barebones Quaker home took place as soon as the doctor could arrange it. Pearl and Rose were their only witnesses. The four of them had traveled by trains, boats, and carriages to the northern haven that was beyond the reach of American warrants. For so long, hope had skittered around them like a bird out of reach, but as Nora and Benjamin exchanged their vows, hope settled on all shoulders. The Quaker clergyman declared Nora and her doctor *mari et femme*. Husband and wife. Benjamin brushed aside a tendril of Nora's upswept hair, took her face in his hands, and kissed her tenderly. When he finished, she grasped the hands still cupping her cheeks and tried to say how much she loved him, but she was so choked up all she could get out was a croak. The light in the room changed to the kind of pink-gold light that one sees when sunrays hit the clouds at a certain angle late in the afternoon, a sign to the Irish girl who still believed in faeries that most everything that was to follow would be bathed in colors like this, the colors of hope.

Pearl completed every kind of education that the Quakers could find in English and became a teacher in a school for the children of former enslaved people. Over time, she mastered French. When her hair jewelry income surpassed her teacher's income, for she was the only supplier of *art de cheveux* in a city in which fashions and fads arrived a year or two after their American and European peak, she employed her graduates in her workroom. Rose kept track of inventory, deliveries, and hearts that needed encouragement. For several months, she and Pearl mulled over which last name to take — Simmons, Rush, Liberty, and Donnelley were considered — and in the end chose one that all four runaways agreed was perfect: Allegheny.

Months after the former Captain Wells began a twenty-year jail sentence, the *Remy Martin* was incorporated into the U.S. Navy's African Patrol. No slaver vessel ever outran her.

AUTHOR'S NOTES

This novel is a work of fiction and none of the characters are real persons living or dead, but many of the details of this novel are based upon actual places and events. A historical fiction author can get lost in research; indeed, she can be so wrapped up with discovering anecdotes and remarkable people that she's at risk of never getting around to writing the novel. Worse, she writes the novel and shoehorns in too much of what she's found, which annoys readers. Elsewhere, say at social gatherings, she must not share too many of these factoids, which others might not find as fascinating as she does.

Certain facts I unearthed are interesting by any measure, though, and so I thought I'd share a few with you.

The sack that Rose gave to Pearl when she was sold away is based upon a real sack that is on loan from Middleton Place Plantation to the International African American Museum in Charleston. The sack surfaced at a flea market in Tennessee in 2007, and its purchaser gave it to Middleton Place, a former rice plantation near Charleston, where it was displayed until 2013. The sack, made from the same kind of linen from which enslaved people made their clothing, probably held rice, seeds, animal feed or cereal. Its heartbreaking historical significance is made clear by the embroidered words on one side:

"My great grandmother Rose, mother of Ashley, gave her this sack when she was sold at the age of nine in South Carolina. It held a tattered dress, 3 handfulls [sic] of pecans and a braid of Roses [sic] hair. Told her It be filled with my Love always. She never saw her again. Ashley is my grandmother. [signed] Ruth Middleton, 1921."

An anthropologist's attempt to reconstruct the sack's provenance can be found in the November 29, 2016 issue of *Southern Spaces*, which is an open-access journal published by the Emory Center for Digital Scholarship. The anthropologist speculates that Rose and Ashley were most likely owned by Robert C. Martin, a wealthy Charleston merchant and planter. Rose is listed among his inventory of slaves in the Charleston Estate Inventory Book 1850-1853. His Charleston home at 16 Charlotte Street was the model for the home where Nora overhears Captain Wells's plot to bring Africans across the ocean to sell into slavery. Robert Martin's plantation in Barnwell county (Millberry Place) is the model for the Millberry Place in the novel, where my character Rose lives all of her life until Pearl buys her freedom.

The Irish have played a significant role in the history of South Carolina for more than three hundred years. In *Shamrocks and Pluff Mud: A Glimpse of the Irish in the Southern City of Charleston, South Carolina,* author Donald M. Williams describes their contributions, tragedies, and sacrifices. I'd like to thank Mr. Williams for granting permission to paraphrase his work in the following paragraphs:

The first wave of Irish immigrants in Charleston arrived in the mid-1700's. Overcrowding on ships and captains' reductions in the passengers' food and water were too often a reality. Illness and death were the result. In 1765 a ship from Belfast arrived in Charleston (then Charles Towne). One hundred passengers (out of 450) had died during the voyage. The survivors were so sick the wardens of St. Philip's Church were called upon to help them. Many of these immigrants were indentured servants and many ran away. Their masters pursued them just like runaway slaves, placing ads in the newspapers giving physical descriptions and reward amounts.

The Hibernian Society of Charleston was founded in 1799 to give aid to Irish refugees. The Society did not require any religious qualification for membership, and its members were Irish Catholics and Irish Protestants. Hibernian Hall, a beautiful Greek Revival building, was built in downtown Charleston in 1840 and, having survived earthquakes, hurricanes, the Civil War, and the society's members, is still the site of the society's meetings as well as public events. An Irish harp is carved in the panel above the main door and another in iron has been placed atop the iron gates at the sidewalk.

After the War of 1812, new ship designs and navigational instruments enabled ships to rely less on the winds and currents that had brought European vessels to Charleston, and so New York became the more common landing place for Irish immigrants.

Charleston needed Irish laborers after the U. S. Congress banned further importation of Africans in 1808, which sent slave prices soaring. Although Charleston had large numbers of slaves because of the number of plantations that had prospered since the middle of the seventeenth century, many owners sold their slaves to meet the demands of the new cotton plantations of Georgia, Alabama, and Mississippi, thus driving prices even higher. Plantation owners sought other workers who weren't their property for the most dangerous tasks. Enter the desperate, cheap, tough Irish immigrant. In Columbia, South Carolina, Irishmen dug a five-mile canal from the bridge at Granby, a treacherous job, especially in the summer heat. Many of those who died were buried in the walls of the canal.

Irish laborers also constructed the South Carolina Railroad between Charleston and Hamburg in the 1830's. They rebuilt Charleston after the fire of 1838, built the facilities used by the then-new Charleston Light and Gas Company (1848), and in 1852 began excavation for the United States Customs House at the corner of East Bay and Market Streets. No job was too risky for the Irish laborers.

Plantation owners also used Irish labor for construction projects. In 1843, forty-three Irishmen built a dike for a rice field on one of the plantations along the Cooper River. The hot, humid climate that was so different from Ireland's and Yellow Fever outbreaks year after year took their toll.

Despite this and the warnings from Bishop John England of Charleston (a native Irishman) to stay away, thousands of Irishmen came to Charleston and other parts of the South in the years leading up to the Civil War. Between 1830 and 1849 (this novel is set in 1849-50), the poor house in Charleston admitted 4,047 foreigners with forty-eight percent coming from Ireland. Much of the influx was fueled by the failure of Ireland's potato crop (1845–1847) and famine. One million Irishmen died of starvation and disease; another one million Famine Irish immigrated to North America. The Hibernian Society did what it could to give them money, food, and shelter. At the time of the Civil War, the Irish were the largest foreign-born group in the South.

In 1856, American landscape architect Frederick Law Olmsted visited Charleston and wrote: "I saw as much close packing, filth, and squalor in certain blocks inhabited by laboring whites in Charleston as I have witnessed in any Northern town of its size."

The Marine Hospital in which the fictional Dr. Frederick Simmons worked does exist. It was designed by Charleston native Robert Mills (responsible for the Washington Monument in Washington, D. C. and numerous other buildings) whose pattern for his Charleston hospital was used to build similar hospitals around the country. Of the nation's original thirty Marine Hospitals, Charleston's is one of eight still standing. Located at 20 Franklin Street, today it is used as the offices of the Housing Authority of Charleston.

The recipe for cooking rice birds (and the alarming instructions on how to eat them) was originally published in *Carolina Rice Cook Book* compiled in 1901 by Louisa Cheves Smythe Stoney. It was re-printed in *The Carolina Rice Kitchen: The African Connection* (Hess, Karen. *The Carolina Rice Kitchen: The African Connection.* © 1992 University of South Carolina). The author writes: "The rice kitchen of Carolina was the result of myriad influences — Persian, Arab, French, English, and African — but it was primarily the creation of early African-American cooks. Although it was the presence of the black cook that was responsible for the near-mythic reputation of Southern cookery, the historical role of these cooks in shaping the palate of the South has never been sufficiently acknowledged."

In Mrs. Stoney's cookbook, she shares receipts (the old-fashioned spelling of "recipes") that have been jealously guarded. She begins by explaining the glory of the famous Carolina rice:

"At the head of fourteen hundred varieties stands Carolina Rice. Richer in fats, more highly flavoured than any other variety of Rice known, it is today the standard of excellence amongst rice consumers not only in this country, but throughout the rice countries of the world. . . . The peculiar advantages of our soil and climate, which seem to develop the grain to its highest perfection have enabled us, for over two centuries, to maintain this high standard, and it is still admitted that Carolina Rice is superior to every other variety in the world."

In slavery times, a portion of Africa's Windward Coast (Sierra Leone) was known as the Rice Coast because Africans had grown rice there for centuries. Thus, South Carolina's rice planters knew well how valuable certain Africans' experience in rice cultivation was. About forty-three percent of Africans taken to South Carolina came from the Rice Coast of West Africa, including Sierra Leone. The planters specifically sought people from the River Gambia area. They knew how to construct canals and dikes, plant and hoe the rice, flood and drain the fields, and harvest and pound rice. The women, for example, brought the practice of planting rice by pressing a hole with the heel and covering the seeds with the foot. When the women tossed grain into the air to land in flat baskets, they and their ancestors had made those baskets according to an African design. Thus, the basket-weaving skills that Nora saw at the fictional Oakland Plantation had originated in Africa. (By the way, some of these baskets have turned up in Newport, Rhode Island antique shops because Charlestonians took their slaves with them when they traveled to their homes there.)

About one of every twenty Africans taken across the Atlantic went to North America; the remaining nineteen went to the West Indies and Brazil.

A number of authors have written about the true story of the racing yacht *Wanderer*, which brought an illegal cargo of approximately four hundred Africans to the United States, landing at Jekyll Island, Georgia on November 28, 1858. It flew the New York yacht club's flag.

There was also the schooner *Clotilda*, which smuggled one-hundred-ten people from the African kingdom of Dahomey in 1860. The sordid story began when a wealthy Mobile, Alabama landowner and shipbuilder wagered several northern businessmen that he could bring in a cargo of Africans into Mobile Bay. Purchased for $9,000 in gold, the human cargo was worth more than twenty times that amount in 1860 Alabama.

He won the bet. The *Clotilda* was the last known ship to bring people from Africa to the United States. After unloading the Africans, the captain set her afire to hide the evidence. In May 2019, the remains of the *Clotilda* were discovered in a remote arm of Alabama's Mobile River following an intensive yearlong search by marine archaeologists.

South Carolina's rice plantations took their last gasps after the Civil War, but their profitability had been declining for sixty years. Beginning in 1800, the European rice market turned to cheaper Burmese, Japanese, and Indian rice. By 1865—the end of the Civil War—the war had destroyed the South's infrastructure and emancipated the labor force. Louisiana, Arkansas, and Texas took over America's rice production with machinery that lowered labor costs. Finally, a series of hurricanes from 1893 to 1906 destroyed what was left of South Carolina's rice fields. For years the embankments melted into the creeks, the wood trunks rotted in their beds, and rice stalks grew tall and haywire, some of them faithfully continuing to offer rice. Eventually northern wealth saved the old plantations. In the early 1900's, industrialists bought them as hunting estates, many times in their thousands-of-acres entirely, saving the grounds from being divided. Today, some are still privately owned, some have become non-profit institutions, and others have become gated communities.

ACKNOWLEDGEMENTS

I would like to thank the historians, academics, naval experts, editors, and friends who helped me shape this novel and ensure its historical accuracy. In the earliest stages of my research, Nic Butler, Ph.D., historian at the Charleston County Public Library, kindly shared his extensive knowledge of Charleston history, particularly regarding enslaved people and the Irish immigrants. The insights of Ista Clarke, Operations Manager of the Old Slave Mart Museum in Charleston, were equally invaluable.

I am indebted to E. Moore Quinn, Ph.D. Professor of Anthropology, Department of Sociology and Anthropology, College of Charleston, who suggested academic publications on the cultural and economic experiences of Irish women arriving in America in the late nineteenth century. Her book, *Irish American Folklore in New England,* was a great resource for Irish culture, i. e., superstitions, curses, food, songs, and women in the labor force.

Shamrocks and Pluff Mud: A Glimpse of the Irish in the Southern City of Charleston, South Carolina provided a great education and I thank the author, attorney Donald Williams, for allowing me to cite sections of his book in this book's author's notes.

I'm most fortunate that *The Market Preparation of Carolina Rice: An Illustrated History* was published shortly before I began my research. Authors Richard Dwight Porcher, Jr. and William Robert Judd created an extremely thorough description of rice harvesting, milling, and threshing before the Civil War.

I thank Vice Admiral Douglas C. Plate, U. S. Navy (Ret.) and Lt. Col. Mike Kobold, USAF (Ret.) for helping me understand how a mid-nineteenth century United States Navy sailing ship would maneuver in the Charleston harbor to fire upon a suspected slaver vessel.

The valuable editorial assistance of Ronlyn Domingue and Vickie Lane who reviewed and edited the earliest versions of the manuscript is gratefully acknowledged. Likewise, I'm grateful to my friends Lisa Cornelius, Kari Swanson, Elizabeth Raub, Ann Robichaux, Pam Levi, and Dellita Kobold for reading the near-final manuscript and offering suggestions for improvement.

Finally, I'd like to thank Michael Nolan, Executive Editor, Evening Post Books, and Elizabeth Hollerith, Managing Editor, for selecting *The Rice Birds* for publication. Thank you for believing in my novel, giving it your care and expert editorial guidance, and bringing my Irish girl's story to a wide audience.

CPSIA information can be obtained
at www.ICGtesting.com
Printed in the USA
BVHW042035260422
635376BV00018B/1686